NAZI GOLD

LATITUDE 55

A. JAY COLLINS

 FriesenPress

One Printers Way
Altona, MB R0G 0B0
Canada

www.friesenpress.com

ISBN
978-1-03-830119-2 (Hardcover)
978-1-03-830118-5 (Paperback)
978-1-03-830120-8 (eBook)

1. FICTION, ALTERNATIVE HISTORY

Distributed to the trade by The Ingram Book Company

NAZI GOLD - LATITUDE 55

a novel by

A. JAY COLLINS

Correct a fool, and he will hate you.

Correct a wise man, and he will appreciate you.

—Morgan Freeman, 2017

Table of Contents

Preface

"Nazi Gold" is the term most commonly used to describe the gold assets nefariously confiscated by Nazi Germany from victims of its conquests during World War II to financially support its war efforts.

It has been estimated that some eighty-four million ounces (over twenty-six hundred tons) of gold was looted during the war—more than one year of production from all the gold mines in the world operating today and worth some $120 billion at today's market rate. In those days it was worth more like $3 billion when the price of gold hovered around $34 dollars per ounce. Most of that gold is claimed to have been looted from the individual victims of the war—most notably the members of the Jewish faith, as well as many other types of people from the countries Germany invaded. Much of the "loot" was already in the form of refined ingots that came from banks, safety deposit boxes, and safes of corporations. The balance was either converted into rough ingots or simply bagged and stored for future refinement, with the identifying tags of where it had come from.

There are many stories that combine fact with the fiction in this history of "magic" that saw the gold disappear into so many places—some accounted for and most not. Some groups and organizations were clearly complicit but not brought to justice, and others have been able to maintain their invisibility for over seventy years.

While the Nazis exchanged some of the gold at Swiss banks in exchange for currency during the war, a lot of it was supposedly hurriedly spirited away to overseas locations controlled by German nationals and their foreign accomplices as the war started to come to an end and panic ensued.

The story of gold movements within Europe during WWII is complex, and there is no intent here to reiterate any of the methods and tactics used to move gold from one country to another. These methods and the movement of gold during those war years have been well-documented in books such as George Taber's *Chasing Gold*. This novel is simply one of a number of fictional possibilities of what may have happened to the looted gold.

The present whereabouts of the bulk of the Nazi gold that disappeared during the 1940s has been the subject of a number of books, conspiracy theories, and a well-documented civil suit brought in January 2000 against the Vatican Bank, the Franciscan Order, and other defendants.

That the Nazi regime maintained a policy of looting the assets of its victims to finance its war efforts, collecting them in central depositories and then transferring them to banks outside the Third Reich in return for currency, has been well documented since the 1950s. The identity of collaborative institutions and the precise extent of transactions, however, continues to be denied.

Some of the thousands of gold rings confiscated by the Germans from the exterminated Jews "left over" after the war and discovered by the advancing allied forces—with so much more available from the frames of eyeglasses, necklaces, brooches, charms, and teeth.

Eyeglass frames of Holocaust victims

In January 2013 Germany's central bank cited the need to build trust and confidence domestically months after federal auditors questioned whether it had verified the existence of bullion holdings overseas. It planned to withdraw 300 tons of gold from the Federal Reserve in New York and 374 tons from the French central bank in Paris, where, apparently, it has been held for decades.

In August 2017 the Bundesbank, Germany's central bank, announced it had completed another program to repatriate gold bars worth nearly $31 billion from storage locations in New York and Paris.

Some 2,000 tons of gold remains unaccounted for—over 64,000,000 ounces, or more than $100 billion, using a conversion rate of $,1500 per ounce, a figure that has been dwarfed by recent accounts.

It is incredible to think that a large part of our global humanity even thought about, let alone attempted to strengthen itself through the psychological and physical defeat of others for the sake of survival, power, and greed. But given what we have experienced and witnessed over the last twenty years at least, it should surprise no one that something like this could happen again.

The perpetrators of the crimes, and now the inheritors of those crimes, continue to make use of the illegal haul and have never sought to repatriate the loot to the relatives of the original owners or their representatives.

This is not a conspiracy theory. It just makes for an intriguing, if not a tongue-in-cheek, fictional story that provides some out-of-the box thinking to end the seventy-five-year circle of questions and conspiracies.

The repatriation of a portion of the gold by Germany, to Germany, over the past decade resulted in my desire to provide closure—fantasy or not—and to create a storyline around the offences just to deal with the frustration I feel for the real but unfinished story. There is a reasonable mixture of fact with fiction here, but whichever way you cut it, it is a sad story that must have an ending, and the culprits must be brought to justice at some point in time.

The search for answers continues.

1

Black Mike

"Hold on, woman!" Black Mike shouted as the two of them crawled onto the crude raft with the last of what they could salvage and clutched at the fragile ropes holding it all together. They were rounding the first bend in the rush of the spring freshet that was finding its way down the myriad of routes through the forest. It was an unforgiving experience, as the turmoil of the unpredictable waterways refused to give them sufficient relief to think about gaining any more of a solid handhold.

It wasn't much of a raft, but it was all they had time to put together as the water around them gained velocity and volume, mixing with the debris it had scoured from the upper reaches of the Toodoggone as the snow and ice melted faster from the higher elevations than they had anticipated. A half dozen small-diameter trees had been uprooted by the rush of water from the melting snow and been dumped onto the bank close to them, and Black Mike and his wife had managed to lash them together to provide a flimsy platform to hang on to as it made its way to lower levels, where the water would eventually spread out and could tip them out onto firmer land—if they were lucky enough to survive the harrowing journey.

"I am, god damn you!" Mike's wife shouted as she was flung from one side of the flimsy raft to the other and clutched for the few strips of rope they had used to tie the logs together. Her face and hair stripped back in a look of angst and near toothlessness as she strained to retain her hold of the ragged loops of rope on the raft's sides. The strain on her face stretched to her arms and the angularity of her hands as they grasped for anything they could grip.

Why hadn't they prepared themselves for this? Why had they waited so long? Why did they even spend the winter in this godforsaken country? The least they should have done was to make their escape while everything was still frozen. However, the temperatures in the mountains had taken a sudden turn with the southern winds, and the snows were melting faster than they had anticipated. But they just kept hanging on, their greed provoking them to collect more and more of the gold dust, particles, and nuggets they could scrape together from the small cave they had managed to carve out to expose the veins. But they had waited beyond what nature had intended. It had warned them, but now it was too late. It had told them the nights were getting warmer and temperatures were over zero. It had told them as the first of the leaves on the deciduous trees started to bud and show themselves. It had told them as they worked in their shirtsleeves instead of quilted vests.

"Throw me the sack!" Black Mike shouted as they started their harrowing journey in whatever direction the flow would take them. She pushed the sack over, and Black Mike clawed at it with his fingers. Only when he had it secured in his hand did she let it go.

The sack contained all they had to show for the months they had endured in the Toodoggone mountains searching for the gold he knew was there from his first trek into the mountains and through all the bar talk back in Prince George.

As the rushing water gained in volume, it gathered more water from the ice melt and found its way between trees and hills and onto lower land while Black Mike and his Mrs. continued to cling on. They were hurled through the shallow but strong rapids as the water found its way around and over the obstacles in its path, creating eddies that twisted and turned them. Low-hanging branches scuffed their bodies and knocked them back and forth, but still they hung on. It became impossible to think. There was no plan. The waters were rising as their raft threw itself farther down toward the valley and was continually caught up in the swirling whirlpools.

Little by little their personal baggage got tangled and ripped apart by overhanging branches and was tugged away from the raft despite it all having been secured to the sides with string, nylon, and rope. They fought with all their might to cling to the sack and themselves. In the end, the sack was all they had left, but a mighty smack into a collection of logs blocking the route pushed the front end of the raft up into the air and upended them. It took all their strength to hold on for their lives, let alone the sack. It disappeared, washed down and beyond their reach and eventually sinking somewhere in the myriad of alternative routes the water surged through. It was impossible to see through the muddy waters, and they had already been pushed too far in the few seconds it took for them to realize the sack was gone. It was too late.

"Hang on, woman! Save yerself!"

The raft threw its way between the trees and down farther into the lower lands with the two exhausted, soaked, bruised, and battered bodies holding on for dear life.

Black Mike and his wife made it, but only just, dumped unceremoniously onto the shallow delta as the flood water spread out over the valley, and the raft grated onto solid ground. Black Mike was not sure whether to be thankful or not.

They had lost everything but their lives.

They made their way on foot back to Prince George, but it was the mid-1920s, and life was as hard for Black Mike and his wife there in the city as it was in the outback. Come to think of it, they were probably better in the outback. At least they could find a way to make money there. But that was the way gold played on a person's mind. It was truly a fever, except that in the case of Black Mike, he knew where the gold was, and there was nothing feverish about that.

They never discussed the loss of the sack, and it was only rumor that told of the small fortune in gold that went to the bottom of the thrashing freshet waters. Still, they came out with their lives. Unknown to Black Mike, his wife had managed to hang on to a small pouch of the fortune by tucking it into the belt she wore to hold up her knickers.

Before they had met, it had been a long, hard struggle for Black Mike McClair to get to this point, ever since he had blown into Prince George back in the late 1920s with the equivalent of $50,000 in today's value of gold dust in his poke and with stories of the Toodoggone mountains in northern British Columbia, well beyond the 49th parallel and on north into Canada. It had been the focus of professional gold seekers of every description, but none had ever discovered the root of the fever: the mother lode. Large, small, male, female, rich, and poor alike ventured to the region searching for their lucky strike. No one ever discovered it, and most never got further than a month into the outback.

"Fuck, I know this is where the mother lode has to be." Every exploration-ist, panhandler, gold gambler, gold lover, gold hater, lover, and dreamer was convinced. Most had never tried to venture into those godforsaken forests and mountains. They just lived vicariously through the stories of others, and Black Mike told the best. Unfortunately, he had no gold to prove the truth of his claims. But it all sounded so feasible, and they all needed the stories to be true.

One typical evening in the local bar, Black Mike was surrounded by more than his fair share of an audience. The beer flowed, and the flames of the log fire seemed to leap higher as the stories unfolded.

"That there Toodoggone is enormous. It takes guts to venture there and fight off the wildlife, the weather, and the mountains. But I did it. All by meself," he had proudly proclaimed. "But you know what? It's there; I feel it in me bones. I seen it with my own eyes as the fingers of Mother Nature beckoned me to share the riches and dreams, if only I was willing to play with Lady Luck awhile." His audience stared at Black Mike in silence as he stretched a beckoning hand out as though he was Mother Nature herself, inviting him into her world.

The innkeeper put another log on the fire, crackling it back into life and sending sparks out onto the floor, and flames licking up into the soot-covered chimney.

Black Mike looked around at the staring faces, their eyes bulging in antici-pation, their hands wrapped around their mugs of beer, not daring to move them in case they disturbed their concentration and they missed a word.

"There's fabulous wealth out there, my friends, if only you have the courage to go find it." Some squirmed in their seats, as though acknowledg-ing they were the ones Black Mike was referring to.

While Black Mike gloried in the attention his stories brought, he had earned his poke the hard way, and he wasn't about to disclose the secret of its location to any man he had met so far in his life. He was one of the very few who had backpacked into the wilderness, using only a compass as his guide, searching for the lost lake that some said was located at the base of a mountain in the Toodoggone. A seemingly impossible task was met by Black Mike's ferocious optimism and ego. He had hooked up with a couple of Natives who, for a pittance, tracked for him through some of the most difficult terrain until eventually making it to a lost lake. It was hard to know if they were in the right place, but Black Mike's optimism took control again and he staked the area at the base of the mountain.

Black Mike watched as the innkeeper pushed more mugs of beer around the tables, set some plates of food in front of a few, spiked two more logs onto the fire, and invited Black Mike to share more stories.

"Well," Black Mike didn't need to be invited more than once, "I sent the Indians off back into the forests and spent a lot of time panning, tilling, pickaxing, and trench digging before I realized I was close to where I wanted to be."

"Where was that?" a toothless young admirer asked without thinking.

Everyone turned to him. "Where the fuck do you think he means, you prat?" Almost everyone joined in the admonishment. "Near the mother lode!" they shouted in unison.

"I was following my nose." Black Mike touched the side of his nose, and everyone knew it as a universal sign of personal knowledge. "Hunches, small signs, the color of the soil, the feel of the gravel, the look of the plants, the word amongst the Indians, panning—lots of panning." Black Mike paused and seemed to go deep into thought as he took a slug of his beer.

"What'd you do?" It seemed to be a group question.

"Well, I built a small cabin from local trees that first year and stashed some tools and all the supplies that remained. I planned on heading back the next year." Black Mike could see the looks of amazement in the faces around him. Most could not fathom one visit to that land, let alone two.

"With winter approaching, I needed to head back. I wasn't equipped to stay in the wilderness with those wicked winds screaming their way down the mountain."

Black Mike didn't tell them he took with him a small pouch, or poke, of gold flakes and nuggets he had panned from the streams to get him through the next season. That's what he had on him now as he looked around and spotted what he thought was a female sitting two tables back, close to the fire, a beer in her hand and a look of awe on her face.

"I know," he carried on, "you have to remember that this is one fuck of a hostile place, not a soul living there, other than some Indians out hunting and a couple of beaver trappers who don't stay there year 'round. Then there are the grizzlies, moose, wild goats, and marmots and such. The nice thing about winter though is that all the critters that might eat you are asleep." Everyone laughed as though to break the concentration. They all needed a little time to sip their beers, have a bite, and push each other around in friendly rivalry.

The party started to break up as smaller groups gathered to discuss their bravado with the rhetoric of getting together to go find the mother lode. Plans were being made to head out before the next freshet. None would go beyond the bar, other than for the voluptuous redhead with her hair piled high in a beehive of a structure. She was the only one to approach Black Mike with any kind of proposition.

"Any room on yer venture?" She was bold, loud, up front, and straight, and she sucked at her clay pipe, blowing a cloud of smoke at Black Mike.

"Fer what?" Black Mike was taken back by the woman in front of him. She seemed determined, strong, loud, and probably good company.

"I think I can do it."

"Do what?" Black Mike asked.

"Get the mother lode, of course. What else do you think I mean?" She didn't smile. She just looked at him as though he was the idiot of the two. Another cloud of smoke.

"Think you know what you want?"

"What are you talking about? Are we lookin' fer gold or not?"

Black Mike liked this woman. She had a mean streak that he needed to help deal with others. She was built for fighting. Her gnarly red hair was a plus although somewhat frightening, as all red-haired people tended to be. Her face was twisted in a strange way, and the well-worn crinkles around her eyes put one at ease if one were thinking of putting his or her future in her hands.

It didn't take much longer for them to tie the bond. Sex was a part of it, although Black Mike wasn't sure who was the strongest, but he didn't think that mattered. What really mattered was whether she was able to keep up with him, fight the outback, wrestle with the weather and the mountains, and be, at the very least, his equal.

They spent the next few days planning their venture. He didn't share all his secrets with her. All he had was a crude map that only he could decipher, but he had enough in his poke to get their supplies organized and make it up to Fort St. James. Black Mike had decided not to hire any local help this time around. He felt confident that he and his woman could haul everything they needed into his camp on sleds. Besides, the fewer people who knew where he was, the better.

So off they went from Fort St. James. There was no fanfare, no dogs to pull the sleds, just two people pulling waxed-rail sleds through the forest as they followed whatever paths had been trodden in a generally eastern direction toward the mountains. It was grueling as they trudged through the unbroken forest floor, through the streams and the sand that had accumulated through littoral drift to the inside bends of the waterways, through the overhanging branches of the firs as they reached down to the forest floor in search of water, around the bear dens, the moose herds, the marshlands that had hidden themselves in the tall grasses, and the mud that surrounded them in every direction.

It took them some thirty days to reach the lost lagoon and find the cabin that Black Mike had described to his audience in the saloon on those comfortable, beer-numbing nights in Prince George. But there they were, at last.

She was impressed to the point of scrambling to establish themselves at the cabin, climbing over the base of the mountain, rushing for water supplies, and generally making camp. Clearly, she was a strong person. She would be his soulmate. One night he told her of his find and the amount of poke he had accumulated. She loved him even more and demanded less. The moment they shared was a moment to be treasured, and she wasn't about to lose it.

Black Mike and his wife scrambled across the mountain scree looking for signs of water that could show them the entrance to what they were looking for. The marmots stared at them and then dodged back into their holes in the mountain, not wanting to give up their secrets. She was the first to find it and dig her way through to a gravel-covered entrance in the mountain that was neither rock nor silt. It could be a natural portal to the mother lode.

"Hey! Hey!" she called out to Black Mike. "I think I found somethin'." Seems to me there's more water comin' out through 'ere than anywhere else. What d'ya think?"

Black Mike scrambled over to her and started to pick-axe his way through the scree. "Think yer right, woman. Could be somethin'."

They scratched, pick-axed, and dug their way forward until their bodies ached, their fingertips were bleeding, and their laughter expressed their exhaustion and joy.

It was late in the season, the snows would be there soon, the streams would freeze, the wildlife would hibernate, and the world around them would become enshrined in a stillness that only a frigid climate could provide, but greed overcame them, and they decided to stay while their stocks of dried meat and fish lasted and grind their way through the scree looking for signs of gold.

The gold veins started to appear on the more solid side walls of the opening as the scree was scraped away. Gradually, they opened a portal they could squeeze into and enlarge and pick at the gold. The veins disappeared into the mountain, but they knew they had made a strike.

They crawled back out of the portal and almost rolled down the scree slope, holding onto each other for support until they reached their cabin. There was no music, but they danced, laughed, drank the moonshine they had brought with them, and then collapsed onto the bedding on the floor and rolled over and over.

"I think we got it, woman!" Black Mike was exhausted but not too tired to celebrate. She kept up with him, and they rolled and laughed and drank until they slept.

But it was winter, and while it was possible to get the gold, it was clear they could not sustain themselves on the rations they had through such a harsh environment when hunting and fishing weren't possible, unless one was a Native.

And so it was that their greed overcame their logic for a while, and they stayed longer than they should have. They had collected a small fortune in gold, tied up into a small sack attached to one body or the other. But it never wandered. And it stayed that way until the freshet came with a sudden rush that they should have foreseen and prepared for.

And so it was that they made their way back to Prince George to tell their tale. But while Mrs. Black Mike wasn't so sure about going back again the next season, Black Mike was going regardless, and he rounded up three companions and two Native guides willing to accompany him.

The next spring, six of them took off with their dogs into the forest. Only Black Mike had the map, although he had left a crude copy with his wife.

It didn't suit everyone, and within two weeks one of the two whities arrived back in Fort St. James to report that he had been overcome by a spiritual experience that told him that only the ancestors of the Natives could visit the area. For whatever reason, it seemed believable, and he went off in search of his soul, although no one ever heard of him again.

A second whitie returned after three days to tell terrible stories of grizzlies that surrounded them and gnashed and threatened and thrashed to the point he could no longer resist and returned terrorized by the images. Again, everyone believed him, and off he went to find his soul. No one heard from him again either.

There was something about that group of men Mrs. Black Mike had never trusted, so it came as no surprise that two weeks after the second person returned, she received news that Black Mike and the last of his cronies had met their deaths on a scree slope avalanche en route. The two Natives with them had survived with badly scraped bodies to tell the tale, and the Black Mike legend became a pub story that would live on without explanation.

It was a short and unsuccessful season, and Mrs. Black Mike could only wonder what had happened. But it was of no use. It was what it was, and her man was lost in the dreams of their golden future.

Mrs. Black Mike had always known the Toodoggone was not a place for the faint of heart. There were other places in the world where gold was easier to access, but the word was that Toodoggone held far richer reserves, if only one could access them. Some had tried, at high costs, with short runs of luck.

What she couldn't have known was that over the years that followed, some companies would try to make a run of things, and some would lose geologists and surveyors to helicopter crashes as they fought the updrafts of the unscrupulous and unforgiving mountainous terrain. Some small processing plants were built using rough gravel airstrips for access and crude equipment, but their ability to withstand the costs of managing the difficulties of isolation, harsh winters, and floods in the spring, combined with the susceptibility to the markets and commodity prices, made them candidates for bankruptcy. Overall, it was the terrain that remained the most unforgiving to those who were unprepared.

2

Mrs. Black Mike

Mrs. Black Mike sat with her "Biggles" helmet set on to top of her fiery red hair, the flaps over her ears, and her hands gripping the straps in the back seat of the Universal Fokker as it trolled over the backcountry of the Toodoggone area of northern British Columbia. They flew low to the ground, as low as the pilot dared, about fifteen hundred feet, to avoid the turbulence coming from the ground that could tip them over in a second.

"Lower, lower!" she yelled through the helmet intercom. "Get lower. I can't make out a fucking thing from here. It all looks the fucking same. Get fucking lower!"

She was as much searching for the sack of gold as she was for the mine. In the back of her mind, she knew the sack would be elusive, but there was still a hope. The mine should have been more apparent, but it wasn't.

The pilot gave no response but merely dropped his plane a fraction. He was not happy, but he liked the money and decided to take the risk. They flew over the treetops and covered an area that was as much as his fuel and her budget would allow.

They found nothing.

Their aeronautical search failed again and again, and she finally gave up after a week of flying in, around, and out of the Toodoggone. It was too vast an area with repeating topography and thick areas of wild forest covering much of it. From the air, one valley, mountain, and stream looked like another, and she hadn't spent the time on the previous trip to take much notice of her surroundings. She thought she knew, but she didn't. She had left that to Black Mike. But he had left her only a rough sketch of the terrain with a few strange notes that only he could understand.

There was little more she could do. There was no way she would be able to retrace the path to the mine; she had no idea where to start, and she sank back to her thoughts of the lost fortune, only to find comfort in the possibility there could be more gold out there and that she could still be part of a grand adventure. She had caught gold fever and had spent the little bit of gold hidden in her knickers, but like most other women of that age, the reality was she couldn't do it without a man. There was no way she would go into the backcountry by herself like the male gold diggers.

Time passed, and Black Mike became a part of Toodoggone history, but neither the man nor his story was forgotten.

Mrs. Black Mike returned to Prince George a disappointed, disgruntled, and angry person. Her stories were never as interesting as Black Mike's had been, and she resented that. She wanted someone to believe her, but how could she do that with no proof, no gold, and no map? Besides all that, she was a woman.

3
Dirty Tommy

1930s

Some say that Tommy Thomas was called "Dirty" Tommy Thomas because he was just that—dirty. Dirty in every way. From his early childhood when he would collect worms in the pockets of his shorts, to the times when he would eat dirt as a dare, to the times when he would show his privates to anyone who wanted to see them. That included his teacher, Sister Anne, who was not impressed with his desire for recognition or the look of his genitalia.

"Dirty *little* Thomas, you come here!" she shouted as he shoved his shirt back into his pants. She then slapped him on the wrist and the backs of his legs with a leather strap. He would just grin in nervous anticipation, so she would slap him again until he stopped.

Hence, he acquired the name Dirty Tommy. It stuck, and somehow, he seemed proud of this significant and unique qualification that set him above others of singular, uninspiring Christian names.

Dirty Tommy was the son of Mennonite parents and raised in a small community in the backwoods of Alberta. It didn't take long for him to escape his roots. By age fifteen, he had made it to the logging camps up north.

"Ever heard of Black Mike?" a gruff voice asked, interrupting Dirty Tommy's thoughts as he sat at a bar in Red Deer. It was a rough place where one either worked or was passing through. Dirty Tommy was doing neither just then. He was merely resting in between thinking about his future.

"Nope," was all he could muster in response.

"Well, the way I see it, you may want to take some notice as a boy who don't know what he wants to do."

Dirty Tommy turned toward the owner of said voice. "Now, what makes you say that?" He would have put it in stronger language except that the person beside him was huge. Even his hands were larger than the plate of food in front of him. Dirty Tommy knew better than to antagonize a brute.

For some reason he listened, though he wasn't sure why. The story the big guy was telling him was intriguing, and something about it inspired him. Before Tommy knew it, he was hooked into the possibility that there was gold out there. All he had to do was to find it.

"Why don' you go an' look fer yerself? Why tell me?" Dirty Tommy asked.

"I bin lookin' for Black Mike's gold for too many years," the stranger said. "I'm ready to cut a deal with anyone who wants to follow on, and it may as well as be a young un' like you."

They exchanged more words, but Dirty Tommy was already hooked. He had nothing, but that's more than it took for him to come to an agreement with his new acquaintance. Thirty-sixty was the split, with sixty going to Dirty Tommy if he found Black Mike's gold. He thought it was just talk and didn't think about it much more.

One day a month or so later, Dirty Tommy drifted into a bar in Prince George and heard about Black Mike and his map again. Black Mike had become a legend and his stories had grown into something close to fantasy. But Dirty Tommy had been thinking about Black Mike and his adventures since that talk in Red Deer with that stranger, and after a little digging, he figured out that if anyone knew the location of Black Mike's cabin, it would be the Natives of the Toodoggone, the Sikamni tribe, and maybe Mrs. Black Mike herself, if she was still alive, although he wondered why she hadn't already acted on it if she knew something that was worth knowing.

Dirty Tommy may have been dirty, but he wasn't stupid. He asked around and found out that Mrs. Black Mike was still thriving, sort of, and living in the same old place. It seemed that she was a regular at the Red Bar Saloon on the edge of town close to her home and had taken up permanent residency in a booth close to the back entrance, where she was free to come and go.

"Any chance we can sit and talk?" Dirty Tommy was never backwards in coming forwards.

Mrs. Black Mike looked at him, squinted, then took a slug of beer. "Do I know you, sonny?"

"No, but I know you. Buy you a drink?"

"Course you can, but don't be gettin' no ideas." Mrs. Black Mike had no problem taking drinks from strangers.

"Heard you came close to the mother lode up in the Toodoggone."

"You heard right, sonny. Me and my man found it and lost it, but I know it's there. Why? You itching to try your luck?"

After a lot of drinking and talking, Widow Black Mike, who was now somewhat frail and given to forgetfulness, gave Dirty Tommy a sketch copied from the map that her man had made. Of course, she couldn't read, so she was clearly at a disadvantage, like most of the explorers at the time. But Dirty Tommy could read, and he could also make some sense of what he was looking at.

He questioned the widow as best as he could, with little success. But she was able to point him in a generally northern direction to Fort St. James, and that was enough for Dirty Tommy. The map would help do the rest, and he would get the Natives to help him out.

"I never took no notice in which direction we was going nor what we were passing, but I know enough to tell you we headed to some mountains due northeast from Fort St. James," Widow Black Mike rambled on. "There's a lake and a cabin. Might even find the sack we lost on the way there."

Dirty Tommy's ears perked up. "Sack?"

"Yeah. Our stash. Fucking water smacked us around so much we lost it. It's out there somewhere. Jus' don' know where."

Dirty Tommy thought it might be a plus to find it, but he wasn't going to count on that. His focus was on getting to the cabin. What it did tell him though was that the stories were very likely true.

"Tell you what, Mrs." Dirty Tommy was going to make a last play in case there was anything else he could get out of the old lady. "Anything I find we split. Sound good?"

"Sounds good to me, sonny, provided I ain't dead by the time you do that." She snickered, and Dirty Tommy smiled.

"Anything else you can tell me?"

"That's all she wrote, sonny. Ain't nothing more I can remember, 'cept the portal is about fifty feet up the scree slope from the cabin."

That was good enough for Dirty Tommy. He knew he had to start at Fort St. James and just hoped the map and what the old lady had told him was all true.

It was another two years before Dirty Tommy made it up to Fort St. James to make contacts, raised enough money to provide supplies for four months, and figured out who in the Sikamni tribe he could trust and was willing to take him on his journey through the backwoods.

A few members of the Sikamni tribe were living in the area around Fort St. James. After all, that's where the saloons were, and the Natives gravitated to them, especially during the winter months when it was almost impossible to hunt.

It didn't take long for Dirty Tommy to strike up a discussion with a few of the tribe members who sat huddled with their beers in the corner of one of the saloons near the outskirts of town.

"What ya doin', stranger?" the biggest of the threesome asked, giving Dirty Tommy a suspicious look. "Don' see many strangers 'round these parts this time of year. They generally comes up in huntin' season to bag themselves some grizzly and moose. What about you?"

Dirty Tommy sat down in the booth, and one of the Natives shoved over toward the wall a little to let him spread out.

"I was lookin' to do some fishin' in the backwoods. Place called Lost Lake."

The three Natives laughed. "They's all called Lost Lake, mister," the big one said. "Ain't one that ain't lost."

Dirty Tommy grinned. "I guess yer right. The one I'm lookin' for is way over in the Toodoggone."

"Wow," one of the other Natives interrupted. "Yer gettin' serious, my friend. Ain't many fish lakes over there. Maybe one or two, but you really have to search."

"I got a map." Dirty Tommy put his scrap of paper on the table, smoothed it out, and used his beer to hold down one corner. They all stared at it.

"That's way over," the third Native said, sticking his face close to the map. He seemed to be studying the details more than Tommy would have expected. "I know this place," he exclaimed, prompting the other two to put their faces close to the map. The three heads banged together, but none of them moved.

The big Native pointed his finger at the lake and the mountain above it and followed the trail back through to where it hit the road near Fort St. James. "That's Sikamni country, stranger. What ya looking there fer?"

"I told you. Fishin.""

"I don't think so, my friend. That's dead fish country. Ain't none up that far. Well, maybe some lonely bull trout but nothin' worth eatin'."

All three turned their suspicious eyes on the stranger.

"OK, I'm lookin' for Black Mike's cabin. Satisfied?"

"Ha! Now that's more like it, friend. Everyone's lookin' fer Black Mike's cabin. Ain't no one found it yet, so what makes you think you're going to do any better?"

"I got this map."

All three stared at the map again. The big Native stroked his chin. The others followed suit.

"Maybe you got somethin', stranger. This is more than the others had."

"Can you help me?"

"How much?"

That's all it took, and the deal was on. The Natives weren't interested in the legend of Black Mike. They were interested in money.

So off they started one miserable rainy April morning as the spring freshet was just threatening to start. Dirty Tommy hoped to make it to the cabin before it took over the forest. The Natives weren't concerned as long as their money was safe.

But they had to go immediately. Winter closed in fast in that part of the world, and it was not at all uncommon to have snow falling by September, with consistently sub-zero temperatures by the end of that month. That gave them four months unless they wanted to fight with nature even more. With Dirty Tommy in tow, the Natives worked their way across the untouched wilderness at a steady clip of about 8 to 12 miles each day for the 160 miles or so from Fort St. James before coming to what they described as the "remains" of Black Mike's cabin in something like thirty days. The walls and the roof were still somewhat intact, but the place had been overrun by vermin, animals, and weather. The bush had closed in around it and grown through the openings into the living area. Garbage was strewn around, and the paper was brittle or rotten, but it was enough to excite Dirty Tommy into believing the stories he had heard were true enough to mount a much larger campaign.

Dirty Tommy let his Natives friends drift back off into the forest with promises of payment once they got back to Fort St. James. They knew he would be true to his word. After all, he was in their country, and they knew he couldn't cross them for fear of retaliation.

Dirty Tommy made the trip into Toodoggone twice more, during which time he excavated the areas that Black Mike and his widow had started, including enlarging the portal and getting farther into the gold seams and veins. Black Mike's stakes were still in the ground around the site, and it was clear that he had whittled his options down to three locations, with the portal being the main marker, before he and his fellow miners had disappeared.

Dirty Tommy watched the water from the various streams as the freshet was coming to an end and panned for gold as he tried to identify which carried the most. He wanted to confirm that the portal was the point of interest. The most likely one led him back to the base of a mountain, and he followed the highest volume of running water up to a few spots where Black Mike had figured the most likely spot to be some fifty feet above the base. His widow was right; that was where it was.

Dirty Tommy scratched around and came to focus on one of the spots in the cave as the most likely target. He had brought enough dynamite to blast, and two weeks after he started, he hit the first large vein some twenty feet into the mountain. From there he branched out, following the vein and then the sub-veins. Over the next two months, he blasted out another thirty feet and piled the waste outside the rough portal. What he exposed was a vein structure that clearly—to him at least—was never-ending and reached out like tentacles into the mountain, with gold gleaming all over it. It was panning out to be a one-ounce-per-ton property from what he could tell, far richer than most.

It was time to get better organized. He needed men, tools, and equipment. His two seasons in the backcountry had paid off, and he was excited to move on to the next stage. He took enough gold to bankroll the next season, and off he went, leaving behind a well-hidden portal, having spread the waste into the streams that would carry it down to the valleys below.

Dirty Tommy returned to Prince George, gold nuggets shining in his eyes, and promptly dropped dead. He had managed to describe his findings to only Black Mike's widow, who cursed his dead body for the bad luck of him dying just when it seemed that she was finally going to get payback. No one really understood how or why he died, but most folk suspected that Dirty Tommy had discovered the mother lode and had given the widow a better map, but she never told.

4
Lucky

1940s

Lucky Luciano languished in the oppressive heat and stench of the six-by-nine-foot cell in the town jail with three cellmates. Once again, he had been caught cheating at poker in the local saloon. Everyone did it, but Lucky did not live up to his name. He was just plain unlucky and spent at least 50 percent of his time incarcerated. He didn't really mind. His meals and accommodations were free, and he didn't carry a permanent record.

He had come over from Italy—Sicily, to be more precise—and had been searching for his Italian roots in the Canadian north. There weren't many, and what there was seemed to be more in northern Ontario, but Lucky didn't like that climate or the people he had met there, despite being family. That part of the world was way too harsh. He hadn't cared for it at all and had drifted west in his search for a better climate and a more hospitable family connection.

Lucky slept the sleep of one who didn't give a damn when one day a compatriot of his from the mother country plonked down next to him in the town jail.

"Hey. You gotta be Lucky!"

"Oh yea. I'm lucky ... really lucky."

"No, I mean Lucky Luciano. We been lookin' for you everywhere, man."

"What?" Lucky looked over at the guy, who grinned at him with a screwed-up grin. "What the fuck you talkin' about?"

"You the Lucky with the map?"

"Whaaaat?"

"The map. The Dirty Tommy map."

Lucky had the map but had never understood what it meant. He wasn't a miner, but he sort of appreciated the significance of the find.

Lucky Luciano was a religious man with strong ties to his old country, his church, and to the gangs that controlled everything. He knew a few of the middle management but had never really clicked with the mainstream and seemed to fall naturally to the bottom of the Mafia pile. He needed to get out and had prayed for a solution. Now there he was at the lowest point of his miserable life, a criminal, and a small-time one at that. He was broke, albeit with a little of the cash he had stolen squirrelled away in a box buried in the church cemetery, drinking alone at the bar and praying for a sign to show him the way.

It was then that an aged Mrs. Black Mike had plonked onto the stool next to him and ordered a whiskey—two fingers. While she cuddled the glass, Lucky leaned over. "Life's the shits, ain't it, honey?" he said in his best American/Canadian accent, which had become strangely quirky when combined with his southern Italian dialect.

Mrs. Black Mike turned and stared into his eyes. Raising her glass to her lips, she took a slug of whiskey and then slammed the glass down on the bar.

"I'm not your honey, honey, so go fuck yerself."

From that moment on, the two became friends of a sort, tied by the respectful bonds of misery and bad luck.

But as it transpired during that drunken night, Lucky became acquainted with the name Dirty Tommy and learned the story of what had happened with Black Mike, the mine, the Natives, and the map.

Without fully understanding why, Mrs. Black Mike started to think through the haze that perhaps Lucky had been sent to her by her dead husband and then Dirty Tommy as a way to a brighter and wealthier future. After all, Lucky looked to be able to take care of himself, was smooth-talking, seemed to really appreciate women, and was as passionate as one could expect in the circumstances of those times and in that godforsaken arsehole end of the world. She was still a handsome woman by some standards, especially there in the outback at a bar all by herself in the mining community with one hand on an axe and the other on a shotgun.

Lucky was not a gold digger in the sense of hard work and sweat. He was more the type who looked for opportunity, and Mrs. Black Mike had a story worth listening to. She had described the gold deposit, crudely exploited by Black Mike, then exploited further by Dirty Tommy. According to Dirty Tommy, the gold was not only visible but also contained in narrow veins that seemed to go on forever. Both Black Mike and Dirty Tommy had brought some gold back with the intent of bankrolling a more substantial trip into the bush the following season. Now both were dead, and she was the only one with the secret and a small stash of gold that could maybe bankroll another venture and maybe more, though she was not about to reveal these things just yet

After an eventful, energetic, and fruitful night of drinking and debauchery that lasted into the next day and early evening, Lucky came away with the map in exchange for a promise to Mrs. Black Mike that she would profit from their liaison, provided there was profit to be made. But his luck ran out on him again the next night when he got involved in another poker game. He was winning but not the right way, and, once again, he got caught and hauled off to jail. That's where he met the ragtag bunch of would-be miners who knew he had the Dirty Tommy map and what it could mean.

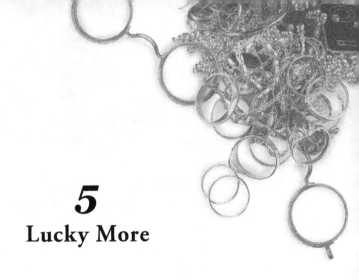

5
Lucky More

The following week, after a few more nights of rolling and tumbling with Widow Black Mike in a slow but thoughtful way as the two aged, she bankrolled him with the last of her gold to search for the treasure.

Lucky made his way up to Fort St. James with a group of suspicious would-be miners planning on setting off into the bush on varying expeditions with grandiose gold schemes of their own. They made it to the only bar in town, the Zoo, three days later and talked for two days about their plans to discover their mother lodes. There was a lot of BS and a few truths... but mostly BS.

All described their lackluster experiences, embellished by optimism. Each had their own idea of where and how, but all had a common purpose—gold. Only Lucky was not a would-be miner, as far as he could tell, but they didn't know that, nor was he about to divulge his ownership of the map.

"Eh, Lucky, tell us about yer find. What's goin' on? Is there anythin', or are you just full of bullshit, same as everyone else?" Greg was a toothless but friendly type who wanted to be a friend but wasn't sure who Lucky was. "C'mon, Lucky. Let's do it."

"What d'ya mean 'let's do it'? What the fuck does that mean? Let's do it?" Lucky leaned back with his beer.

The loose lips were starting to get more lubricated as the beer flowed.

"C'mon, man, you know what we mean. The gold, for chrissakes. Where the fuck is it? You got the map, an' we all knows it." It was Gerry St. Germain. He was just a loser, another one with few or no teeth, not much of a nose, and a little less than two eyes but always ready to give it another go. Why not? He had nothing to lose.

"We know what you know, man."

He didn't, of course, but that was the talk. He supped another couple, then got up and left.

There was only so much they told him but so much more to tell.

"Ain't you gonna take any of us, Lucky? I mean, we really wanna go and find it."

"Any idea where it is, Donny?" Lucky asked, staring at him.

"No, but I'm OK with following, if you know what I mean."

"Why don't you guys go off and do yer own thing? Y'all seem to know what yer lookin' fer, so go find it, and don' bother me." Lucky was not getting any more patient with these guys. In fact, he just wanted to cut them loose. A couple of them got too close, and he felt uncomfortable as they pushed their way into his space. It didn't take a lot more for a fight to start in the clearing close to the front entrance of the bar, so Lucky could make his thoughts better known and for his groupies to back off.

A couple of days later, the sheriff was looking for whoever may have seen a vehicle mowing down two of the outsiders on the road into town about two miles south. No one knew anything about the incident, but the sheriff didn't dwell on it. Both of the outsiders seemed to have wandered drunk into the middle of the road.

Lucky had listened to everyone's advice as best as he could and absorbed what he was able, but he was determined to search out members of the Sikamni tribe who might be able to guide him to the cabin. He had the map, but he didn't have the confidence to set off into the unknown wilderness by himself, and he didn't trust any of the miners who were left in the group that had followed him north. He was more of a city—or, rather, village—man himself, and the backcountry was an uncomfortable wilderness for him. He wasn't exactly sure where north was or whether he could use it as an internal compass, and he sure wasn't trusting in the miners who wanted to follow him. None of them seemed to understand where they were, let alone where they needed to go. Sunrise and sunset didn't seem to mean anything to them in terms of times of day, and they needed to go. All they seemed to want to do was to look for something, somebody, anything, to latch on to that might lead them to success.

Lucky stayed around the bar for a few more days and talked to some of the locals while the others just seemed to drift off and latch onto other folks who seemed to be optimistic about finding something. None of them were serious participants, and none of them had ever been on a true expeditionary journey into the north. Good riddance.

Within a few days, a couple of local Indian band members who hung around most of the time seemed to listen to his fabricated plight to find the cabin of his dear long-lost friend Black Mike, and his desperate need to pay homage to his memory by placing a Bible on the last spot he was known to have been. But as they listened, with a gleam in their eyes fired up by the beers, it wasn't the plea that made them interested—it was the money, and money was scarce in a little town like Fort St. James, especially outside hunting season when it was everyone for themselves until the next year.

It took almost a week for Lucky to separate what he thought were the good Natives from the not-so-good. He knew they were all after the money and didn't give much thought to Black Mike, but he needed those he could trust would guide him there and fend off any predators.

Lucky had no resources in the town and was staying at the local motel adjacent to the highway. There was a knock at his door one night, and a couple of local Natives filled the frame, side by side. Benny and Jimmy had met up with Lucky a few times in the bar and claimed they could help him find his way. They sat on the bed and drank some warm beers while Lucky laid out his plan.

"An' the money? What about the money?" Benny asked.

"Yeah, the money, Lucky. When do we get the money?" Jimmy echoed.

"Listen, you guys, I got money, but it ain't here. It's in the bank, and that's where it stays until the job's done."

Benny and Jimmy looked shocked.

"Don't we get any now?" Jimmy asked.

"I'll give you an advance. Let's call it a deposit, and we're going to have to pick up supplies and things, so we need to do some shopping over the next few days." A couple more beers were cracked open as they made a list.

It included everything from sleds to food, tools, gunpowder, and tents. They would only be able to manage what they could fit on the three sleds, and each of them had to pull them through the bush.

Once equipped, with the sleds packed up and the dogs that Benny and Jimmy had brought along from the reservation running all around them, they began their long assault into the bush. The Natives had no need of the map, but Lucky followed it so that he could remember the landmarks, the twists, the turns, the creeks, and the valleys, and he added notes as they went.

There were a few loops of lost meanderings as they closed in on the cabin's location, but all in all, Dirty Tommy's map was good enough to guide them. And at the end of the route, he had drawn a gold bar, outlined with stars and exclamation marks.

It took nearly three weeks to make it to the cabin. After the first night of rest there, Lucky persuaded his guides that they could leave while he would stay for a few days to soak up the memories of his dear friend.

Lucky paid his trackers half of the money and told them who at the bank in town they needed to see to get the rest. He gave them a note to take with them for the banker, who would have a similar note to match up. That was his only guarantee they would not turn on him in the wild and leave him for dead after they took the money. It all worked out, and everyone seemed happy. The Natives knew where he was in the event the other half of the money didn't turn up, and that was all the surety they needed to treat the relationship as successful.

6

Lucky's Moment

Lucky didn't want to sleep in the remains of Black Mike's cabin, not that there was anything of comfort left there after so many years. Instead, he slept in a pup tent off to the side.

It took Lucky a few more days of living rough and searching before he discovered the mine portal in the scree partway up the mountain that Black Mike had started and Dirty Tommy had blasted out. It hadn't been totally hidden from view, and, with a small amount of effort, Lucky broke through the pile of stones and brush that had been piled in front of it before he fell into the narrow decline. He crawled through on his belly, a flashlight tied to his old pit helmet, to where the decline widened enough for him to squat on the soles of his feet and look at the walls and roof around him. His eyes took a while to adjust to the shadows that were cast across the angular rock faces, his light bouncing off at different depths and rock faces. He slowly acclimatized to his surroundings, albeit uncomfortable in a permanent knee-bent stance, but his butt settled into a natural position that balanced the rest of his body. His excitement mounted as he realized what was in front of him. There was no doubt about it; the gold veins were prominent and narrow with a small cluster of nuggets located sporadically along the length of the strike. As he moved forward in a crouch, scraping his flattened feet across the uneven floor, the space became larger, Dirty Tommy having followed the veins that branched in several directions into the walls and roof, resulting in an open space of something like fifty feet long and about six feet wide. It was a cavern with multiple gold veins striking in all directions on the walls, with some ending or disappearing into what had yet to be explored.

Six hours later Lucky crawled out of the cave, delighted with his find, and congratulated himself on having had the strength, endurance, and will to get to this point from the oppressions of jail in Prince George, let alone from his little village in Sicily. He had already made up his mind to sketch out the cavern, show the veins, describe them in terms of thickness and potential, and establish their directions. He was no geologist, but he knew the discovery was substantial—perhaps not a world-class mine but certainly one that could provide a good living for a poor, neglected Italian boy so far from home. He felt that he had suddenly become something, someone who could make a difference, someone people would talk about.

He often talked to Black Mike and Dirty Tommy as though they were watching.

"If you guys could see what's here, you'd be blown away. But you did it—or we did it—when no one else could. We made it. We struck the mother lode."

He was sure he heard them talk back to him on occasion.

"About fuckin' time someone found it. It's been lying here for a million years, and that goddamn Dirty Tommy could have got it if only he had tried harder." That was obviously Black Mike. But maybe it was just the wind as it howled through the portal and down the adit toward him. But Lucky didn't complain. He was sure they were with him, and that was all that mattered.

Over the next two weeks, Lucky went back underground each day, spending six to eight hours in the dark with just his headlamp to guide him, and plotted and noted his findings. He thought about his next steps and how he was going to keep the secret until he could record the land in his name and gather the financial resources he would need to develop the mine. Sure, he could take enough gold out to get things going the next season, but, according to his rough calculation, it was going to take quite a bit to get the capital he would need to get into any kind of production that made sense at thirty-five dollars per ounce. Going back and forth every year for what may prove to be just pounds at a time was not going to be sufficient to pay for a mine to be built. That would require more like four and a half tons of gold.

No, the best way forward was to solicit help from his Sicilian friends. They could be trusted, and they had the money to help, and he was desperately looking to use his newfound knowledge to raise his stature with them. Surely, they would be excited with the prospect of owning a gold mine. He had to get back to civilization.

His confidence over the weeks he had been in the bush had risen enormously, and the discovery only heightened his sense of invincibility as he made his way back to Fort St. James with a small pouch of gold nuggets. He fully intended to keep the secret for as long as he needed to get things organized, including land title. He made his way east along the logging trail to Prince George and the minerals title office to register his claim, all the while keeping to a low-level dialogue and not once claiming to have discovered anything. It seemed that little in the Toodoggone area had ever been entered into title. He had expected the licenses to have at least been filed but lapsed after both his predecessors had died. But no, it seemed as though neither had taken the time to get them registered, so it was easy to conceal the importance of the find to the title office. It was not that they were particularly concerned with land value, but if someone who worked there knew about a gold discovery, word would spread quickly.

7

Lucky and Sicily

Lucky sat at the same bar he had sat at before his great adventure waiting for Mrs. Mike Black for four days. She never turned up, and word was she had gone off with some gold digger to Dawson City, hoping to make it big. Apparently, she had already written Lucky off after a few nights of sex and hadn't fully realized how serious he was, although she was mad with herself for giving up a copy of the map just for sex, even though the sex was good.

"Too bad," Lucky said to himself after waiting, hoping she would turn up and remembering the fun they had had and the promises he had made. He fondled the pouch of gold nuggets in his pocket, having intended to split them with his benefactor. Perhaps they could have gotten drunk together again.

The next day, Lucky went over to the telegraph office and sent a note to a friend in Sicily whom he knew was well connected. He just didn't know how well. The response wasn't positive. No, they weren't interested in developing a gold mine in some godforsaken area in northern Canada! Money was a lot easier to come by than through honest means, and where the hell was Canada?

This isn't going to work, he thought, judging the telegraph to be a useless instrument for communications that demanded more emotion. It showed no excitement other than the use of apostrophes, exclamation marks, question marks, question marks, more question marks, and all-caps. He needed to go to them and explain what he had found—and take some proof.

Lucky had enough gold to make the trip, stay a while, and return to Canada if he needed. He wasted no time and telegraphed for a sleeper on the train to Montreal and his cabin on a Marseilles-bound ocean liner. He felt elated, successful, and full of enthusiasm about the future. He also thought about whether the Mafia would take up the challenge or not. And what if they didn't? What if they thought it was a lousy idea and sent him packing? As all those thoughts floated through his brain, something was gelling that could be the answer for a back-up plan. If they didn't like it, he would find a way to go it alone no matter the costs. While that frightened him, it also invigorated him. He needed that way out whether it was truly feasible or not.

The trip back to Sicily was nerve racking. All he could think about was the gold, the adventure, the excitement, and the wild enthusiasm he was going to be met with once he laid everything out. He couldn't fathom the ultimate extent of the find, but his imagination envisaged such an incredibly huge potential, with himself sitting on top of a stack of gold ingots, a ginormous Cuban cigar poking out from the side of his mouth, a Panama hat tilted to the side of his head, and women hanging from both his arms—the epitome of success!

In most ways, Lucky was not a big thinker when it came to the world at large, but he did have the savvy of someone who watched out for an opportunity. While he was not a gold digger by nature, he was a person who listened and watched within his fraternity for an opportunity of some kind—any kind—to present itself.

Lucky's telegraphed message had climbed its way up until it reached Meyer Lansky who, coincidentally, had been searching for an answer to his "problem"— where to stockpile the hundreds of tons of gold the Napoli branch had been handed as WWII came to an end. The message languished there on Lansky's desk with a paperweight holding it down. It was always in his vision, but he wasn't a trusting person by nature, and Lucky's message didn't seem to solve his problems. But as he rolled through the potential solutions, he concluded the Vatican was definitely out; they wanted too much of a fee. Banks were not trustworthy, and the Swiss—well, the Cosa Nostra despised the conservatism of the Swiss and their haughty, snobbish attitude to anyone outside their world. He was playing with the idea of splitting the loot up and hiding it in several places around the world.

8

Lucky and Lansky

"Who da fuck is dis Lucky Loochiano? Do we know dis guy? What'd he want?" Lansky was fingering the message Lucky had sent. Now that Lucky was in town, it seemed he needed to pay some attention to it.

Lansky spiked another ball of spaghetti on the end of his fork, twirled it, and pushed it into his mouth. He didn't chew much, letting it all slide down his throat in one lump. That was how it was done in Sicily. Not a lot of taste so much as texture.

Lansky sat at a restaurant with his associates in the village square. Mama made the food. The note from Lucky wasn't much to go on, but for some reason Lansky was intrigued and began to form an out-of-the-box thought. He thought and thought some more. He made thinking faces, stuck his bottom lip out, picked his nose, scratched his head, and got up from the table.

"Bring dat sonafabitch to me," Lansky said to no one in particular.

* * *

Lansky's problem had started as the war was coming to an end and the fleeing Nazis sought to hide what looted art and gold riches they could.

It was already well known that as much as one hundred tons of gold, which was being kept in the Reichsbank, was moved by rail when the bombs started falling. Some of it was stashed in a potassium mine 200 miles southwest of Berlin. That was recovered by Patton's troops when workers at the mine told them what lay within, and other smaller lots found their way to other hiding places.

Despite all the rumors of gold being dumped into Lake Toplitz and small finds, such as watertight casks of Nazi gold being discovered in other lakes in the mountains of Austria and new discoveries being made every year, even in dormant accounts in the Bank of England, there remained a holy grail for the treasure hunters. Even the whereabouts of Peter the Great's Amber Room seemed to have been resolved—although, for some strange reason, not yet officially confirmed and never considered to be a part of the war loot included in the 84-million-ounce tally.

But the majority went missing, and the Allies had no clue where it went and instead speculated who was likely involved, including Argentina, the Vatican, the Cosa Nostra, and, of course, the German and Swiss banks. The interconnections had been unraveling over the last seventy-five years, but in 1944 it was Lansky's problem to find a safe storage location away from the prying eyes of some of the most sophisticated government and private agencies in the world, led by the UK and the USA. Both were doggedly persistent, and both knew the rough value of what they were looking for. The very least they had, as the war ended, were many of the records from the Swiss banks and a lot of talk from the banks in Berlin, Munich, and Frankfurt, not to mention the concentration camps that kept meticulous records of their work, including the gold shipments. The remnants left behind presented the tip of the iceberg of what was out there.

Gold and currency that had already made its way into accounts in neutral countries, such as Switzerland, simply kept moving. A US Treasury agent's report that was filed in 1946 (and declassified fifty years later) indicated that millions of dollars in gold coins wound up in a numbered Swiss account belonging to the Vatican. And in January 2000, a civil suit was filed against the Vatican Bank, the Franciscan order, and other defendants.

By far the largest amount of gold ended up in the hands of the Cosa Nostra, which had commandeered the gold through their eventual control of the German banks through intimidation, blackmail, and murder. It was there that Meyer Lansky played a pivotal role in managing the gold. He and his associates had strong connections to the Swiss National Bank, and Lansky provided them with the way to launder hundreds of millions of dollars in gold into their anonymous accounts, including a substantial amount to the Vatican for safekeeping.

But Lansky was a sly fox. He and the brotherhood siphoned off most of the gold before it made its way into those anonymous accounts, but he still needed to figure out how to keep the bulk of the gold away from prying eyes.

*   *   *

Lucky came face to face with Lansky within the hour of his summons. The restaurant was deserted, and they sat at a small table in the most discreet part of the room with a bottle of grappa between them. Two of Lansky's henchmen, Alfonso and Giuseppi, sat facing them but at the next table leaning over the backs of their chairs, watching. Lucky hated grappa but took a slug regardless, and to please Lansky, of course.

"What is this to-the-dog-on?" Lansky waved a heavily gold-ringed hand at Lucky, who had seemed to shrink some in his chair. Lansky slurped a knot of spaghetti into his pliable mouth. The first plate had gone cold while he waited for Lucky. But then, he always had time for pasta, followed by a two-hour afternoon nap.

"Toodoggone. It's a gold area in northern Canada."

Lansky wiped his lips. "Where is dis Canada?"

The conversation wore on, and eventually Lansky understood. He sat back in his chair, tipped it onto the two back legs, and stared at Lucky. His mind was gearing up to speed. This could be the answer he had been searching for. This to-the-dog-on underground mine could be the ideal "safe" for the Nazi gold.

"I like you, Lucky. You're a guy close to my heart. Do you feel it?"

"I do, I do," Lucky replied, not quite sure what he was responding to, but it seemed to be the right thing to say under the circumstances. He wasn't sure whether to trust this guy or not. There was something about him, but at the moment he wasn't in any position to negotiate or look for an alternative.

"Lucky, I think you can be very useful to us. Now tell me more about this too-dog-gone thing, and maybe you and me can put a plan together."

"Well, I found it when no one else could, and it seemed to me that we could make use of it. I'm not the brains here, but I figured someone could do something with it. You never know... maybe it's a gold mine, and we could work it. But I dunno. I just wanted to bring it to you."

"Glad you did, Lucky. It seems like it's a good find, altho' I have to admit I don' know where the fuck it is." He laughed, and so did everyone else, including Lucky. "But let's suppose it's a good find. What we gonna do with it?"

"Store the gold, boss?" Alfonso looked at Lansky and shrugged. "Could work, boss."

"Yeah, I think so too, Alfonso. Let's think about that." Lansky was happy, and the guys were happy. Lucky wasn't quite sure what they were talking about, but it sounded good, so he was happy and just wanted to get out of there alive at that point.

"Listen, Lucky, we're goin' to be friends. I can tell you dat, an' you are gonna be one of my lootenants." Lansky grinned from ear to ear, as did Alfonso and Guiseppi. This could be the solution to the problems that had been nagging them for a while now. "I'm a gonna make you in charge of dis caper once I get de nod from Napoli."

"Sure, boss." Lucky was hesitant, excited, happy, and reluctant all at once. What if the boys in Napoli didn't want him to be a part of the team? What if they decided to take the mine for themselves and cut him out? But he had no choice but to stay with the plan and hope that his knowledge was enough to carry him. He didn't realize how much influence he really had, but his confidence hadn't built yet to the point that he knew how to control his future.

Lansky patted Lucky on the back, put an arm around his shoulder, told him to stay close in one of the pensiones in town, and promised to get back to him within the week, or maybe a month. He liked him, Lansky had told him, and Lucky felt charmed. This was going to be his big breakthrough into the Cosa Nostra. The man with the big ideas. The "Golden Man," they would call him.

*   *   *

Lansky needed to educate himself more on Lucky's information before he could take the idea up the chain of command. There were a couple of alternatives. From what he could figure out, they could either build a mine and store the gold there, or they could just store the gold there. He didn't like the idea of having to build a mine at all. Too much work and too much attention. In any case, why build a mine when they had all the gold they needed without lifting a finger other than to store it?

Lansky visited Rome to talk to some better-educated folks about Canada, building a gold mine there, the possible costs, and how he could go about creating a legal entity to shelter the operation in a cloak of legitimacy. He didn't like what he heard. All of it was way too much work. Then he needed to better understand the logistics for getting the gold over there, including shipping routes, costs, and what it would take to round up the equipment and crew needed. He liked that idea, and it all seemed reasonable and feasible to his simple money-making mind.

Once Lansky had put his ideas together, he pitched the scheme at a meeting of his local Cosa Nostra membership in Palermo. They weren't impressed and seemed to be hung on to the remoteness of this too-dog-on location and their lack of knowledge of where the gold would be going and the potential for getting involved in a legitimate project that would raise the attention of people they didn't want to get involved with. No, they weren't impressed. Not even as a safe haven for the gold. Way too much could go wrong. And where was this Canada? It sure wasn't in Italy, and that was a problem for them.

Lansky was disappointed but encouraged by what he was discovering, and at that point he really needed to find a way out of his dilemma. Not only were the Swiss and the Vatican pressuring him, so were the top brass of the Cosa Nostra in Rome as well as New York—and that was pressure.

Lansky took Lucky with him to meet the Napoli branch. Lucky lent a sense of reality to the plan. He had been to the mine. He knew how they could do it. He also knew what the risks were: none. Neither of them advocated for a mine to be built. They had put their eggs in one basket and went for the storage option. They even had a plan of how to filter the gold out to the market as needed.

The Napoli branch liked the ideas, but they all agreed "We no build nuttin'," and that was that. Clearly, they saw no reason to make an investment in mining gold from scratch when they already had a substantial stockpile of their own that needed little additional investment other than for storage and security.

Lucky was somewhat disappointed, but Lansky was elated. He really didn't want to get into a mine construction and operation business. He preferred making money the easy way—through crime. Lucky, on the other hand, had raised his own profile with the Mob people who mattered to him, and his name was referenced whenever the subject of Nazi gold came up.

The Napoli branch was tough but eventually agreed to a practice run to figure out the logistics before thinking about whether it was practical and cost effective to move all 2,000 tons of the gold into such a remote area, where it could remain for quite some time. And moreover, they especially wanted to know how easy it would be to get their hands on it when additional money was needed.

After several more days and some long nights of planning, Lucky took the Napoli branch through his plans and promised that he would have more definitive answers after he completed the practice run.

Lansky convinced the Napoli branch that it would be better than a bank vault, hidden from prying eyes with a tag of legitimacy that no one would argue with. And no fees. This was a property that, if played right, could leach gold into the outside world forever and never be questioned. In those days, while Lansky and Lucky didn't know it at the time, there was no Securities Commission, no regulations, no shareholders breathing down your back, no NGOs that gave a darn about grandfathered prospects, and no government interference to worry about. The Toodoggone mine supported a potential underground mine development that could be gradually enlarged to store the looted gold.

Lansky had really come to appreciate Lucky, although not enough that he would try to salvage him from the vindictiveness of the Mob if something went wrong with the plan. In fact, Lucky was his potential foil.

Lansky nominated Lucky as the coordinator of the venture. They were both sure this was the solution to their problems of gold storage for the long term. They could avoid Argentina, circumvent Vatican interference, cold shoulder the Swiss banks, and hide amongst the weeds of post-war investigations by the Allies. This was the real deal. This was big. Bigger than the Mafia had ever been involved in, and it dwarfed their other ventures to the point that they never appreciated what was truly involved. Billions of dollars in gold that they never had to lift a finger to get and always ready if and when they needed it.

9
Lansky's Plan

Prince Rupert is located on a deep, undeveloped fjord about five hundred miles as the crow flies northwest of Vancouver. Canadian Customs paid little or no attention to the comings and goings in that part of the world. In fact, it had often been a resting place for German submariners during WWII who crossed through the northern reaches of the Arctic to avoid detection by the US as they made their way south and then turned at Tierra del Fuego to the Atlantic and headed north, looking for easy prey. The US had never bothered to set up any sophisticated submarine detection systems on their west coast. That was where America had felt most protected during the European war, and the likelihood of a Japanese invasion never really crossed their minds. It was too far—or so they thought. Of course, that was a serious mistake.

Nazi gold would flow beyond the borders of Europe to South America, around Cape Horn, through Drake Passage, and north to Prince Rupert on the west coast of northern Canada, where Lucky would take over. It would be a forty-five-day journey (there was no Panama Canal in those days) covering some 14,750 miles, a huge undertaking but not an uncommon one.

Anyone linked to the transactions, other than Mob members, were dispensed with, and Lansky started moving the practice shipment of one hundred tons of gold offshore.

"Dominici, my friend." Lansky appealed to his boyhood friend who had risen to become a young but influential part of the pontiff's advisors. He was certainly moving on to having a role in the Vatican Bank, and the Cosa Nostra knew this. "This will be good for our church, for our people, and for you. We

38

need the seal, and we need you to do what you have been trained for."

Dominici was in his late twenties and still impressionable, but he knew where his allegiances lay. Plus, his family was at stake, and he was reminded of that every time Lansky or one of his people contacted him.

"Please don't worry, my friend," Dominici said, breaking out in a sweat, as usual when Lansky called. "I will get the seals and add them to the paperwork and talk to the officials. Where are the containers going?"

"Just tell them the freight will be going to Canada. Tell them Montreal."

It didn't matter to the Italian customs where exactly the shipments were destined for. The name of the country was good enough. It was common for trans-shipments to happen when containers could be redirected at the will of the freight forwarder.

"You will not regret this, my friend. The fee will be transferred as soon as the shipment leaves Italy." Lansky hung up his phone and smiled.

So now the Vatican was part of the plan, and Lansky had an agreement in place to act as the conduit for the gold heading to Canada under the Vatican seal. Lansky was happy.

The Vatican never knew where the final resting place for the gold would be. They were guaranteed their cut, as were the banks and anyone else involved in the transfer. The Cosa Nostra could settle back with the knowledge that they were well funded forever to take control of governments and power brokers when the time came. The remainder of the scurrying Nazis had no time to turn back and search. They carried armfuls of loot—as much as they could handle—and headed offshore, most notably to Argentina. The influence of the Germans had matured there over the years through investments, influence, and control of places such as Patagonia, a remote mountainous paradise filling fast with Nazi refugees.

During, and long before, WWII, Argentina had an open-door policy on immigration. In the aftermath of the war, Argentina's door was opened even further and to a much more sinister group of people: Nazis and their collaborators fleeing Europe to escape trial (or, one supposes, a bullet in the head courtesy of Mossad) for their war crimes.

Despite an official position of neutrality, Argentina actively supported Germany during the war after Juan Perón traveled there in 1943 to discuss the possibility of an arms deal between the two countries. Following the war, Germany worked with the Perón government when he became president and organized the emigration of multitudes of Nazis to Argentina. They included Josef Mengele, Adolf Eichmann and his adjutant Franz Stangl, Erich Priebke (a former captain in the Waffen SS), Klaus Barbie—also known as "the Butcher of Lyon" (a former captain in the SS and a member of the Gestapo)—Ustasha Dinko Šaki (the former commandant of the concentration camp that was nicknamed the "Auschwitz of the Balkans"), and many, many others.

The fleeing Nazis were given landing permits and visas, and it has also been claimed that many of them were even given jobs in Perón's government.

No one asked questions in Argentina, and the Germans headed to Patagonia to hide out in luxury. But in all the panic, the Germans had lost track of the gold. It certainly wasn't coming to Argentina, and they had no idea where it would end up.

And so it was that by the fall of 1944, Lansky and Lucky had marshaled over one hundred tons of unrefined gold ingots of varying sizes and shapes and transported them from the shores of Europe to Prince Rupert, on the west coast of British Columbia, Canada's westernmost province, with the Pacific as its shoreline.

The gold was transferred to five flat-bed Mack trucks for the eight-hour journey to Fort St. James, over 350 miles away, before being hauled on tractor-hauled skids along the rough track through the outback that had been cat-skinned by local Natives and two old but serviceable Caterpillar 60 rubber-tired dozers into the Toodoggone area, 160 miles into the dense forest. The local Natives had no problems. This was what they did. Sometimes they skidded camps in for would-be fishermen and their chalets, sometimes for hunters or miners, and sometimes for their own kin to spend some time hunting and fishing. It was all in a day's work, and when they were finished, they went back to the reservation and waited.

It was a wilderness with no easy ground access and likely never would have. It had no settlements and was generally of no interest to anything other than moose, grizzlies, wolves, wolverines, and marmots.

Even then they needed two local Native-operated dozers to travel ahead of the tractors and trim corners and small rock outcrops and create creek crossings from locally felled timbers for the sleds. The going was rough. There was no asphalt, only logging roads, gravel, mud, marsh, and sometimes nothing but forest. That initial journey took almost two months, but once the first load had been transported, the dozers continued their work to create a more passable, but still very rough, route through the forest, deliberately made to prevent trackless vehicles from using it.

It was a long, tough, but worthwhile task. To all intents and purposes, the gold had disappeared from the face of the earth. No one knew other than the few, and all of them were somehow related to the Cosa Nostra. No one else—not the Vatican (or at least most of them), the highest-ranking German Nazis, the SS, or the banks knew what had happened to that one hundred tons. There was simply no accounting of the total magnitude of the plan. The gold had simply disappeared while the Allies were only just starting their search but still coming up empty and finding but a few gold crumbs by comparison to what had already disappeared and what was about to.

Lansky had taken a huge risk on the relatively unknown Lucky Luciano, but Lucky had come through. He led them to Fort St. James, then on to the mine, and there it was, a cavern just as Lucky had described. Large enough for the initial haul at least, and if it wasn't, then, hell, they would make it so.

Lucky was charged with the responsibility of governing the "vault." He had a couple of mobile trailers hauled in and set up for a bunkhouse and cookhouse. He also brought in dogs, equipment, and provisions and staked his spot in the wilderness with a few of Lansky's most trusted Mob members. They brought in supplies and building materials and strung a roll of barbed wire fence around the property. The entry was marked by two oil drums ten feet apart with a tree trunk resting on them.

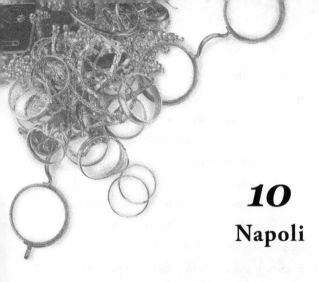

10
Napoli

Lansky had gone back to his Mafia contacts in Naples and reported on how well things had progressed with the initial one hundred tons, from transporting to storage at the mine. He had photos of various phases, including the mine site and the gold ingots being taken underground. Lucky posed on one of the gold pallets as it was being unloaded from one of the tractors at the site. Clearly, he was pleased with the venture, his thumbs tucked into the loops of his suspenders as though that was the mark of success. Lansky described the storage area and the rock that had to be blasted to make room for the complete gold hoard. It was all possible, and costs would be reduced now that he knew what needed to be done and how to reduce the time needed for the complete cycle, from loading to storage. Lansky persuaded the Napoli chapter that with improved access and sources now established for Native labor and equipment, future loads could be transferred in about four weeks less time, and maybe faster if he could improve on transportation efficiencies.

Napoli was as happy as a Mafia chapter could be and decided to move the rest of the gold into hiding in discreet amounts of one hundred tons per month. Encouraged by Lansky, they agreed that would allow the site-based people to enlarge the cavern for loads as they were received. The campaign took two years to complete before all 2,000 tons or so of gold, including an assortment of sacks of gold paraphernalia, were neatly tucked into the side of the mountain at Toodoggone, one of the most remote regions on earth.

* * *

The gold arrived as certified ingots that had been looted from banks. It included crudely made ingots comprised of melted gold rings, teeth fillings, earrings, ornaments, cutlery, and other paraphernalia contaminated with bone fragments, other jewelry ingredients, adhesives, and, of course, fake gold and knock-offs. Also included was gold taken from bodies and stacked together in skips and sacks.

At first Lansky didn't comprehend the complexity of the issue. All he knew was it was gold, but clearly his managers wanted more. What kind of gold? Was it marketable? Could it be sold? What about the bone fragments? It was quite a dilemma for Lansky, and he was beginning to wish he wasn't the prime mover. But he had taken on the task of storing the gold, and he felt he should at least better understand what was needed to put the gold on the market once any of it was released. It wasn't that he felt obligated so much as it had to be better understood if his Mafia friends were going to be involved. And they were.

He knew the certified ingots were already 99.9 percent pure and stamped with authenticity numbers; he had seen them. The crude ingots were more like 35–45 percent pure with no stamps other than perhaps a marking that showed where the gold came from, whether that be a death camp or a foreign source. The original crude gold was a mixture of 14 to 24 karat. Each karat is equivalent to 4.167 percent gold, such that 14 karat gold contains 58 percent of gold, while 24 karat is considered to contain 99.9 percent gold. Some of it had already been mixed with various alloys depending on what the end product was intended to be. Jewelry represents the single largest use of gold, and because gold is soft, it is mixed, or alloyed, with other metals to provide the requisite hardness and strength. Typical jewelry alloys are gold-silver, gold-copper, and gold-silver-copper.

The lower the karat rating, the more alloy had been introduced. A rating of 14 karat meant the piece contained 14 parts of gold (or 58 percent pure) and 8 parts of another metal or metals to improve its physical properties or add color. For instance, white gold is an alloy created by adding palladium, but federal reserves and banks want 24 karat gold with a 99.9 percent purity, so everything but the gold content had to be removed from the haul.

Through his discussions with a variety of banks, Lansky realized that all the gold had to be refined, including the certified ingots that needed their stampings replaced before it could be distributed for full value without penalties. The task had to be undertaken by a certified international refiner at some point.

Lansky didn't know much about gold to start with, but he was learning. The gold industry was still a fledgling in Lansky's days, but there were some rules in place, and Lansky sought out help in understanding some of them from his Swiss banking associates.

Only so many gold refiners in the world were accredited by the London Bullion Market Association (LBMA), the center for gold transactions even in those early days. Gold produced in any of the accredited refineries was acceptable on the world gold trade markets. Each ingot needed a unique serial number embossed on it along with a certification paper. There was little room for forgery.

The logistics of certifying the amount of gold involved with the release of the Nazi loot onto the market were going to be challenging, but with the help of the Swiss bankers, Lansky became somewhat educated. At the time the top seven refinery groups in the world had a combined gold refining capacity of only 5,500 US tons per year—just over twice the total capacity of what had to be stored in the mine. Lansky was still a worried man. He was now well outside his comfort zone and had no idea which way to turn for help. But he was a fast learner and realized that if only one- to two-hundred-ton batches of gold were released for refining, it was something the refining industry would be able to cope with, provided the arrangements were made well in advance. After all, a release that would mean a cash payment in the order of $5 billion to $9 billion each time was significant enough to get the attention of any refinery, especially if their fee was double the usual amount.

Most major banks have a gold business side that never sleeps—as one market closes for the day, another elsewhere in the world is opening. One gold bar, with a value of around £430,000, is currently held in a London vault. The bar comes from Krasnoyarsk in central Russia, which is also the name of the refinery. It is stamped with a unique serial number, a stamp that includes the refinery's logo, the refinery's identification number, a number that denotes purity (in this case, 99.99 per cent, as pure as it gets), the assayer's stamp, the year of manufacture, and the gross weight of the bar—in this case 12.124 kg (26 lb).

None of the crude gold bars had anything like these markings and essentially only had the markings of where the bar was cast or which concentration camp the loot came from. On average their ingot product was just above 9 karats apiece (around 37.5 percent pure). It was a telltale of what the Nazis were really getting for all their atrocities.

Without a hallmark, gold cannot be legitimately and certifiably sold.

To date, some 170,000 tons have been mined worldwide—which would fit in three Olympic-size swimming pools—but there are only 90,000 tons of known resources remaining. This means that at current extraction rates, the world will run out of gold in thirty years—unless there is an alternative supply—and that is likely best filled to the largest extent by recirculation of the product.

Gold never corrodes or degrades, which means all the gold that's ever been mined is technically still in existence—the ultimate recyclable product.

With mining companies going to increasingly exotic and politically risky areas for decreasing gold grades that need higher processing costs, from the far northern reaches of Canada to 17,000 feet above sea level in the Andes, exploiting such sites requires massive investment before mining can begin. For instance, in northern Canada, gold miners could find themselves 500 miles from the nearest road.

What could be better, more profitable, less aggravating, and less costly than having a ready-made product at hand with relatively little costs, other than for transporting and refining?

Gold was the product that everyone trusted, yet it was controlled by those who had no propensity for population health, safety, or concern. It was just a tool used to control. And neither the Cosa Nostra, the Vatican, nor the global oligarchies had any appetite for adding value to the welfare of the general population. They just wanted and wanted more. Power was everything, and everything was power. Gold was just a tool, and Nazi gold was free.

Initially, Lansky thought they should build their own refinery, but as he educated himself more into the complexities of doing so, it was clearly too much to take on. Hauling in acid, creating sufficient power, not to mention the toxicity of the fumes that would be given off in the process, made them rethink the plan. At the time of the original planning, they hadn't even considered what was needed to authenticate the gold bars in terms of ingot stamps and papers. It was all too much to think about for them. There was no way they wanted that challenge compounding what they were already tasked to do: store the gold.

They decided it would be more efficient, and logistically simpler, to refine the gold after each batch had been hauled away from storage. There were enough locations on the way back to Europe, as well as in Europe, where the gold could get refined and stamped even in those days.

Better to leave it to the future to make whatever arrangements had to be made. Of course, at the time they were debating the issue, the involvement of Global Gold had not been solidified, but in the end, it would be them who would handle the refining aspect, and they would do so as a bonafide gold production company with the same connections as anyone else in the industry.

While Lansky and Lucky didn't have the foresight to know this, they felt comfortable with their decision. Their task was to store the gold until it was needed.

Lansky was not stupid enough to think he could just "get by." By the time the gold needed to be moved to market, someone else would be responsible for refining it, and Lansky would likely be dead. His problem right now was getting it to storage and keeping it safe from prying eyes. That's all he wanted to focus on. It was enough.

11

Matthew Black

Vancouver—Today

It was a beautiful spring day in Vancouver as Matthew Black sat on his balcony overlooking the ocean with his bedtime sidekick, Emma. They watched the container ships as they curled through their moorings, depending on tide and current, with the laser sailing dinghies and small sailboats dodging around and between them. The girls went by on the boardwalk below in their skimpy summer outfits, their male followers trailing behind.

Matthew and Emma sipped their tall iced-vodka Americanos as they thought about what to do with their time off. Summer on the west coast offered so many choices for recreation, from sailing to skiing to mountain biking to hiking, browsing stores, bar and gym hopping, eating, or lying around reading, thinking, or just going blank.

Matthew was in his early forties, athletic and fit, with a reasonably well-sculpted body and short, curly black hair. He was intelligent, and he had a quick wit and was an easy conversationalist. His natural charm, white teeth, smile, and square jaw disarmed most people, but he was not narcissistic to the extent that he couldn't be constantly alert to his surroundings and ready to spring forward to react to any threatening situation when needed. Emma was not only his favorite lady, she also happened to be his favorite co-conspirator and the daughter of his boss, Murray Stockman. They had worked on a couple of projects together, sometimes with Emma just watching from the shadows in case he needed help and sometimes with her front and center.

Emma was single, athletically constructed, fit, and in her early thirties. Her everyday style preference was for short-cropped black hair cut in a pixie style for easy management and minimal makeup. Clothing was optional, but her preference was for black jeans, a short high-collared white shirt, and high-cut ankle boots. She could always camouflage herself as a feminine female any time, but it was not what she was comfortable with, although she was one sexy lady with no lack of libido.

Matthew looked over at her as though comparing her with the girls on the boardwalk. He wasn't, but that's how it might look to anyone else. He really liked and respected this lady, and while they were not romantically engaged in any long-term relationship, they were each other's go-to whenever they needed it, but they weren't tied. If the situation presented itself, there was always the potential to take it in stride, and they often did, for the sake of the project as well as... well, just because. They often shared their experiences, but most times they did not.

Their thoughts were disrupted by the ringtone of his cell phone. Not only did the tone, which replicated the barrage of cannons from the 1812 overture, reveal the caller's identity, but the 357 area code meant it could only be Murray Stockman calling from Cyprus. Mathew gave Emma the eye, and she understood that it was her father on the phone.

"Hey, my friend. What's up?"

Even though they had known each other for more than a decade, there was no small talk. That could come later, but for now they both reserved phone time for short, pointed information with no names.

"We've got a live one. Better get yourselves over here so we can go over things with the crew." Murray clearly knew that Emma was at shoulder length from Matthew, which was just fine.

"Where's here?"

"Ankara—Friday morning. I'll have you two picked up from the usual place. The rooms are reserved for Thursday and Friday night. But you will have to decide for yourselves what to do after that depending on how things go. I'm sure you won't have a problem figuring that out." There was no sarcasm, just the facts. That was Murray.

The line went dead. Matthew's incoming email already had the reservations confirmed for their business-class seats on the next evening's Lufthansa flight out of Vancouver to Frankfurt and on to Istanbul and Ankara. The decision on what to do with their summer was no longer in their hands. Emma unwound herself from her lounger, downed the rest of her drink, then pecked Matthew on the cheek and let herself out of the apartment.

"See you at Departures tomorrow."

She headed back across town to her own place to prepare herself mentally and physically for their next project.

Murray managed Matthew's activities as well as his daughter's in the world of industrial sabotage and manipulation, and he had done so since he engaged Matthew ten years earlier when he was a young, energetic, clever exotic metals welder with a mechanical engineering degree in the petrochemical world and was tagged even then as a potential saboteur operative. Matthew was recruited as an agent for ORB, the Organization for the Reorganization of Business, created by Murray to intercede wherever in the world it was needed to "redirect" business, political, or religious efforts that were considered to be off course or going off course. Sponsorship came from governments, corporations, and charity brokers as well as wealthy individuals dedicated to maintaining the status quo. The validity of a cause was considered and voted upon by a group of twelve selected by the sponsors.

Emma was just as qualified as a saboteur and held her own easily in the male world of welding, anything from tanks to piping, tubes and pharmaceutical-grade metals. Her father adored her, and her fit with Matthew was perfect and natural. She was clever, intuitive, and ready to react to whatever the situation required. She never failed, and she was never demanding. It helped that she adored her father and truly cared for Matthew.

Matthew had become a seasoned professional saboteur with a wealth of practical qualifications that few could rival. He may not have the skill set for political restitution, but he certainly had the ground domination needed in the practical world. His relationship with Emma had grown exponentially since their first liaison when she was a mere shadow of his activities. Now she was a formidable force and an expert physical saboteur in her own right. Matthew and Emma had come together on that first project, but they knew each other from their previous work when Emma was merely known as "E" from the weld symbol she had to emblazon on her high-pressure welds in the petrochemical industry.

The following evening, Mathew and Emma headed to the airport in separate cabs. They had one carry-on each, a Canadian passport, a spare UK passport, some US dollars and Turkish lira, and a brief on where they needed to go and what the arrangements were. There weren't many. He had done this all before, and Emma was no redneck.

They both traveled in business class but never conversed or exchanged glances. That was the primary rule. Do not be seen to be together. Often they traveled on different carriers, but in this case their schedules didn't allow that point of safety.

Esenboğa airport is located twenty-eight kilometers northeast of Ankara, the capital of Turkey, but is still not considered an international airport to the extent that one would expect. Besides Turkish Airlines, only Lufthansa, Austrian Airlines, and Swissair offer direct flights from their European hubs. For other carriers, flying through İstanbul is the only choice.

Ankara, the capital of Turkey, sits in the north-west part of the country on the Anatolian Plateau at an elevation of some 3,000 feet above sea level. A lexicon of races and religions mixed up in one of the greatest human melting pots on Earth. It's where east meets west, where the tentacles of the old Silk Road trade routes were used as a passageway for merchants moving from one country to the next with their wares. Where ideas were exchanged along the route, and spices traded for wines and silver, silks for wools, precious stones for rugs, and where animals from all over found their way to new worlds. It's a place where religions have fought for hundreds of years. Christians and Muslims continuously at odds, until the Turkish Ottomans were eventually defeated in 1918, three years after their victory at Gallipoli.

While Ankara languished for several centuries following the Ottoman defeat, it became an important center again when Kemal Ataturk chose it as the base from which to direct the Turkish War of Liberation and create the modern Turkey we see today. It has stayed on the map of international politics ever since.

No other country shares a claim of being part of two continents. Turkey has embraced the situation with a comfortable grace and attitude, often running from one to the other depending on the politics of the day. But the one thing it has never achieved is acceptance by the European community as being one of them. Turkey is still considered somewhat barbaric, too "Third World." Politics, that's what it really was.

Matthew and Emma flew from Vancouver by way of Frankfurt and Istanbul on Lufthansa before eventually arriving in Ankara with Turkish Airlines—more than twenty-four hours of traveling from the Canadian west coast. They were tired and ready to head to the hotel, even though they would like to have played a little. They took separate taxis to the same hotel.

The Hilton—or "Heelton," as the taxi drivers called it—would make a welcome break until the morning, when a driver would pick them up from the hotel lobby and take them to meet the others. But that was ten hours into the future. For now, Matthew and Emma relaxed in the lounge bar on the ground floor and sampled the local cold beer, Efes, and the usual roasted nuts. Both of them surveyed the property, keeping their eyes open for anyone who might be tailing them, but his jet lag got him before he could finish a full surveillance, and he had to head up to his room. Emma and Matthew cheek-kissed on the fourteenth floor as she got out, and he carried on to the sixteenth. No one appeared to be following, but at that point he wasn't overly concerned, sleep being his main priority.

For now, some bottled water and two melatonin pills were what he needed—with a shot of Laphroaig, of course, and then, hopefully, some quality sleep. Emma called as he climbed into bed, but it was brief, just to say goodnight, that all was good, and that she was also headed to bed.

Matthew had a restless sleep. He dreamed of covert assailants from his past, of would-be assassins from his future, of difficult people who had made an indelible mark on his subconscious, and of impossible situations. They were all mixed up in a crazy concoction of ridiculousness contrived to impart a feeling of undermining his reality. Truth was too difficult to deal with. Reality was hard to differentiate from fantasy, but that was the overdose of melatonin working. Reality was confusing and unreal. In the morning, he struggled to wake up and throw off the dreams. Today was another day.

12
The Turks

The shiny black Mercedes E550 picked Matthew and Emma up in front of the hotel at 10:00 a.m. and then artfully navigated its way through the considerable traffic. About thirty minutes later, it slid onto a badly maintained side road followed by a narrow gravel track with high hedgerows and gnarled, stunted oaks that threw their shadows over the path. Occasionally, Matthew saw a backdrop of fields of high grass and the city in the distance. Sheep littered the track but gave way easily to the Mercedes and a prod from the herder. No one was going to travel very fast there, but then, no one had to.

On the outskirts of Ankara, about forty kilometers from the "Heelton" and over an hour through the loud, unruly congestion of traffic, into the village of Pecenek, two of the most powerful and well-connected Turkish ex-politicians lived a rural but luxurious life nestled in the privacy of a small but ample house in a well-contained area at the end of the gravel road that led through a settlement of no more than 200 people. It was a poor community of farmers eking a pitiful living from the dry soil but happy with the prospect that they had survived the growth of the sprawling city contained to the other side of the highway. They were also thankful to their political benefactors, who now lived among them, providing them with advance notice of approaching vehicles and generally providing them with ever-watchful eyes.

The Mercedes edged through the tiny village, almost scraping a stone wall here and there as the way narrowed and then widened. The smells in the air were of the moistened earth as the sporadic rain rattled down in five-minute bursts. Rainwater collected in pools as the car splashed the sides of the road.

Within a few minutes of each downpour, the water evaporated in all but some of the larger ponds, where holes in the tarmac were left in disrepair and ducks would waddle over for a refreshing bath.

As the Mercedes approached the old wrought-iron farm gate that sat askew with one hinge slightly out of whack, a peasant woman in a headscarf appeared and tugged it open. It groaned under the movement, and the car slipped through and parked on the lee side of the house, away from prying eyes.

As Matthew and Emma emerged from the car, they heard the gate groan again as it closed. Then the old woman trudged over to them, head slightly bowed, eyes averted, and held a hand out in front of her to show the way around the corner of the house to a neatly manicured garden, concealed from view by two weeping willows that reached their tentacles down to the grass on all sides. Between the trees were three tables set with plates, some cutlery, and baskets of bread. Some iceboxes were set on the ground, and the old lady pointed toward them as if in invitation.

Matthew reached out to one of the boxes while looking up at the old lady as though seeking her approval and opened it to find a variety of bottled soft drinks sitting in ice. He took two without further invitation, snapped the caps off both with a twist of a nearby spoon, handed one to Emma, and then chugged at his bottle. As he lowered it to the table, people started to come out of the house. He spotted Murray Stockman in the middle of the bunch. He never seemed to change and was always a welcome sight.

Murray came forward and grabbed Matthew's right hand. "Good to see you, old boy. Nice drop of rain, eh?"

Matthew smiled. "What are you—or should I say *we*—up to this time, Stockman?"

They both laughed as Murray caught hold of Matthew's shoulder and turned him around to face the others.

Murray put his arm around his daughter's shoulders and hugged her. He kissed her on the forehead, and she held him close.

"Hello, Daddy."

Murray gave her a squeeze and then smiled as he turned his gaze to his other guests. "I'd like both of you to meet some of my friends."

There were six of them. It was difficult to tell if they were all Turkish just from their looks. The cross-breeding over the years, combined with the integration with the Silk Road travelers, had resulted in one of them with blond hair and fair skin, another with a decidedly Slavic look, two others with a Parisian look that seemed as though they had just stepped out of a European café, one who retained the angularity of the Turkish nose and jutting chin that so often gave Turkish people that noble, proud look, and the last with an olive complexion, curly black hair, and a prominent nose. He seemed unfamiliar with those around him, following them at a distance.

"My friends," Murray said, "this is my beautiful daughter, Emma, who is on the team, and this is my friend Matthew Black, who I have mentioned to you occasionally. I have had the pleasure of working with Matthew on a number of extraordinary projects just like yours." Murray bowed his head as he turned from the group to Matthew.

As each reached out a hand to Matthew, the group introduced themselves one by one, as though rehearsed, in perfect English.

Emma remained subdued and decided to introduce herself to each person after Matthew had done the rounds.

"Hello, I'm Misha. It's very good to meet you, Matthew. Welcome to our home," said a well-maintained, older, aristocratic Turkish lady with coiffured graying hair, expensive jewelry and clothes, brushed makeup but not overdone, and an experienced look in her eyes. She waved her arms at the house and the garden in one continuous, fluid movement. "It's small, but my husband and I love it here. Away from the madding crowd of the city but close enough to those we love, and we so enjoy it here in our little oasis." Her English was perfect. She smiled as she held out her arms to Matthew as though waiting for him to come to her.

"It's a pleasure to meet you, Misha. You have a beautiful place here, and so peaceful—especially compared to what I've just traveled through." He moved a little closer, gave her a bow, and turned to whom he assumed was her husband, a large, balding, mustachioed, barrel-chested man who held his hand out and took Matthew's. He put his arm around Matthew's shoulder as though he had known him for years.

"She could never leave all this, Matthew. She was with the government overseas for years, and I'm afraid this is now and forever more her retreat, her hideout from everything and everyone." He laughed gently, not taking his eyes from Matthew's.

"I am Eric—a pretty dull name for a Turk, I'm afraid, but it has made me feel at home in so many countries. My birth name is Kemal, but Eric seems to be more of a universal name from the Scandinavians to the English to the Americans and those darned Germans—but perhaps not the French. But then I hate the French, so it doesn't matter!"

"Oh Eric," Misha said as the others laughed, "you can be such a bore at times. The French are fine—as long as they keep producing good wine, food, and, of course, clothes." Her comment was met with more polite laughter.

"Come, let me introduce you to the others." Eric turned first to the other two ladies, extending his palm to one of them. "This is Helena, our token purebred Turk, who has never enjoyed the pleasures of travel to other countries and so can easily imagine a Turkish empire again."

Helena smiled and gracefully shook Matthew's hand as Eric turned to the other woman. "This is Sophia—our guardian angel who watches over us to make sure we never drink too much and tell tales that are too tall."

Sophia was not backwards in coming forwards. "Please forgive us, Matthew. We could have all met on Zoom or some such thing, but what would that do for us? We need to see, touch, and feel, and this is still the only way we know how. Would you like some refreshments before we bore you with the last of the introductions?" She ignored the open bottle on the table in front of Matthew as though that had not been a part of her rehearsal. Nor did she wait for an answer but turned instead and waved gently toward the house. A man and a woman emerged laden with trays of more social drinks and appetizers. Everyone waited until the refreshments were placed on the table and each person was given a napkin and small fork. The two turned and went back toward the house, splitting up before they entered as the man headed toward the side entrance where a barbecue had been set up. He doused the coals with some fuel, then struck an overly large match and tossed it into the center. There was a brief explosion of flame before it settled down to turn the fire into glowing embers.

"And this is Murat." Eric had guided Matthew over to the next member of the group, who held his hand out and smiled effusively. He grabbed

Matthew's hand with both of his and shook it excitedly.

"I am so pleased to meet you, Matthew. Murray has talked a lot about you—all of it good, I must say."

Matthew smiled back. "That's good, Murat, but I hadn't realized there was that much to say. It's a pleasure to meet you, and thank you for the welcome."

Matthew turned and walked toward the next to last person in the group, an elderly, short, robust Turk with dark-set eyes, a balding head, and a large, open smile.

"I am Mustafa—the dwarf with a dream." He shook Matthew's hand as vigorously as Murat had.

Matthew smiled. "What is your dream, Mustafa?"

"To be as large as my wife and take her to bed over my shoulder instead of her doing it to me!"

Everyone laughed loudly and clapped.

"Ever the optimist, our Mustafa," Misha said, having recovered first. "But then, we are all optimists, which is why we have asked you to join us, Matthew."

Matthew looked a little bewildered but had learned over the years that when dealing with Murray, there were always surprises. Matthew enjoyed surprises, but more often than not they came with risk.

He looked at each member of the group, who stood smiling before him. "Thank you all so much for your warm welcome. I hope I can live up to your expectations—whatever they are."

He turned to the last quiet, suspicious-looking member of the group with a questioning expression on his face and held his hand out.

"I am Yousef, a friend of the family," the man said as he shook Matthew's hand, leaving his introduction at that. Matthew raised an eyebrow but decided not to venture further.

"Good to meet you, Yousef," Matthew said as he pulled his eyes away from the suspicious look.

He turned his head to settle his eyes on Murray's. The discomfort he had felt with Yousef subsided but didn't quite go away.

"Come and sit down, everyone." Murray put his arm around Emma's shoulders, whispered something in her ear, then led the group over to the willows, waving toward the trees as he guided each of the ladies to their seats. The men fended for themselves.

The sun had come out again, the clouds had scattered, and the evening was starting to settle in. Not a sound around them. No traffic. No children playing in the alleyways or the road. A high wall overgrown with ivy surrounded the property, and Matthew noticed cameras aimed in a variety of directions mounted on poles strapped to the inner part of the wall, hidden in part by the tangled growth around them, all of them turned outward.

Murray looked around at the group before him. "It's always difficult to start, but let me do so by inviting you to listen to a seventy-year-old conspiracy story that has matured into something that is real and requires resolution. It's why I'm here with Matthew and Emma.

"I think you all know that when Hitler came to power in 1933, the German treasury was bare. The government was running scared, and that's why they became looters on an international scale."

Murray allowed himself an ironic smile. "They quickly learned that Germany's financial security could be improved with the gold stolen from Holocaust victims and the civilian populations of occupied countries.

"The Swiss bankers and money launderers took in over four billion dollars' worth of gold at 1945 prices, or about eighty-four million ounces, which would amount to a value of about one hundred and twenty billion dollars using current prices. That's more than one year's total global production of the yellow stuff by today's reckoning."

Murray waited for his audience to take in the magnitude of the numbers before he continued. "You can imagine that the SS started exterminating people just to loot their personal jewelry, watches, rings, and even their gold dental fillings, many of their victims being Jews herded into notorious death camps, like Auschwitz. It had now become mass extermination for the sake of greed.

"The gold from the internment camps was sent to the German central bank, where it was re-smelted. Most of the plundered gold arrived at the Reichsbank in crates that bore the stamp of the concentration camps where the gold had been confiscated, but by the end of the war, thousands of bags of gold had not been melted down. And then it all disappeared!

"Which brings us to today. The difference is that now we have a pretty good idea of what happened to the gold, and these folks," Murray opened his arms as if to embrace those around him, "want it returned to the rightful owners—or at least to their descendants."

Murray looked at Yousef, and a piece of the jigsaw of whom Yousef was dropped into place as he assumed that Yousef represented the interests of the State of Israel.

"And my good fellow," Murray glanced over at Matthew, "that is where we come in."

"Where do Turkey and our friends here fit into all this?" Matthew asked, looking around the table.

"The Turks had been duped once again by the Germans," Murray said. "The gold hoarding in Turkey was claimed to be their way of eventually repatriating it—with a fee, of course." Murray held his hands up in supplication and shrugged his eyebrows.

"You probably know that Turkey played all sides of the war. First as an ally of Great Britain and then of the Germans. You see, Turkey was the sole supplier of the chromite ore that was used to strengthen the German steel armaments. It was so critical for the Nazis that Albert Speer stated that their war effort would come to a complete stop ten months after the supply was cut off. But Turkey was so desperate for the money that they couldn't stop themselves.

"In the end, Turkey was forced to stop due to continual pressure from the Allies, and the German war machine came to a grinding halt just as predicted. But by then Turkey had lost track of the hoarded gold.

"The Allies pressured Turkey over the restitution of the looted gold but abandoned their position when it became clear they needed Turkey to help them contain Russia. It was just as well because the Turks had no idea where the gold was."

Murray took another sip of his lemonade and looked up at everyone. "Everyone with me?"

Other than Yousef, who remained stoic, the group nodded in encouragement.

"Over the years," Murray continued, "theorists believed the looted gold was funneled to Argentina by high-ranking Nazis. So it was a real twist of fate that while it was Turkey that had triggered the end of the war for their own gain, it was the Germans who had appeared to be the real benefactors—twice. What a coup!

"What we know now is that Argentina was not, in fact, the final resting place of the loot. We also know that the Bundesbank has repatriated seven hundred and forty-three tons of what we believe is the stolen loot over the last ten years."

Murray looked around the table again, meeting each gaze. "There have been so many conspiracy theories on this subject—the Vatican, Swiss banks, the Mafia, Ustaše, the CIA, SS sympathizers... the list goes on.

"We think that one of the most likely scenarios is that under the regime of the Napoli Mob boss at the time, Giovanni Carmino, Meyer 'The Lure' Lansky, stole the gold to finance the Cosa Nostra, or at the very least provide them with an eternal war chest, and the gold was shipped offshore to a secret hiding place.

"Our job is to identify the gold's final resting place and return it to the ancestors of the victims by way of our clients, this group before us." Murray waved his hand to his audience.

"That's where Matthew, with the help of Emma and many others, comes in. Matthew is our main man in the field. His responsibility is to identify the location of the gold and get it out of wherever it's stored and back into the hands of those who own it, or at least their descendants. He is fully supported by our off-site teams, who are responsible for the freight logistics, legal issues, and information of the other groups involved, including the Vatican and the Mafia. I think we have it well covered. Oh, and my job is to keep you all informed." He paused and smiled. "On a more serious note, remember that Matthew and Emma are essentially resources who are acting for us all below the radar. You cannot discuss who they are or what they are."

Everyone nodded their understanding. Matthew raised a hand to attract Murray's attention. "I'm still not sure where Turkey comes into the scene."

"Let me just say that this is really a matter of their acceptability into the European Union," Murray replied. "The next council resolution is in six months' time, and we need to beat that deadline if Turkey wants to become accepted into the Union. It's an unspoken creed and is the last hurdle for them."

The truth was out. It would take more than only stopping the slaughter of cattle on one national holiday each year, but also halting other barbaric habits the EU considered beyond acceptability to the culture of their membership to gain entry into the most prestigious international cooperative—the European Union. The reconciliation of a fundamental international scandal was required to provide the remedy, and they were ready to resolve that issue.

"That's about it," Murray said, opening the floor for the others to respond. When no one did, Murray went around the group, shook hands, smiled, joked, patted shoulders, embraced, and provided words of comfort. The Organization for the Reorganization of Business (ORB) would do the best they could; they always did.

He turned to Matthew. "When you come to Copenhagen, we can talk about the how, when, and where." He shook Matthew's hand firmly and slapped him on the shoulder. "Chin up, old boy. It's never a problem working on the right side of life!"

With that, Murray disappeared through the gate and into a waiting car that whisked him away, leaving Matthew to consider what he had just heard. This was a truly complex matter of personal and business identity. Matthew always tried to err on the side of business, but his personal feelings also came into his decision making. The project also had to meet his internal moral compass. The mix of the two values was where his true identity lay. But for a moment at least, he could relax and take in the culture and listen to the gossip of politics amongst his new group of friends.

Emma seemed intoxicated by her new acquaintances, and they were obviously drawn toward her. She was delicious, engaging, and educated. She talked to them about their discoveries, doing a far better job than Matthew could have done. He was ecstatic that she was working with him in the open. She had discovered so many details as a woman that a man could never discover.

He and Emma left the small group a couple of hours after Murray. They had made some new friends they could count on in the future. Yousef remained a ghost, but while he never opened up to them, it was clear he was on their side. He wanted what they wanted, and if they needed an attack force, he could arrange it, no problem. Just give him a few hours' notice.

Their car was ready, and they sped back to the Hilton where they would spend just a small part of the night before catching the early morning flight to Istanbul.

Matthew and Emma relaxed in the lounge bar and talked about what they had heard.

"Any thoughts, Emma?"

"I think we need to find that fucking gold and get it back to the Turks, although I think that creepy guy, Yousef, is very irritating and could… let's just say… be Mossad."

"Me too. I like him." Matthew sipped his Efes. Emma looked at him as though he had something missing.

He finished his beer, kissed Emma on the forehead, then headed up to his room to freshen up. Emma tucked her legs under her on the lounge chair and called for a raki and ice. She wasn't ready to leave just yet.

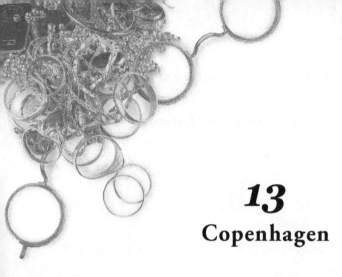

13

Copenhagen

The Scandinavian Airlines 767 circled Kastrup International Airport in Copenhagen twice before coming in to land and taxi toward its Terminal 3 slipway. It had been an eight-hour journey from Istanbul through Frankfurt. Along the way, Matthew and Emma had managed to get some rest, read, and consider their situation. He was about to get involved in yet another ORB venture, and he needed to get into the right mindset to accept that. He shared his concerns with Emma, but she was somewhat thoughtful and distant, and he understood this to mean he should take it all in his stride, and she had her own issues to worry about.

It was a rare pleasure for Matthew to visit Copenhagen, although it had always been on business trips, but he had learned to stay away from the crush around Tivoli Gardens and instead head for the luxury of a boutique hotel near the ferry terminal where the boats came and went to and from the rest of Scandinavia. It was Emma's first trip to Copenhagen, and it would have been much more of a delight for her had she been able to take more advantage of a trip through the incredibly tasteful and beautiful sights of the city with the myriad of cyclists who naturally carried out their daily chores in suits and office wear.

During his first few visits to the city, Matthew would take a cab from the airport, but now he had learned to take the train directly from Terminal 3 to Kongens Nytorv St. and walk to the 71 Nyhavn Hotel at the end of the canal near the ferry terminal for Malmo. It was such a pleasure to walk along the canal and be surrounded by the colorful four- and five-story houses, the bars, the boats, the noise, and the scenery, with young people spilling out of the pubs with their sandwiches and beers.

The 71 Nyhavn Hotel was such a cozy place to stay. Located away from the madding crowd, it was still just minutes from the hubbub of the bustling pedestrian and cyclist-driven city center dominated by the royal palace.

The hotel had started life in 1804 as a warehouse and eventually developed into a charming, romantic getaway complete with Pomeranian pine beams and small but luxurious rooms where one could happily romp in bed all day or sink into the soft pillows with a book. Ideal for a weekend retreat—or for someone looking for a hideaway with a view of the ferries or the canal. Matthew and Emma luxuriated in the comfort and relaxation of Matthew's room, knowing it could be their last of such nights for a while.

Matthew showered, shaved, downed a gin and tonic, chewed the lime, plonked down into the small but comfortable chair by the window overlooking the wharf, put his feet up on the windowsill, and pulled out a file to read the descriptions of his fellow conspirators. He browsed the profiles, recognized a couple of the characters, and stored the rest of the information in his brain for the morning. Emma did the same but with a naked vodka. They didn't talk, just took in information from what was in front of them.

Matthew prepared his clothes for the morning, set out his man products, kissed Emma on her eyelids as they stretched out on the bed, and then threw his arm across her as she stroked him. The warning signs were there, and there was no point in fighting nature, but he needed to. It was already late, and they had lost nine hours through time zones. Emma's body was warm and tucked into his side. She was so delicious, so beautiful, and so incredibly comfortable. But before they could drop into the snore zone, Emma got up and headed to her room down the hall.

* * *

The Pakhuskælderen Restaurant, or Packhouse, as it was known to the locals, was located in the hotel's cellar level—an intimate, low-light atmosphere where booths provided privacy and comfort, and the chefs had mastered a refined combination of honest Danish cooking with an eclectic mix of dishes from around the world. The wide selection of wines was notorious throughout the city for its variety and caliber and was displayed on the walls around the perimeter of the seating area.

Murray was at the restaurant bar to meet Matthew at 8:30 a.m., sipping a tomato juice while he waited for his breakfast session and taking in the headlines of the *International Herald,* a favorite of his whenever he traveled. What a troubled world it was. There seemed to be no end to conflict in every direction. The Middle East, Africa, Pakistan, Indonesia—all caught up in religious fervor. Shiite versus Sunni, Muslim versus Christian, Chinese versus Tibetans, Indians versus Pakistanis—if it wasn't some fallout over religion, it was a more serious fallout over cricket. Then there was Iran versus the great white Satan, and Israel versus almost everyone. Extremists, fanatics, junkies, drug lords, pedophile priests, lesbian lovers, gaylords, single mothers, the CIA, the FBI, subversive this and subversive that, and that didn't include the latest acts of God with floods, fires, hurricanes, and earthquakes. What a world it had turned into.

Murray skipped some pages and went to the Sports section. At least there was some respite from the world. But the first gay hockey player? Okay, that was part of the new age, but Murray accepted the changes with great interest and support.

Murray folded the paper and laid it on the bar. He looked at his watch as Matthew came down the stairs and extended his hand in greeting.

"Haven't seen you for ages, old man. You're looking good." A broad grin broke Matthew's tired face.

"Very funny," Murray shot back, shaking Matthew's hand vigorously. It had been almost two weeks since their meeting near Ankara, and he and Matthew had been on the trail in different directions. He pulled Matthew over toward a door in the corner of the restaurant.

"This seems to be a strange one for us to handle, Murray. This is hardly a business that must be reorganized. It's more like a few countries!" Matthew looked at Murray as they stopped before they reached the restaurant door. ORB usually carried a trademark method of high-level interference using government and private consultants to "reposition" certain companies within the global community when the companies were incapable of doing so themselves. Successful and smooth, they had a membership of un-linked professional individuals who were not always armed with the full story—just enough to do their portion of the job. In the case of the Nazi gold, ORB was getting involved in the business of countries and criminals, not just companies.

"Look at it like this, Matthew," Murray said, glancing back at him with a twinkle in his eye. "All we're doing is repositioning a group of companies at the same time. They just happen to be called Cosa Nostra, the Vatican, and the German banks, not to mention others that will certainly be impacted!"

Murray sauntered into a small, secluded private dining area at the back of the room. "Let's meet the others."

They were faced with a small group at a rectangular table already well into their breakfasts—open-face sandwiches, a few beers, a Jägermeister or two, and coffee. Emma sat at the end of the table, just one of the boys, chatting to everyone. She knew them all, and they all knew her—not just as her father's daughter but as a real activist with ORB. She brought value, and they all knew that. She was not shy about telling everyone that. But then, they were all like that. Matthew and Emma felt as though they needed to hide their intimate association from the group, although the consensus appeared to be that everyone knew that something was going on, but nobody cared as long as they did their job.

Like the other meetings, there were no formal introductions, just a wave, a nod, or a smile from each member of the group. Matthew noticed the two faces he already knew apart from Emma and gave them a nod and a wave. He didn't dwell on his lack of knowledge of the others. Their bios were enough, and, in all likelihood, they would not be meeting again unless something dramatic happened to change course. He trusted Murray implicitly to coordinate them. All Matthew needed to understand was what other bases were covered and what his resources were when he needed information or help.

Murray closed the double doors behind him and pulled curtains across to muffle any sound and provide an additional barrier against any intrusions. He went to the far end of the table where a laptop and projector had been set up. He slipped a memory stick into the laptop and pressed a key.

"I know you have all looked over everyone else's bios, so you should already be up to speed on where each person's strengths lie. You all have a binder that summarizes a lot of the things we don't need to cover here, but it's all good background that you need to understand. I have kept the details to a minimum, but if you have any questions, make sure you contact me.

"Most of you know Matthew, and I'm pretty sure you all know Emma, my daughter, both of whom have been on a number of projects with me as well as in the company of some of you. Mathew will be responsible to complete the physical transaction, and the rest of us will provide the support. Emma will support Mathew in the field, as she has done before, but this time she will be more, let's say, visible." Murray pointed to his daughter, who nodded. "I remain the overall coordinator, and you all report to and through me."

Murray clicked on his remote, and the screen lit up at the end of the room. He let the words "Nazi Gold" on the screen sink in for a few seconds. One more click and then two photos. One was of a large skip containing gold rings and the other gold-rimmed spectacles.

"These are facts, everyone, but it's just a small sample." Murray lingered for a moment while the group took in what they were looking at. "About hundred and twenty *billion* dollars' worth of gold, by today's reckoning, was snatched, grabbed, ripped, and stolen from Holocaust victims and the populations of invaded countries by the Nazis and their friends during WWII—with a haul over twenty-six hundred tons. Can you imagine?" He stopped and looked around as the numbers sank in.

"Of course, these photos," Murray pointed at the screen, "show the worst of the atrocities, where personal effects were ripped from the bodies of their victims. The vast majority came from the looting of homes and businesses, including banks. Some of the gold has been accounted for, but most has not.

"We already know that Germany has repatriated nearly seven hundred and fifty tons of the loot over the last eight years to prop up their debts to the European Community after bailing out the poorer countries, but something like two thousand tons of gold has never been accounted for, and that's what we are looking for. We've narrowed the location down to somewhere in northern British Columbia—that's in Canada, in case you don't know. More specifically at a latitude of around fifty-five degrees north.

Murray wasn't ready for questions, and the group knew that. He flicked to the next slide, which said, "Bundesbank—Vatican—Mafia."

"These are the three major culprits in the scheme, but read the dossier I've given you. All the details are there. Who are our clients and why? Who did the looting? Who was involved in spiriting the gold out of the country? Who's looking after it right now? Where we think it is roughly located, all that stuff. I prefer you to get educated enough to ask me questions that you consider are pertinent to what you need to do.

"What we know, in general terms, is that our clients have confirmed that the Mafia, the Vatican, and the Swiss national bank, acting for Nazi Germany, are the culprits in this conspiracy. However, we don't believe the Nazis were capable of organizing such a complex, large-scale project as making some two thousand tons of gold disappear as the panic set in near the end of the war. We are, however, sure that with the Vatican's help as a conduit using their sovereign seal, the Mafia managed to make the gold disappear, and none of the others knew what happened to it.

"Why the Vatican? you may ask. Let's remember they were almost bankrupt at the start of the war despite the opulence they display. The deal with the Cosa Nostra meant they got a fee for every ounce of gold that passed through their hands, and they probably kept a few ounces on the side. But, as it happens, the Cosa Nostra needed the Vatican to help contain the Catholics as much as the Vatican needed the Cosa Nostra."

Murray clicked to a photo of an overweight, cigar-smoking, hooligan-looking guy with an Italian look. The caption beneath the photo read, "Giovanni Carmino."

"Some people estimate that during the last months of World War II, the Italian mob boss at the time, Giovanni Carmino, had close connections within the Swiss national bank and the Vatican. It was Lansky who initially 'lured' the Nazis into handing over more than one hundred tons of the looted gold for 'safekeeping' with the Vatican. That never happened quite how the Vatican thought it should. The gold disappeared into the Mafia's hands.

"That got the ball rolling for the Cosa Nostra. The clients of the Swiss banks had little choice but to use them to move the gold. Some of the gold was tracked, but most of it was not. This all happened during the panic of war."

He moved to the next slide, which was titled, "2000—Vatican Legal Case."

"In a 2000 court action against the Vatican, they did not deny that a large shipment of gold arrived in Rome in 1946, but they claimed sovereignty and wriggled their way out of any kind of liability, but we are pretty sure they actually made away with well over two billion in 1945 dollars. No questions yet, guys—let me finish." Murray held up his hand, looked down at his notes, and moved to the next slide: "Tracing the Gold."

"Our Turkish friends traced the gold shipments that had arrived in Frankfurt about eight years ago back to a Brazilian refinery, Queiroz, to the south of Brasilia. one of the largest in the world. The paperwork and stamps verified it. The gold had been trucked all the way from Callao, a port south of Lima, Peru, to the refinery. They discovered that the shipment had arrived in Callao from Prince Rupert, a small port on the west coast of British Columbia. It didn't take much more of an effort to discover those containers were delivered to the port from someplace called Fort St. James, a desolate frontier town on the fifty-fifth parallel in the outback of British Columbia. The tracking goes cold before that. What we have to do is to figure out exactly where the balance of the unshipped gold is, get to it, and repatriate it. Sound easy?"

"I guess that would be Argentina, boss," a team member named Colin said, stating the obvious.

"Not quite," Murray replied, moving to the next slide: "Argentina or ???"

The group sat in stony silence as they waited for the next shoe to drop.

"Now, some might suggest, like Colin, that the gold was stored in Argentina. After all, that's where the high-ranking Nazis all made off to at the end of the war. But these days we don't think that's realistic. You see, gold mining was in its infancy in Argentina in the forties, fifties, and sixties and never gained a foothold until much later, so the idea of storing large amounts of gold there never gained traction, or should one say, would have gained too much attention! But storing gold in Canada, in one of the most prolific gold-mining areas of the world—what a concept! And then releasing it into the market as they needed. Simple plan, run by an unscrupulous Mafia-controlled group collectively known as Latitude 55, coincident with the general location of the loot.

"But even in those days they knew they needed credibility. Lansky contacted his Cosa Nostra cousins to find out who in their organization might qualify to be the figurehead for the property and eventually leach the gold out into the market without raising suspicions.

"The name Theodore Munch popped up—a Hungarian Jew and Canadian citizen and one of the wealthiest people in the world. He was CEO of the largest gold-mining corporation in those days, Global Gold Inc., which was founded by some Russian oligarchs. It also happened to have a few senior members of the Cosa Nostra as majority shareholders, although they kept their profiles very much below the radar. Munch and Global Gold had the pedigree to facilitate the property in British Columbia, and when tucked into their portfolio, it never garnered any attention.

"On the basis of all we knew, we narrowed the prospects for gold storage to the Toodoggone region east of Fort St. James as being the most probable fit. We think the specific location had been identified by an old miner, Black Mike, back in the 1920s, and eventually passed on to Lucky Luciano back in the late 1940s, and he was the Mafia connection. But we must remember that we are dealing with myths, legends, and perhaps reality here." Murray shrugged and smiled, then carried on.

"This is one serious location, everyone." Murray looked around at the group. Most had never ventured farther than the forty-ninth parallel, and the idea of there being anything of worth beyond never gained traction. "If you want to get into the site, you will need dog sleds or, better still, bulldozers. It would take two to three weeks to make the trek through the bush from the nearest almost habitable place, Fort St. James, which has only just come out of the bush itself. The specific location still eludes us, but we *must* find it. That's where Matthew and Emma come in.

"Now, we know that one hundred tons of unrefined gold made its way from Europe to the west coast of British Columbia sometime in 1945 or 1946 and onto trucks up to Fort St. James before the shipment disappeared into the forest. We also believe it was followed by a lengthy campaign of freight being taken into the same area.

"Recently, when Germany repatriated some gold in 2013 and again in 2017, Tom and his IT guys discovered that substantial amounts were paid into the Mafia and Vatican banks in the late 1940s as well as when these recently reported amounts were repatriated. We think they were the fees for the gold transfer back to Germany.

"So what does all this mean? Well, we have learned that these days a little man named Marino De la Hora is our key to unlock the gold's whereabouts. Since the death of Lucky Luciano and Lansky, both in the 1960s, there have been a number of gatekeepers of the gold-laundering movement, but none as clumsy or as greedy as De la Hora. He works out of Global Gold's Vancouver office. As far as our informants tell us, he has zero social skills, zero sentimentality, and zero consideration of others, but he does have an insatiable greed. De la Hora is unscrupulous but a little sloppy after all this time when it comes to managing a secret so old and so valuable. The probability is that he has no idea how it started and has zero concept of regret. But he is still a Mafia man and answers directly to his handlers in Italy.

"Let's assume we locate the gold, seize it, and turn it over to our client in Turkey for them to repatriate it. Let's also assume that we go one step further and implicate the Vatican such that they have no choice but to submit to international financial rules and not only release whatever gold they have in storage but also submit to the scrutiny of criminal investigations for their participation in the biggest money-laundering scheme in history."

Murray paused and looked around the table. "Tom, you and James need to work with the same banks as De la Hora, all of which are headquartered in Switzerland, are gold carriers, and are open for business to the Mafia. I'll confirm the bank names and best contacts for you after this meeting.

"Gerry, you need to look at how we may be able to ship directly from the Canadian coast over to Izmir on Turkey's west coast.

"Bernard, coordinate with the Turks about how to receive the gold and get it through customs and into the refineries, which our client will arrange. We have some excellent contacts in the freight business in Izmir who are on board. Also, find out what you can about the gold-refining business and who is who in that world.

"Daryl, make sure we are legal in every direction. We need the right paperwork, clearances, transfers, etcetera. Start with the Turks in Ankara. We may need to set up a separate import-export company and transfer a few dummy shipments to make things legitimate. But we can't just transfer a ship full of gold out of Canada and into Turkey without it being a legitimate corporation.

"Colin, find out everything you can about Global Gold—their board, the board members' friends and family, histories, financial situation, who's trading, who controls the stock, all of it. Matthew will handle Global on the ground, but he will need support.

"Matthew, you need to work on a couple of fronts. Get to Vancouver to see if you can rattle any information out of Global Gold and then head up to Fort St. James. See if you can get eyes on that gold and make all the necessary arrangements to get it out of there and over to Turkey. We'll talk more about that as we go forward. Emma, shadow Matthew in Vancouver, but you need to be his go-to person once he gets into the field. I'll expect you both to work on that.

"Gerry, make sure you line up contact names in the Fort St. James area in case Matthew needs support. Visit the local port at Prince Rupert as well as labor and equipment brokers. You will find the Natives to be the best resource for both, and they're not likely to gossip to non-Natives."

Murray lowered himself into a chair and faced the group. He nibbled at some toast and sipped a beer as he looked furtively around at the faces concentrating on him.

"We'll need a contact list," Gerry said, "as well as passports, money, and—"

"All arranged," Murray said. "As usual, you will all have credit cards that access a communal bank account, multiple passports that will give you entry almost anywhere in the world, visas, and contact lists for each of your tasks as well as one for each other. The code name for this operation is NG-Liberate2000. That's also your password for access to all server information and background on what you need. Make sure you dump all your information into the server files that are already set up with your file names. I'm always available on my encrypted cell. Matthew and Emma, you will both communicate via satellite phone, unless you're in a city. Anything else?"

Everyone looked around at each other and shrugged, then shook their heads.

"Let's get started," Gerry said. "Once we get the tools, perhaps there will be more questions."

"No problem," Murray replied. "If there are, make contact through me, and I will send a circular out if the information needs to be known by anyone else." Murray raised his eyebrows. "All clear?"

One or two people got up to leave. Others finished their breakfast or just sat and talked to each other. They were all aware of the confidentiality rules. No one talked to the others unless it was through Murray.

Murray got up, tapped Matthew on the shoulder, and then strolled out the door.

"Are we good?" Murray asked once they were in the lobby.

Matthew nodded. "For now. But I'm sure things will heat up soon. Had a good talk with the Turks after you left, and I'm pretty sure where to start. I think a trip to Global Gold's offices in Vancouver is my first stop."

"OK. Let's circle back in a month or so once we see where we are with things."

"Any timeline?"

"Yes, two. The European conference is in September, so Turkey needs to know where they are placed. That's five months from now. I also think De la Hora is going to move fast now that he knows there's a problem. He's going to want to either move that gold out of there or remove everyone who gets in his way so that he can continue to store it. So the faster we move the better. No time to waste on this. We don't want our target to get ahead of us. Questions?"

Matthew knew what his marching orders were, and he didn't need to question them. He needed to take out De la Hora, neutralize Global Gold, identify where the gold was stored, and then get it the hell out of there. Everything was as clear as he needed it to be, including the fact that he had five months to pull it off.

"Nope, no questions," Matthew said as he and Murray shook hands and then walked off in different directions.

14
Back Home

Matthew flew back to Vancouver from Copenhagen through London.

The scenery through the cabin window never ceased to delight him as they circled over Vancouver Island, flew relatively low over the Strait of Georgia, and headed toward the runway at Vancouver International. They had managed to take in the sight of the multitude of islands in the strait, lying like jewels in a basket of blue water, and the rather brown contrast of the mighty Fraser River as it dumped its sediments into the delta close to the airport. The ripples of the waves made just enough crests to give the water a shimmering look as a few boats sped or sailed from one side of the strait to the other and the occasional ferry transported passengers between various islands and the mainland. It was a beautifully clear day, and the coal mountains at Point Roberts Terminal stood high against the backdrop of beauty as another train pulled in to dump its latest load from one of the coal fields in eastern British Columbia, to be shipped to China.

It was always a delight to be back in the fresh air and head home to his place in Crescent Beach, just outside Vancouver. The place was secluded, overlooked the strait, and was framed by the majesty of 200-year-old firs and cedars. He had designed and built the 7,000-square-foot house, complete with pool, bar, billiard table, and theater and all the amenities that a large family of wealth might need. The only trouble was, he didn't have a family, but he loved the space, the tranquility, the view, and the feeling of being in the country without being overly isolated and with easy access to the city.

But he was not going to be relaxing for long. He needed to catch up on jet lag and then gather himself to enter the business world of mining. The first thing he wanted to do was start buying stock in Global Gold, sufficient to get the attention of the executives and open the door to the board room. After that he would head north to Fort St. James and do some legwork in the backwoods.

When his home's security system didn't beep when he opened the front door, he raised an eyebrow in question. Instead, he heard a female voice from somewhere upstairs.

The words "Welcome home" lingered in the air as Matthew was left to guess at who had invaded his space. The voice sounded friendly and was definitely female.

Dusk was starting to settle in, and it would be dark in another hour. He pressed some light switches, and low glows turned on in various corners of the main floor. So far so good as he made his way to the stairs, dropped his bag, shrugged off his jacket, undid a couple more buttons of his shirt, and reached the upper level. A drink was waiting for him on the upper landing. He picked it up and sniffed. It smelled right. The view of the ocean was stunning, and the garden below was decked out with the usual beautiful birds as well as rabbits and squirrels chasing about, looking for anything they could eat. It wasn't hard for them to find something. His gardeners kept the place immaculate and fed the wildlife, while a handyman took care of the maintenance inside and out. The house and the grounds were always in an immaculate state and ready whenever Matthew needed to enjoy them.

Matthew sipped his drink as he peeked through the open bedroom door and watched as a mound under the eiderdown moved and moved again. No body part was showing as he slowly wandered over to the side of the bed. As he placed his glass on the night table, a female hand slithered out from under the bed cover and gently grabbed his leg. The covers were thrown back, and a female form displayed itself to Matthew.

"For chrissakes, Emma! How the hell did you get back here before me?"

Matthew let his hands wander over her slender naked body.

"I caught the midnight Air Canada flight. But I just had to come over, Matthew. Daddy asked me! Wasn't that nice of him? Of course, I'm not sure that he really needed to ask me, but on the other hand, I would have waited an eternity if I waited for you to ask!"

Matthew stripped his clothes off and dropped them at his feet. He didn't bother to gather them up and fold them, as he would normally. What was in front of him was far more important than a bunch of clothes—and God, he needed it. He bent over the bed and took one of her small, dark nipples in his mouth. He went from one to the other as though searching for something. Emma didn't move, just allowed Matthew his moment as he slithered into a prone position next to her.

He moved one arm under her waist and pulled her into a position parallel with his own body while the other arm reached out for the bed covers and pulled them over, as though hiding from the outside world. It didn't last long, as the heat from their bodies made Matthew throw the covers off, and for a few minutes they wrestled with each to get into a comfortable position. As Emma landed on top of Matthew, she smiled before lowering herself down on him. He felt her pubic hairs and was again surprised at how silky they were—he would always remember that for some reason. There weren't any in the landing strip, just enough to help guide him to the terminal.

"That's nice," Emma said with a naughty, angelic smile on her face.

It was a perfect fit as each relaxed into a position of emotional intoxication and moved gently to absorb each other in the consensual feeling of the moment. To enjoy and embrace it. Moving with a rhythm that only came with comfort and trust. They moved without talking, without needing to. He needed it. She needed it. Moving slowly, one on top of the other and back again, rolling from one side of the bed to the other as they jostled for position in an extremely personal moment that only their two bodies, so familiar with each other, understood and truly appreciated. A moment of feeling and the kind of love that didn't come other than through a strong feeling of compassion and need. A gentle giving and a gentle receiving—a thank-you for sharing. An appreciation of giving a little of oneself in a moment of heat and subdued passion.

They played that way for almost an hour before Matthew finally pulled himself up and into the shower. Emma joined him and helped clean his body. Then he helped her.

"I have to do something," he said, looking over at her.

"I hope so," Emma replied coyly.

"Not that! I have to do something before the markets open in the morning. Let me get my laptop and a couple of drinks. Come and join me on the patio, and bring something to wrap us up in. It's beautiful out there, and we can watch the lights of the traffic across the flats."

Emma brought some bed covers and headed downstairs to the patio. He collected his laptop from his briefcase and put together a couple of Ungava gins on ice. It was his favorite type. A Canadian Arctic yellow clear blend of juniper, cloudberry, wild rose hips, and crowberry. He pushed open one of the sets of French doors that led out to the patio overlooking the bay and the hills beyond with the lights from the highway between and the curving rail line that followed the bay below.

They settled next to each other on the deep cushions of one of the rattan sofas and arranged the bedclothes around them as they sipped their drinks and smiled at each other. It was a beautifully clear night with a huge array of stars and a classic quarter moon throwing soft shimmers of light on the waters in the bay. It couldn't have been a better background to have returned to after the trip to Turkey. Emma touched and felt him playfully until he tapped her hands away. Matthew fired up the laptop, looked over at her, and smiled. She knew it was work, and she loved him for his underplay. Emma just looked over his shoulder. She was incredibly bright and followed his every move without question. She knew what he was doing.

Global Gold was held tightly with just over 300 million shares outstanding and a price of $16 per share. It was a real steal these days with the somewhat depressed gold price. They had been trading at $54 per share just three years earlier, before the commodity market started to bottom out. Like all the other gold plays, Global was suffering huge losses and reduced dividends. But perhaps with the Nazi gold sitting off to the side, it really didn't matter to them what the gold price was.

The market value of Global Gold was almost $5 billion. The prospect of buying a controlling interest through stock purchases would be impossible. Not only would it be expensive—about half a billion dollars for just 20 percent to show any serious intent—the likelihood that one could even purchase that amount from such tight control was next to zero. There had to be another way of getting the interest of the Global executive and somehow establishing with a better degree of certainty that what ORB suspected was true—that Global was a cloak for the Nazi gold.

Matthew tapped out a message to Murray asking for some background from Colin, who had been charged with looking under Global's hood. A lot of good information came back—stakeholders, bios, investment partners, likely associations, capital structure, and organization.

Perhaps the threat of a hostile takeover might do it. It didn't have to be pursued, just raised enough to get in the door and see the whites of the eyes of the group that controlled Latitude 55. Perhaps one or two of the board members would be willing to relinquish their positions if threatened with prosecution over some trumped-up or, better still, real charges and subsequent leniency related to the handling of the stolen gold. Once Matthew had the background on the company, perhaps the maybes would turn up something that could be turned into a positive for ORB.

Meanwhile, Matthew decided to place some buy orders with his broker for 50,000 shares each day for a week just to see if there was any reaction. It was a drop in the ocean compared to the company's value, but at least he would start by nibbling around the edges and have a reason to get his name in front of the president or chairman of the board. He placed the first order at a value close to $850,000 and then rifled through the information on the company, including members of the board.

Ian Burvill, a well-known psychotic Aussie, was the CEO of the company, but the information beyond that was limited. According to a three-year-old press release, Burvill had been parachuted into the top position by an unnamed entity. It seemed that Giuseppe Bonafacio was the president and had been for almost ten years. Interestingly, there were clearly Italian roots there that intimated there could be continuing ties to the Mob. The rest of the board had similar backgrounds, from education to professional status—mostly money men and mostly lawyers. One stood out, the chairman, likely not Italian, but with a diverse background in international executive positions within the mining industry over the past forty years. English educated, worked in finances with some major companies, and now lived in Monaco with his French wife. A tax haven exile protecting his assets and answering to very few. Peter Barnham had impeccable credentials, was retired, and served on the boards of five diverse mining companies operating in eight different countries between them. Was he connected to the Mob? It was difficult to tell, but it gave Matthew a possibility to consider.

Latitude 55 was mentioned almost casually in the company bio and buried in the narrative of annual financial statements. The reference was minimal, noting that the mine in northern British Columbia continued to be a small producer and almost insignificant to the company's bottom line. The mine's output or its life expectancy were never mentioned. Matthew found no press releases, no names to attach, and nothing else that might suggest it was anything other than a pimple on the butt of the Global Gold elephant. Their assets were primarily in offshore locations, including Africa and Central America, both of which were difficult areas to investigate and devoid of news. It appeared as though Global continually kept themselves below the radar, created no waves, were good citizens, and filed all their reports with the security commissions they were responsible to on a timely basis.

Emma slipped her hand over Matthew's. He set the laptop to one side, wrapped a bed cover around them both, and pulled her into him. They sipped the gin and stared out at the darkness filled with millions of pinpoints of light and the magnificence of the quarter moon. Emma would be gone soon, and he would sleep until noon the next day as he tried to shake off the jet lag that seemed to adversely affect him more with each passing year.

When he woke the next morning, Emma had vanished without a hint of her having been there at all. She needed to go to her own place to prepare herself for the future.

Matthew checked Global Gold's stocks, but no one had bitten on his offer to buy.

15
Global Gold

Trading volume was thin. It took two days for Matthew to secure the order through the prestigious Canaccord Group for 50,000 shares, even at market. As soon as it was completed, Matthew put a repeat order in, this time at two dollars above market. That one took three days to fill. Few people were selling, but he knew one. ORB had been at work and approached Andy Kazmera, a sleazy Global Gold shareholder based in Denver. Kazmera was an easy target and was suffering from a great deal of hidden devious exploits and debts. It didn't take a lot to convince him to sell.

Another order went in for two dollars more and another after that for a two-dollar premium over the last order. It took fifteen business days and around $5,000,000 to complete the 250,000-share purchase he had targeted. The price was now showing as a little over twenty-two dollars per share. Hopefully, that would catch the attention of someone at Global. By then Matthew had heard back from Murray.

Colin had reported on Global, to the extent he could uncover anything in the time he had to dig into what was a well-guarded secret. But with the passage of time, Global had lowered their guard a little and over the years had become a little more loose-lipped about its business dealings, which were, to a large extent, above board, though somewhat immoral. But then, immorality was not illegal, and there were enough companies in the mining industry that suffered from the same affliction.

Many of the juniors held completely frivolous land positions, hyped them to get the stock price up, only to cash in to raise sufficient funds to pay themselves and settle back into an obscure position until the next time they needed money. The stock price would go down, and they would purchase their stock back and wait for the next time they needed cash. The sad fact was they really had nothing other than a promise, some exploration licenses, soil samples, and, if they were lucky, land positions close enough to more promising deposits to claim theirs was simply an extension of the one with proven geology. Often there was little similarity but lots of hype, no action, and management was quite happy to live off the drippings of those that had been touched by the fever enough to buy in. It was a cycle that had endured over the last sixty years in the industry and was likely to live on. Every now and again a junior would get more excited and issue press releases to get the word out sufficiently to raise some more serious funds by floating flow-through shares that offered tax-free investments. They would always get a hit of some kind. Flow-through meant exploration, and exploration meant the potential for possible good results—and it was tax-free income at work.

Colin had discovered that one of the shareholders in Global Gold, Lapa Investments, had built its equity in the company to over 55 percent with a well-known prime objective of buying distressed mining companies. Rarely had they ever actually developed a property beyond the theory, and never had they put a property into operation, whether it had been there before or not. Their modus operandi was to create an independent corporation for each of the distressed properties with no legal ties to Lapa that could be easily proven, develop a mine's potential, or breathe new life into a once-operating one, to the extent of adding value before any real work and money had to be expended on the property; to get to production by getting permits; to plan infrastructure improvements; to establish agreements with governments to participate "for the benefit of the community"; to complete what engineering remained; to establish a proven resource—if there was one to prove, and even when there was none they would pump up the prospects of there being one by continually lowering the cut-off grade and increasing the probable category of reserves; and to generally mitigate risk.

Success meant selling the shovel-ready properties off at huge premiums based on the value of ounces—or pounds, in the case of copper—in the ground plus a premium estimated based on supply and demand. When they couldn't turn the distressed property around, and they couldn't unload the property on some unsuspecting but optimistic company that defied the odds, they used Global to fund the purchase of their stock in the failed companies and tucked them into a portfolio of losses to be used as capital losses against Global's gains.

Like many Russian billionaires, Mr. Ivanovich also held German citizenship and lived in Switzerland, having made his fortune amid the breakup of the Soviet Union in the 1990s.

Ivanovich grew up in the shadows of the Russian Mafia with family ties that reached back to their Italian ancestors who had fled their birthplaces when the Germans first invaded Italy. He had Mafia blood in his veins, and Colin had surmised that he may be the one who held the secret of the Nazi gold that had been passed on through his family over the last seventy years— or maybe not. While Theodore Munch had originally taken on the task, it was now Ivanovich's job to protect it, and the modern way was through business—his business. Unfortunately, he was now saddled with Ian Burvill, the erratic, disturbed, psychotic, but validated president of Global Gold. It had been an oversight Ivanovich had regretted over the years, and when he died in the 1990s, he left no clues of his past.

Burvill threw up his hands from across the table where Giuseppe Bonafacio and Peter Barnham sat looking bewildered at the short, curly haired, almost-bald man who seemed to be constantly on the verge of an apoplectic fit. Burvill was given naturally to theatrics, and this time his body language seemed to be asking a question.

"Who the fuck is playing with us?" He held his hands out across the table, palms up. "Who the fuck pays nearly 20 percent over market for a handful of our shares when we have no news out there, no short-term prospects, and no fucking likelihood of ever wanting to sell our shares to some unknown shithead at market prices?"

No responses. Just stares. Burvill's eyes bulged further. "I'll tell you who would do that!"

The others waited.

"Someone poking around for a way in. Someone who wants our attention. Someone who may know something they shouldn't. Someone testing the resolve of our investors."

"Let me do some digging around and see what I can find out," Bonafacio said, finding his tongue at last. "We know the trades came through Canaccord. We also know they were all made by the same account holder, so all we have to do is get one of our people at Canaccord to find out who it was."

Burvill relaxed a little and slid his arms back across the table so just his hands rested there. His face was settling back from an apoplectic red to a pale purple and pink, but his eyes still bulged, and he left sweat marks on the table where his hands slid around.

"OK, that's a start, but we have to get to the bottom of this. Where's De la Hora?"

Many stories associated with Global Gold were to be hidden from suspecting eyes, but the most important one was the Toodoggone story. Even Burvill was not sure what it was all about, but he did know that it needed total secrecy—his bosses had leaned on him enough for him to know there was hidden value there that no one should know about.

De la Hora shared space with Global Gold and had a separate trunk phone line hook-up with his own number set up in one of the offices for when he was around. His door was metal and well secured. He never left his laptop around or used paper.

De la Hora had been based in Canada for nearly ten years and looked after the Latitude 55 holdings, which meant the gold at Toodoggone. The rest of the Global holdings he left to others and rarely ever contacted them. He had always viewed Global Gold's ventures as shams to keep people away from Toodoggone—his secret.

He was currently working on moving the gold to the coast for shipping offshore to Brazil for refining and then to Argentina, where it would be "cleaned" through German-controlled banks until the Germans called for it. One container at a time with twenty tons of gold in each marshalled in Fort St. James and then trucked to Prince Rupert where it was transferred to small container ships that carried everything from copper, zinc, and lead concentrates and sometimes timber products down to Vancouver for transfer to oceangoing vessels. The gold was bound for South America for refining, and the twenty-ton capacity standard-size eight-by-eight-by-forty-foot high-value gold container would get lost amongst all the others. Apart from the serial number on the container, the only other distinguishing features on the outside of the gold containers were the triple padlocks. Inside, the container walls, roof, and floor were reinforced with high-strength steel bars running horizontally and spaced six inches apart with heavy-gauge steel wire mesh attached to the inside of the bars on all fronts with a reinforced inner cage door only accessible through the rear doors of the container. Only De la Hora and one person in Brazil had the keys to the inner door.

"My little friend." Burvill touched De la Hora's shoulder and took his hand in welcome as he came through the door to be faced with the three men. He relaxed, although he was not at all prone to panic, and despite his size he was not afraid of many people. Ian was not his superior, but other than the gold, they had no ties. They never socialized, knew little or nothing about each other, and had no idea of what each other was up to during any day.

"Hey, Ian, what gives?" De la Hora was nonchalant, giving nothing away. He glanced from one man to the other and nodded.

"Hey, Giuseppi, what brings you two all the way down the corridor just to see me?"

Looking uncomfortable, Bonafacio put his fingers into his collar and worked them around. De la Hora saw small beads of sweat on his brow, and he wasn't sure if that was the work of Burvill, who had often lost his cool with Bonafacio and generally made his life miserable, as he did with almost everyone, or whether there was something more, and he was about to find out.

Burvill's eyes had started to go back into their sockets, but he was clearly still rattled, his hands shaking slightly.

"Marino." That was a big giveaway to De la Hora of an impending problem. Burvill never called him by his first name unless he desperately needed help. "Has anyone been poking around your territory over the last few weeks that we need to be aware of? Any strange faces or questions? Anything out of the ordinary? Any calls or visits from your handlers? Anything like that?"

De la Hora thought for a few moments and grimaced as his brain locked into gear. One could see him thinking and stretching his memory back a few weeks. He had been up at Fort St. James, over to the mine site, and been in Prince Rupert and now in Vancouver, but everything was much the same as it always was.

Nazi

cretsboldmission

De la Hora had spent all his time over the last decade on just the one thing—Nazi gold. Although the story had become watered down over time, he had very little concept of the origins of the haul. He focused these days mainly on bringing the twenty-ton shipments of gold down, one at a time (only to be reduced to more like thirteen to fourteen tons after all the impurities had been removed in South America), before heading out to Italy. That tonnage still amounted to some 420,000 ounces of pure yellow gold with a street value of something like $600 million for every shipment ending up in the hands of his employers—as far as he knew.

He was also a ruthless person who never forgave and always punished anyone he thought might be, or become, a threat to his mission—that's how he saw it: a mission. In fact, there had been a number of "incidents" over the last few years as the gold started to move when he had to clean up some indiscretions amongst the Natives in Fort St. James and a couple of container retrofitters in Prince Rupert. Their loose lips in the local bars had to be silenced, and there was no other way but a swift end to their lives. De la Hora had a small team of Mafia associates who looked after the dirty work and kept their ears to the ground and their eyes peeled for potential problems. They were not beyond exterminating the loose lips and everyone who encountered them should that need arise.

De la Hora, an Italian American, had been chosen specifically for this job by the Neapolitan Mob boss to succeed the last "manager," who had met an untimely death for asking the wrong questions. De la Hora's last assignment for the Mob had been the unearthing of the whereabouts of the $500 million Amber Room before the Polish government ran over the Mafia group that guarded it when it was discovered hidden behind a false wall that was sealed shut inside an old wartime bunker. The discovery had been kept secret from the outside world, but while De la Hora had successfully bullied, threatened, and tortured his way through to finding the hiding place from the one or two people remaining that had been responsible for the mission on behalf of the Russian government, his fellow Mafia compatriots had not been able to resist the Polish invasion, and the contents of the Amber Room stayed in Poland while unofficially denied the light of day. These days it was considered the Polish financial security vault, and no one talked about it.

De la Hora had inherited the responsibilities for the Nazi gold from the crime bosses in Naples, where only a few knew the original story and where even fewer now lived to tell it. The story had faded somewhat, but the fact remained that the gold was there, and it was starting to leach back to Germany. It should have been divided up amongst the survivors of the Nazi conspirators who had been part of the triumvirate that included the German banks, the Vatican, and the Mafia, but it wasn't. It leached into the German economy, and there were no repercussions.

"I can't think of anything out of the ordinary, Ian," De la Hora confessed. "Nothing more than the usual. No strange faces, not even any loose lips for a while. I guess they learned their lesson." He smiled, a sort of twisted, mean smirk.

"Better be on the lookout. It seems we have a little bird watching us, but we don't yet know why or if it's for real. Could be just a little sensitivity on our part, but I don't want anyone taking things for granted. We haven't seen much interference so far, just a few government folks poking around at our records, but nothing we can't handle. Stay sharp, and report back to me on the slightest thing. You copy?"

Ian looked at both, and they nodded in return.

"Giuseppe, find out who the little bird is, and let's see if we can get to know him a little more. Marino, you're doing a great job, but remember, we want all the gold out of there over the next five years."

De la Hora put a thumb up into the air, nodded, and his visitors left the room. He really didn't give a toss for either of them. They had zero input to his mandate. He would do things his way, although their comments about the possible spying were worth thinking about and making some changes to security.

* * *

"Chris, what do you know about the trades over the last three weeks coming out of Canaccord for Global Gold stock? Seems as though we have a buyer at nearly 20 percent over market who has collected about a quarter of a million shares. I'd like to know who the buyer is as well as the seller. We don't usually have many sellers, so this is important. Someone is trying to raise money by selling our stock at a premium to market. Could be just a temporary thing, and they'll buy it back later when the price settles down, or maybe they just want to get out."

Bonafacio paused to allow the information to sink in to Chris, one of the senior Canaccord traders who had the Global Gold account in his portfolio.

"Yeah, I saw that go through. It surprised me as well, and I did a little checking of my own since it seemed so out of the ordinary. No one has bought any worthwhile Global stock in over three years. Some guy called Matthew Black, right here in Vancouver, placed five orders over ten days for fifty thousand shares apiece at an increasing buy amount to twenty-two dollars a piece. Strange since there were no sell orders at that level, but it did attract one seller. It seems that a certain Andy Kaz something or other was ready to sell. He had the stock for a few years tucked into his portfolio with us, so it was a fast, easy transaction. He's out of Denver, and I have no idea why he sold or if he's intending to buy back in. Want me to check? "

"No, I'll do that, Chris. I know Andy, but get me some details on this Black guy. What's he up to and why? Is he just interested in getting a small stake and holding it, or does he know something we don't?"

"Will do." Chris was a typical broker. Full of confidence, optimism, and expense credit cards. The proverbial slick salesperson. As charismatic as he needed to be to get the deal but incredibly skeptical when someone else was trying to sell him something. He didn't trust anyone—including, and likely more so, his fellow traders. But he did trust Bonafacio; he had to. Global Gold used his services for all their transactions, and that was a substantial account to hold, since they had quite a few affiliated companies.

The line went dead, and Bonafacio sat back in his chair. He had known Andy for a few years. Andy had another quarter of a million shares, and at that kind of a premium he could cash them in for about $3 million over market on the total shares he held. Mind you, he had bought in at an average of $20 as the price dipped to the current level, so perhaps he just needed to cover his costs for now. Still, it was time to put a call in to check on what was happening. The stock was at its lowest point for several years, and selling out didn't make good financial sense.

"Andy, Giuseppe here. How's it going? Haven't talked in a while."

"Hey, Joe." Andy always referred to Bonafacio by his first name, Giuseppe, translated to English. It really bothered Bonafacio, but he never dwelled on it. He just never called Andy unless he had to.

Andy had been with a Lapa Investment subsidiary in Turkey as they turned one of the local companies around and spun it off to a Denver-based mining company. It had gone on to make some good money, but the easiest money was in the pockets of Lapa. They had used Andy to continue to add value to the property, getting agreements with the local community in place that, in the end, meant nothing. Andy was a cunning, deceitful guy who put his nefarious skills to work on the simple dreams of the local village. He had promised to relocate them to new housing where they would always have running water, heat, light, sanitary facilities, and places to grow food and keep their goats and chickens and other livestock. A place where they would have a new school, a new mosque, and a burial site where the occupants of the old cemetery would be taken and where the living would have their own plots—each and every one of them.

He had promised to bring over the latest farming techniques from the US, provide them with winning livestock to procreate and produce the best cattle money could buy, and provide experts in the areas of husbandry. All of this if only they would sign the land-sale agreements he put in front of them. All of it offered through lawyers who dealt with the partially illiterate mayor and his village council. All of it to an unknowing, trusting, but duped group of villagers who constantly lived on the borderline of life and death, well away from the protection of the central government or the militia. Andy's legal team had the agreements drawn up, except that the meaningful language wasn't quite what the villagers had been led to believe. There was nothing more in them other than a promise of a relocated cemetery and the construction of a new road to the area that had been set aside for their new homes—to be constructed by them. Lapa took over when Andy and his contractors came to start construction and found their way blocked by the villagers. Nothing could move forward until Lapa moved in with their own private security forces. Meanwhile, Andy had done his job and moved on to his next Lapa assignment—this time in Armenia—to do it all over again.

"What's new with you?"

"Hey, Andy, I was talking to a buddy of mine over at Canaccord this morning. He mentioned you sold some Global Gold stock and wondered if you were going to buy it back if or when the price came down a little. Any truth to that?"

Andy stalled. He knew this wasn't normal. Brokers shouldn't be giving personal information out about trades, but he also knew that Global wasn't a normal company. Someone had been watching, and he guessed that Burvill was involved.

"Can't do anything in this world without someone watching over your shoulder, Joe. Who was it? Burvill? "

"Doesn't matter. Let's just say the transactions were seen and the news passed on. You know this is a delicate situation. We don't usually see trades like this, especially from our own. That's usually left to the two-bitters who have a few shares and just play for fun with other two bitters. Yours is a half a mil bit of fun, and that's serious stuff for us. Now we have a new shareholder whom we don't know. So what's up?"

"Nothing's up, Joe. Just a bit short and feeling the squeeze with the market the way it is. That's all. Maybe I should have told you first."

"Maybe you should have, Andy, because now I've got Burvill all over my ass wanting to know what's going on, and I don't know—and I should know!"

"OK, Joe, settle down. Sorry, just had to raise a little cash, and this came up. That's all."

"Next time let me know first, or there's going to be a price to pay. If Burvill doesn't like it, neither do I, and there's too much at stake here."

After he hung up, Andy sank back into his chair and steepled his fingers, deep in thought. The visit from a couple of heavy-set, dark-complexioned guys a week earlier had rattled him. He was a wanted man in several countries for his misdeeds where he had cheated local landowners out of their properties, all in the name of the mining companies he had worked for. He was an easy target and easy to intimidate, and the two Turks who came looking for him were clearly very serious. Their threats, just a few words and a chokehold, were enough for Andy to agree to sell his stock in Global Gold when the time came, and it came as soon as Matthew entered his buy orders.

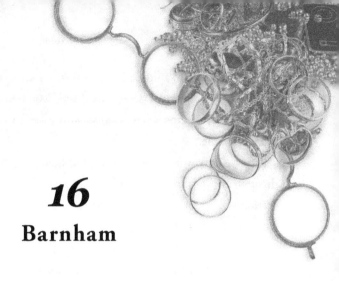

16

Barnham

The Terminal City Club was a prestigious gathering place for business people in Vancouver. It was located at the end of the financial district and frequented by those who needed a quiet, open atmosphere in which to lunch and talk business. It was there that deals were done—outside of the golf course—for those in mainstream business circles not given to the pomposity of hierarchical bastions of more exclusive clubs that still insisted on ties, no women, and armchairs one could snooze in. Those kinds of clubs were more for the retired super-funded these days who had little business interest anymore but a lot of political influence.

So it was that Peter Barnham, chairman of Global Gold, sat on the terrace and looked out over Coal Harbour, the marina below, the seaplanes coming in and out of their new digs near the latest addition to the waterfront convention centers that catered to the ginormous cruise ships and their hordes of tourists, which was more than compensated for by the grand vista of the snow-capped mountains beyond. He was a Monaco man now, but he appreciated his treats, such as coming to Vancouver, all expenses paid, and eating at the finest restaurants. In one of those rare moments, he had decided to take lunch by himself at his favorite spot on the patio of the Terminal City Club, where he might see a few old acquaintances, but if not, so be it. He was there for himself, by himself.

"Is it really Peter Barnham?" a male voice asked, interrupting his thoughts. The individual held out a hand to Barnham who, bewildered, had little choice but to proffer his own and shake hands for a few seconds while racking his brain for the elusive memory of who was before him.

"I can see you're a little surprised, Peter. Don't you remember me?"

"Well, no. Frankly, I don't, I'm afraid. My memory is usually pretty good with faces, but I must admit that in your case I'm at a complete loss. Sorry to sound so rude."

Peter didn't want to be perceived as being overly disinterested just in case this person was important and he had just forgotten ... another symptom of getting older, perhaps. He needed to play with it for a while until he could fathom who this was.

"Did we meet at a conference?"

"No, we met in Monaco at the casino. Don't you remember a few years ago when that Saudi prince dropped a million at the baccarat table, and we fell into conversation about the poor of the world and the frivolousness of the Saudis?"

"I confess I don't remember. And your name?"

"Matthew Black. You can call me Matthew or Matt; I respond to both. Surely you must recall that evening, old chap, although I must admit we likely had a little too much champagne, and the ladies around us were quite stunning and getting most of our attention. But no matter. What are you doing here, Peter?"

Barnham still couldn't place the event or Matthew, but ignoring it might be something he did not need.

"Oh, I'm here for a board meeting, and you?"

"I just happen to live close by, so I dropped in for lunch. Would you mind if I joined you?"

Peter hesitated but decided to play through, just in case.

"Oh, please do." He got up as Matthew seated himself next to his chair rather than across the table. Peter looked a little quizzical but again decided to keep going.

"Isn't this the perfect spot for lunch in the city on a beautiful day such as this, Peter?" Matthew swept a hand across the vista and breathed deeply, taking in the oxygen, albeit contaminated by the traffic fumes from below them. "How's the board meeting going? Finished up?"

"Yes, we'll be going for supper together this evening before I head back to Monaco in the morning. Love Vancouver but quite happy to go back."

Peter picked up the menu and casually looked over it without concentrating. He had lost his appetite.

"Oh, terrific." Matthew didn't miss a beat, carrying on as if he had known Peter for quite a while. "I remember some excellent meals at La Piazza. The best veal-and-pumpkin cannelloni ever! That Orsolini is truly magnificent, don't you think?"

Peter looked Matthew in the eyes and paused for a few seconds as he wondered what trick of memory was causing his to fail. If he couldn't remember a name, he could usually remember the face or vice versa, but in this case, he was drawing a blank. But this man clearly remembered the menu at La Piazza on the seafront in Monaco where the rich and famous, and Peter, often dined.

"Yes, yes, the best. I have to say, he runs a superb establishment and one of my favorite restaurants." He decided to test Matthew. "I would assume you enjoy the casinos in Monte Carlo. I just wish there was a little more culture though." He eyed Matthew for a reaction.

"How can you say that, Peter? It doesn't get better than the Casino Monte Carlo at one end of the atrium and the fabulous Opera Hall at the other end! You have as much culture as you need for a country that doesn't even have forty thousand residents to support itself."

"Well, you have a point, I have to admit, and I can tell you are quite familiar with my hometown. But tell me, are you a traveler? "

"Oh, I get around. A little work and a little play, but I usually manage to combine the two wherever I am. Like now, for instance. I'm going to eat a great lunch in a wonderful location with an old, if forgetful, friend."

"And the work side of that, may I ask?"

"Well, I'd like to suggest a proposition to you, Peter. What a coincidence we're here at the same time. I'd been thinking about Global, and it hadn't even crossed my mind that you were on the board," he lied. "But when I spotted you, I remembered, and as it happens, I have a little Global fever. So here we are." Matthew smiled broadly and held his hands out by way of invitation.

The waiter arrived, but clearly the two had not yet decided on what they wanted. He disappeared, having put the obligatory basket of warm, crusty bread on the table with some butter, fresh water, and ice, with lemon on the side.

"Oh?" Peter looked a little stunned. "What do you mean?"

"Well, it seems to me that we have something in common."

"What might that be, er, Matthew?" Peter hesitated, as though using the other man's Christian name somehow hinted that he knew him—and he didn't.

"Well, my partners and I—who I will only describe as an international group of concerned citizens—are looking for a way to somehow, shall we say, get to know Global a little better, and it seems to me that you might be the very person to help us." Matthew sat back, looking pleased with himself.

"Now how would I do that, Matthew?" Peter asked, smiling sarcastically. "Or should I say, *why* would I want to do that?" He was starting to bristle at the impertinence of this person before him. Clearly, something was going on, and he didn't like the smell of.

"Because at this very moment, your wife, bless her soul, is being held in a secret location in Marseilles. She is likely quite upset and rather confused as to what's happened. After all, Monaco is such a peaceful location for you to be squirrelled away with your share of the take, don't you think?"

Peter's face paled, his lips quivered with rage, and his fingers pressed tightly on the table. He hesitated to make a scene and was holding himself back as though restrained by an invisible force. "What the hell do you mean?" he hissed.

"Now take it easy, old man. We're just having a chat here. Nothing to get overly concerned about. We just need you to get me some meetings with Bonafacio and Burvill—oh, and tell me everything you know about Toodoggone and Latitude 55. Think you can do that?"

"Or?" Peter asked, knowing he was no match for this nemesis.

"Or Mrs. Barnham won't sleep at night, and after a while, neither will you." Matthew grinned. "Perhaps an extra push might help things. Remember when I mentioned your share of the take a minute ago?"

Peter looked puzzled as well as worried.

Matthew nodded, still smiling. "Yes, you remember. The take. You know, the kickbacks you've been getting as chairman of the board from Global all these years to approve the purchase of the unworkable distressed companies that Lapa brought in. Remember that now? Well, we also remember, and everyone in the business world as well as everyone in Monaco will get to remember as well. You don't really want that, do you? Not as well as losing your dear wife, right?" Matthew laid it on thick.

Peter stared at him, thunderstruck and unable to mutter a word.

"Would you like some lunch or perhaps just give it a miss for today?"

Peter didn't respond, just slumped back in his chair.

"So perhaps you will take a few extra days in this beautiful city. Let Bonafacio know that you had met me—the strange buyer of your stock— and fill me in on some details. How about that? Not convinced? Here's a little moment we recorded for posterity of your wife relaxing in restraints, poor girl."

Matthew pulled out his phone and showed Peter a short silent movie of his wife ensconced in what seemed to be a somewhat run-down building surrounded by a scrub. It wasn't clear where it was taken, but it certainly was not at their home in Monaco. Peter's face and body sank further. He needed to think. He needed to check some things. He needed to get out of there.

"OK, now that we've had a little trip down memory lane and you've still come up short, let me give you a clue as to how I really met you. You would never recognize me. I was a little, uh, disguised at the time, but when you were chairman over at Firebrand Minerals, I had to do a little reorganizing, and you got caught in the crossfire. Remember?"

It started to dawn on Peter who he was being confronted by. Matthew had played the part of the president of a takeover company, and it was Firebrand Mining that he wanted. They mined and processed uranium in Kazakhstan for the Russian appetite. Not only did he want it, he wanted to trade it for something in the US—some kind of new technology being used in the petroleum industry—fracking. Matthew had been bold and aggressive. He spread rumors about the board, pushed the stock price as low as he could, and then mounted a hostile takeover. Peter was out, and Matthew was in—or rather, ORB was in. Peter was left out of the whole transaction, having lost the confidence of the shareholders, which was the real reason he had fled to Monaco. That was then, and this was now, and Peter realized he was being used again. Living high and on the edge had its consequences, especially if one didn't continuously look over one's shoulder, and Peter didn't. He relied, naively, on luck, ignorance, and an ability to use his wealth to dodge the bullets. Once again, it hadn't worked.

"Oh, hell," was all he said.

"Don't look so glum, Peter. No one has to know. Just arrange the meeting, and see me at the same time but at Hy's, up on Homer, tomorrow. I'll be in the northeast corner booth. If you're not there tomorrow, I'll be there the next day and the next, but no more than that. The longer you take to make the arrangements, the longer your poor wife—Marion, I believe—will be cooped up with the pigs, the flies, the spiders, and who or what else I really don't know, and you surely don't want that, do you?"

Matthew didn't wait for a response. He got up and patted Peter's shoulder. "So great to see you again, old boy. Sorry about lunch, but let's see if we can do it in Monaco the next time I'm there."

With that, he sauntered out of the restaurant and down the curving staircase to the lobby below. He waited at the desk for a few moments to check the people around him, then strolled out into the sunshine.

Peter remained at the table, dumbfounded by what he had just experienced. He tugged at his shirt collar, which seemed to have shrunk during his ordeal. Thoughts flashed through his head: his wife, Lapa, his wife, his home, his wife, his wealth. The images kept recycling through.

The waiter arrived at the table for the second time. "Ready to order, sir?"

"Uh… I think my appetite has disappeared. It must be the heat." Peter tugged at his collar again, pulled the knot of his tie down, and undid the top button of his shirt. He pushed himself up from his chair, tossed the napkin on the table, and wandered out the door, chased by the waiter who was looking for a signature on the bill.

Peter headed back to his hotel, where he slumped into an armchair in the corner of his suite, took his cell phone out, and called home. Only his own voice echoed back. "Sorry, we're unable to answer right now. Please leave your name and num—" Peter ended the call and let the phone drop into his lap.

"What now?" he mumbled.

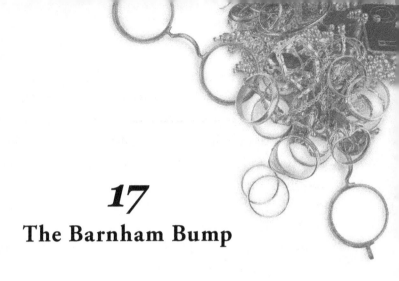

17
The Barnham Bump

"You know, a funny thing happened to me today at the restaurant," Peter began as he sat opposite Bonafacio and Burvill in the president's corner office. They both looked up at him. He had called to let them know he was going to stay an extra couple of days and help with any outstanding business.

"What's that?" Bonafacio asked.

"Well, I bumped into Matthew Black."

Both pairs of eyes and ears focused on him.

"Wow," was all Burvill could say as his eyebrows seemed to move up an inch farther than they usually did when he was surprised by something. His eyes started to pop, and color flooded his face.

"Yes, it happened quite by chance, or so I think." Peter tried his best to seem cool and collected, but underneath he was a mass of anxiety. "I overheard a bit of a conversation at the next table when some guy arrived at their table and introduced himself as Matthew Black. I assumed him to be the same one as we talked about in the meeting earlier. They all shook hands and settled down to lunch. I couldn't hear what they were saying. It was all very discreet, but it seemed like business, judging from the body language. They finished lunch, and Black got up to go. He was the first one out the door, so I decided to get up and follow him. He went into the men's room, and I followed. I didn't have a plan; I was just acting on instinct. But we struck up a conversation as we washed our hands, and I dropped the name 'Global' to see if it would get a reaction. It did."

"And?" Burvill asked impatiently.

"He asked what my association with Global Gold was, and I told him. Then he laughed and told me he had been buying a few shares over the previous three weeks. I looked dutifully surprised and asked what had made him do that, and he told me that he had heard from friends in Europe that Global was a key player in the gold industry, and it seemed as though the company's involvement wasn't always in mining. I looked a little shocked, of course, and asked what he meant. By then we were out in the lobby, and there were people around. He told me he didn't really want to talk about it in the open but that he would really like to meet with you two to throw some ideas around. He gave me his card and then left."

"Wow," Burvill exclaimed. "OK, let's get him in and find out what's going on. Treat him like an interested shareholder who just dropped five million dollars on our stock. He deserves a little attention, don't you think?"

Burvill looked at the other two. Peter fidgeted nervously, but Burvill just shrugged it off.

Bonafacio nodded. "No harm in that, I suppose. We'll give him the five-cent tour and show him the door once we figure out what he's up to."

"OK. Peter, make the arrangements. I'm here for the rest of the week, so any time suits." Burvill didn't wait for either of them to acknowledge his remarks. He just got up and left the room.

"Who do you think this Black guy is, Peter?" Bonafacio asked, clearly more relaxed with Burvill out of the way.

"Oh, I don't know. Maybe just poking around to see if we're a good buy—or perhaps a good buyer! But it can't hurt to see what he has to say and then get him on his way."

"I guess so, but I'm going to run some checks on him regardless. He isn't on our radar, and I thought we had pretty well everyone who counted in this industry on it." Bonafacio sat back, arms folded, suddenly deep in thought.

18

Poor Old Peter

Global Gold's offices were in the old art deco Marine Building in Vancouver, once the tallest building in the British Empire. Their offices took up the three top floors, including the penthouse, which was only accessible by a narrow set of stairs from the twentieth floor.

A previous resident had installed a two-inch thick Plexiglass sheet as the front door to the suite with a halon fire-protection system on three sides for additional security protection. It seems the previous owner was on the outs with the Canadian and US authorities over environmental problems at one of his mine sites in the States, and they wanted him extradited to face charges if the Canadians ever caught him on their soil.

The massive room took up the top layer of the three-layered cake look that topped the building and had a couple of small offices off to the side and up a few more stairs. The view was spectacular from the outside patio that wrapped around the entire floor. The patio was also the most private area in the building.

Peter wandered around the patio, hands in his pockets, deep in thought as he stared out at the Vancouver landscape with no particular interest. He had little choice but to tell Black as little as he could to get his wife back and to elicit at least promises that things would go no further. At least that was his hope.

He carefully made his way back down the steep stairway to the twentieth floor and two less precarious flights to the eighteenth before taking the elevator to ground floor. Normally, he would take great delight in admiring the intricate copper engravings surrounding him as he descended, but his mind was far too occupied, and it seemed like but a second before he reached the cramped lobby and stepped out into the sunshine.

Just a few blocks to the south, Hy's Steakhouse celebrated over fifty years of prime steak cuts for lunch and dinner. Special patrons of the city had their private booths reserved permanently for lunch. Matthew was in a booth in the corner, as he had told Peter he would be. It was just before noon, and he was sipping a virgin Caesar while he checked his messages.

Murray had been in contact with more information on Global Gold and Lapa. Nothing much on Latitude 55, and that's where the bottleneck seemed to be. There really was nothing. No history, no management, no stats, and no financials other than a byline in Global's annual financial reports. That's where Matthew needed to focus. What did Peter know about Latitude 55? He had been with Global for nearly fifteen years, had signed off on the annual reports, chaired the board meetings, but he seemed to be the only member of the board who was not somehow tied to the Mafia. The question was, did he really know anything?

Peter strolled up to the corner table, pulled out a chair, and sat opposite Matthew—no handshake, no head nod, no smile, no acknowledgement of any kind other than a stare.

"You have your meeting with Burvill and Bonafacio. Just tell me the time and date, but it has to be this week." Peter sat grim faced and stared at Matthew, despising him.

"The day after tomorrow at two o'clock in their office. Now, Peter, tell me about Toodoggone."

"There's not much to tell. I've always been kept away from that area of business. I just sign off on the financials, and Toodoggone is such a minor part it really doesn't come in for any scrutiny. Why do you want to know?"

"Just looking at options—maybe a takeover, an investment, or a joint-venture."

Peter stared at him. "Are you joking? They haven't entertained any of those ideas ever! What makes you think they would now? Who the hell are you? Do you know who these guys are? Have you got any idea?"

"Well, we think they're connected to the Mob. We think Global is a front for distressed companies sold to them by Lapa to hide in their portfolio. We think

Lapa is part of the Russian Mob. And we think that Toodoggone is hidden in there somewhere, but no one knows why. Is that a reasonable start?" It was Matthew's turn to stare at Peter as he waited for the information to sink in.

"God almighty, Black. These people don't play around. I've been on the board for fifteen years, shared dinner with these guys, gone on fishing trips, traded stories, and had one or two of them to my home in Monaco, and still I know nothing about Toodoggone. It's been on the books forever and done nothing. Well, at least until the last few years, and then I really don't know anything. But it's not me you need to talk to; it's De la Hora. He's the mastermind behind all that nonsense, whatever it is. But it's all top secret. No one ever discusses it in any meetings or even in the coffee room, so to speak. There's nothing in writing that I've ever seen. De la Hora is the key, not me!"

"It's a start," Black responded dryly. "I was hoping you weren't in the inner circle, Peter. Otherwise, this would have been so much harder."

"What do you mean?"

"Well, if you really were in the inner circle, we wouldn't be talking, and you would have just become a casualty."

"What's that supposed to mean?"

"I want you on the inside. I want you to nose around Toodoggone. I want to know what's going on. If you don't then rest assured that our little conversation here will get back to Burvill, and the Russians will surely have something to say to you about it, don't you think?"

"How am I ever going to do this? And what about my wife? What's going to happen to her in the meantime until you get what you want?" Peter leaned forward in his seat, his elbows on the table.

"Well, as a small gesture of our appreciation, we'll take her home, and you can talk. We'll leave her alone as long as you deliver. We'll leave your reputation intact as well as your finances, your family, and your friends as long as we get some cooperation. Thoughts?"

"I have to figure this out." Peter wiped his finger across his top lip and rubbed his nose, thinking. "Christ, what a hell of a situation. Fuck." He scratched his balding head, held the back of his neck, and rested the side of his face on his hand as he stared at Matthew. "And you'll let her go right away? Right now?"

"Yes, we will, Peter, right now at," Matthew looked at his watch, "8:30 p.m. Marseilles time. What do you say? Do we have a deal?" Matthew held his hand out across the table.

"No way I'm shaking your hand, you bastard. I'll help you but only as long as my wife stays free and all the other conditions are met. Otherwise, forget it, and everything stops the moment you renege."

"Same here." Matthew responded casually as he withdrew his hand. "Shall we eat?"

Peter just stood up without responding. Matthew smirked. "Oh Peter, don't be so melodramatic. You at least need to have a method of contacting me. Here's a cell phone. It only has one number in the call list, and it's all you need. When you call and someone picks up, just ask who it is. If someone says ORB, it's good. If not, just hang up and ditch the phone, disposing of the battery and the SIM card separately. If it's good, just tell me a time and place and we'll meet. Nothing more. I won't say anything other than ORB. Got that? I don't care where in the world we meet. Oh, by the way, I want to buy some of your stock in Global. Seems as though your friend in Denver is fully divested."

"You can't do that!" Peter said, pulling away. "They'll have my guts for garters!"

"That's part of the deal, Peter. We need more shares, and you're the best positioned to sell. Just tell Burvill that a crisis has come up, and you had to raise some capital."

"He'll just tell me that the company would buy them."

"No time to wait for board and securities approval, Peter. You just have to get on and do it—a matter of life or death, my friend."

Peter turned and left, completely dejected, not knowing whether to worry more about his wife, his reputation, his upside-down world, the Mafia, or Black. He had a feeling Black could be the biggest thing to worry about.

19
Global Stock Problems

"Giuseppe, it's Chris."

"Hey, Chris, what did you find out about our little bird?"

"Not much. Sounds pretty independent. No ties that we're aware of. Has had a Canaccord trading account for the last fifteen years and has traded on and off all that time. Portfolio is mixed, nothing special, up and down, all-in-all pretty mediocre. He lives south of the city and by all accounts is single and travels a lot. Beyond that he's a bit of a mystery."

"Thanks, Chris. Got a number?" Bonafacio jotted a phone number down as Chris gave it to him, then dropped the phone back on its cradle.

"OK, Mr. Black, let's see what's going on."

Bonafacio called a couple of his associates across the city who had done work for him before when he wanted to find out the background on people who came sniffing around now and then.

"Hey, Tony, how's it hangin'?" Bonafacio asked, putting on his best New York accent. He loved to do that with the Tonys of the world. It was just one of those names. He was one of those mining promoters who exuded enthusiasm for every venture he was involved with. Most people fell for it, but some didn't, and his reputation was a little on the shady side, to say the least. But he was very well connected and seemed to know everything important that was happening in the industry. He treated everyone as a client.

"Hey, G, how's it goin' with you, boss? Got something for us?" Tony was slouched back in an armchair watching the Packers and 49ers in their NFC league game. His pal, Lou, was in the other armchair manicuring his nails and keeping his eye on the game at the same time.

"I need you to check someone out for me. Matthew Black. Lives just outside the city but has no obvious ties to anyone that I know. He's sniffing around, buying some Global Gold stock at premium prices. He's coming in to meet us, and I'd like to find out a little more about him before he does."

"Sure. How soon?"

"He's coming in the day after tomorrow, so do what you can with that time."

"OK, boss. I'll get back to you tomorrow sometime. This a good number?"

"Better call me on the cell. You got the number."

Bonafacio put the phone down and leaned back in his chair, deep in thought. Hopefully, he would have a little more information before his meeting with Black. He wondered what was up, and he felt a knot starting in his stomach that was usually a sign of something going on without his knowledge.

"Ruth, get me the latest rundown on stock movements over the last two months!" he shouted out to his secretary in the next office. They often communicated that way rather than just get up and go to the other. It was faster, and they had both become accustomed to it. No big deal.

A minute later Ruth dropped a single page onto his desk with the list of trades with broker names. It was a short list dominated by Canaccord and the Black transactions. The others were small-time trades that were piggybacking on the rising value of the stock as Black's trades went through above market. There was nothing special about it other than that.

"Take a look over the past year, and let me know if there've been any trades other than these that have exceeded twenty thousand at a time."

Ruth backed out and went back to her desk.

"Nothing!" she shouted a minute later. "Not a thing. All small stuff. Always is."

Bonafacio went back to thinking. *Now, what the hell?*

20

Nothing to Report

The next morning, Tony called Bonafacio. "There's not a lot to tell on this guy Black," Tony began. "As far as I can tell, he may have been involved in a company takeover a while back—Barnham was on the board at the time. Not a friendly affair, to say the least. Barnham was turfed along with the rest of the board. Management was shaken up, and the company seemed to do a bit of a turnaround. Have no idea who he was working for, but they were a powerful group, by all accounts. It was a short, sharp thrust, and everyone was out. Seems like Black disappeared after that, but I have no idea where he went or what else he got up to. Bit of a mystery man. Could just be a hired gun working for some big boys."

"That's it?"

"Yeah, that's about it, G. Not bad for a half day's work, eh? Could dig a lot more, but I'm probably not the best person to ask at this point. If you wanna know more and get down deeper, maybe Al over at Matrix can help."

Matrix was used by a lot of mining execs to do more forensic digging on potential properties, looking for clues that might be showstoppers. Bonafacio had used Al before. He was the best, but it took time and a lot of money. Money he had, but time he didn't.

"I'll think about that, Tony. Thanks for the info. Could be useful. I may have to talk to Al if the plot thickens."

"What gives, G? This guy Black doing a number on you guys?"

"Don't know yet, but my gut says there's something out there that needs fixing. Maybe I'll know a little more after our meeting, and maybe it's nothing other than an interested party looking to be our friend. But I don't think so. Thanks, Tony. Let's get lunch soon."

"OK."

Bonafacio pondered the coincidence of Black and Peter being involved previously in the same company, wondering if there was anything to it.

21
Global Deal

Matthew sat in a chair in the lobby of Global Gold at the top of the Marine Building. He had arrived ten minutes early, been provided with a coffee, and was now thumbing through one of the magazines spread out on the table before him. He glanced at his watch: 2:15 p.m., and the only sign of life around him was the receptionist who stared at the computer screen in front of her and ignored him following the initial introduction.

"They'll be with you in a moment, Mr. Black," she said eventually, as though she had checked with him before but hadn't. That had been twenty-five minutes ago and still no show.

Matthew could wait. It was important. He curled his strategy through his brain as he ran his eyes over the words in front of him, not taking any of them in.

It was 2:45 before two men approached him.

"So sorry for the wait, Mr. Black," the shorter Italian-looking man said. "You know how it is. All rush." He didn't wait for a response. "Shall we go into a meeting room?" Bonafacio held his hand out in greeting and smiled at Matthew with almost a grimace, not knowing what to expect.

Matthew shook his hand and turned to the taller, partially bald man with short, curly red hair encircling his broad head, who reached his hand out in greeting. It wasn't a warm handshake. More of a distracted, limp one, and Matthew felt his eyes penetrating his as though seeking an answer as to what this was all about.

"Burvill" was all Matthew got in exchange, and a somber statement it was. There was no need to introduce himself. They clearly knew who he was and likely a lot more.

They turned a corner and entered a small meeting room bare of any wall coverings, phones, and anything else other than four chairs and a round table. They all sat as Matthew tossed his raincoat over the back of one of the chairs. Clearly, this was not a room for guests, and there was nowhere to hang a coat, nor did they offer him a drink.

"Many thanks for seeing me, gentlemen. I was very fortunate to bump into Peter the other day at the TCC, and I thought it might be an opportunity for us to meet. I'm sure you're wondering why an unknown like me is buying your stock. Of course, I was lucky there was a seller, I suppose. There hasn't been much movement over the last couple of years, and I guess that intrigued us."

"Us?" Burvill asked abruptly.

"Yes. I represent a group of like-minded individuals who search out potential takeovers."

"What makes you think we're a takeover target, Mr. Black?" Burvill asked, leaning forward in his chair. Bonafacio sat with a stony face, not wanting to add anything yet. "We know about your trades, of course, but we have no understanding of why, unless it's out of portfolio interest."

"Well, it isn't an awful lot of use in a portfolio, is it, don't you agree?"

They both sat back, a little stunned by the statement.

"Let's face it," Matthew continued, "the stock really doesn't move much, which means it all must be held by a few investors, which likely means control. So what would be the point?"

"What is the point then, Mr. Black?"

"To meet with you," Matthew said, smiling slightly.

"Now that you've met us, does it mean you intend to sell your shares back?" Burvill asked.

"I don't think so, at least not yet. You see, we're more interested in pursuing one of the distressed companies you represent. We think there's merit in pursuing it, and this meeting is our way of introducing ourselves."

Both of the other men relaxed visibly. Perhaps this had nothing at all to do with their most treasured secret but was just a play for an acquisition.

"And how may we help you?" Bonafacio asked. "We have a few properties that could be better off our books than on, but why would you want them if we've already put them in the distressed package?"

"Well, I think the equation is fairly simple—acquire mineral rights, build a portfolio of projects, and leverage them forward to bigger ones. Let's face it, it's all a bit of a game, and perhaps distressed to you is not the same as distressed to me."

Bonafacio and Burvill looked at each other and shrugged.

"OK, say we do have some properties for sale," Bonafacio said. Which one—or ones—are you looking at, and what are the terms?" He sat back in his chair as though he had just delivered a minor coup d'état.

"We find the most intriguing one to be your Toodoggone property."

Burvill and Bonafacio leaned forward, their body language giving away their sudden angst.

"Toodoggone?" Bonafacio said. "It's not distressed. It's just a minor producer that we've expanded to its fullest extent, and there's no further potential. You must be mistaken in your research. Toodoggone remains in our portfolio as a poor boy that gave birth to our subsidiary. It's more a question of loyalty that we keep it—although it does pay for itself but only at the lowest of margins."

"Ah, but it happens to be in an area we are very interested in," Matthew said. "You see, we've taken a position in the Lawyers and Cheni properties adjacent to yours and are looking to expand our exploration over the area—at least in the area you haven't already staked. It seems to us that there could be some symbiosis there."

Of course, Matthew couldn't disclose the fact that he really didn't know exactly where their mine property was located, despite several satellite images. It was a huge area, more than half the size of England, and it was heavily forested with a quagmire of mountains, creeks, and valleys, giving nothing away. There were no communications towers, power lines, or roads that could help identify a likely location, but he had to take the chance that their property would likely be somewhere close to known geological outcrop potentials.

"You know the area, Mr. Black?" Burvill asked.

"Of course. We did our due diligence on the area with exploration teams traversing the adjacent properties, taking soil samples, and the like, so, yes, we know the area fairly well."

Burvill and Bonafacio stared in amazement at this man in front of them. Was he serious? How would he know the location? What did he really know, and what was this all about?

"Well, Mr. Black, we're not interested in selling our mineral claims around Toodoggone," Burvill said. "They have served us as well as they could over the years, and while they might not add a lot to our bottom line, we forgive that for peace of mind and out of respect for our former chairman, Theodore Munch. No, we won't sell."

"Well, perhaps I can entice you."

"How?" Burvill asked.

"As odd as it may sound, you see, I represent the Vatican, and they are particularly interested in the Toodoggone area for whatever reason. I must admit that one must wonder whether they really know what they're interested in, but mine is not to wonder why but simply to execute on their behalf. I understand they have investment portfolios, just like anyone else, and this, perhaps, is one investment that is of particular interest to them."

At the word "Vatican," Burvill and Bonafacio seemed to press themselves into the backs of their chairs, their eyes starting to bulge.

"That can't be!" Bonafacio blurted. "There's no way. They aren't interested in Toodoggone. They can't be! That doesn't make any sense. It's a shithole in the middle of a shithole and going nowhere."

"As I said, mine is not to wonder why. But what I do know is that they're serious and anxious to know how to secure the land position at the earliest possible time—with or without your help." Matthew slipped the last few words out with a smile and as smoothly as he could. He watched them squirm. Bonafacio began to wring his hands, a sure sign of anxiety. Burvill sat in glowering silence, his own sign of anxiety together with his popping eyes and red face.

"Perhaps that could motivate you into at least thinking about it. As you know, the Vatican is wealthy beyond belief, so money is certainly not an obstacle. Perhaps there's something you need in exchange?"

"No!" Burvill cried. "We don't care who it is or what they can offer. We will not sell, not even to the Vatican!"

"I'm sorry, Mr. Black, but I believe our meeting has concluded, unless you're interested in any of our truly distressed properties," Bonafacio said, trying to bring the meeting to a close, palms up in supplication.

"Well, I guess I would be if the Vatican was, but it isn't."

"Then I think we've finished our business," Bonafacio said. "If you decide to sell your shares, we ask that you contact us first so that we may have the first right of refusal to buy them back."

"Certainly, gentlemen. But I can't foresee my wanting to do that soon. In fact, I believe we will be continuing to buy. I would urge you to consider your position. Here is my card should you wish to discuss the matter further." Matthew handed over a simple card with his name and a cell phone number on it. He didn't ask for theirs.

They all stood and headed for the door. Neither Burvill nor Bonafacio saw Matthew out. He just picked up his coat, nodded to the receptionist, who managed to look up from her screen quickly in a way that said "Goodbye" as he disappeared through the door and down the stairs.

Matthew was quite happy with the meeting, having achieved what he came for—to see the squirming at the mention of the Vatican and Toodoggone in one sentence. It just about confirmed ORB's suspicions. The Nazi gold was there somewhere. Global Gold and the Vatican were somehow complicit.

Matthew put in a buy order for 50,000 of Global Gold stock for each day, hoping to pick up whatever Peter Barnham had. In the meantime, he prepared to head north. He didn't expect a call from Global about his proposed transaction immediately, and he wanted to let them stew for a while.

22

Burvill

"What the fuck is going on here?" Burvill was livid as he slumped into the corner of the sofa in Bonafacio's office. "Where's this coming from? Who the hell is this guy, and what is the Vatican up to? They know that Canada is Cosa Nostra territory even though they don't know why. We need to get this cleared up immediately!" He thumped the arm of the sofa.

"OK, OK, there has to be some innocent explanation for all of this." Bonafacio stared at Burvill as though he had the answer.

"What the fuck, Giuseppi? The Vatican interested in some goddamn wasteland in the asshole of the world? I don't think so. Something's up, and we need clarity. Clarity!" He thumped the sofa again. "Get a hold of Cardinal Alfonso at the Vatican and find out what he knows about this Black—if he'll even tell us. Someone we know has got to know. I'll contact Napoli and see if they know anything. I can't believe this. What a cluster-fuck it will turn out to be if this is true. Find out if Black is on the Vatican's payroll and who exactly he's representing. I'll talk to De la Hora and find out what he knows—probably nothing, but you never know if he had a change of orders. He's going to flip!"

They both sat in silence as they gathered themselves, trying to strategize on how best to handle the situation.

"What the fuck is going on?" Burvill leapt up from the sofa and strode out the door toward his office, almost apoplectic. A door slammed down the hallway, and Bonafacio was left to ponder. It took him a few minutes to gather himself before he looked at his watch to figure out what time it was in Rome and whether he could get hold of the cardinal now. It was 10:30 p.m., and the cardinal was likely unavailable and in Matins, but he would at least try.

* * *

Burvill couldn't make contact with Napoli, and neither could Bonafacio make contact with the cardinal. It would all have to wait. It was going to be a long night, but at midnight the phone calls would begin.

Meanwhile, Burvill stomped into De la Hora's office. He was still around and lounging back in his upholstered chair staring at the view of Vancouver's harbor.

"Marino, what do you know about the Vatican's interest in Toodoggone?"

De la Hora swung his chair around to face Burvill. "What did you say?" he asked, raising his eyebrows.

"The Vatican. What do you know about their interest in Toodoggone?" Burvill's face was red with anger.

"What the fuck are you talking about, Ian? You gone crazy? The Vatican? You know where they are? Roooommmme! Why the fuck would they be interested in some ass tit piece of land in nowhere Canada?"

"A source told us they *are* interested, and that source apparently represents their interests, or so he says. And that interest right now is Toodoggone. They want to acquire it for some reason that currently eludes us, unless they know something they shouldn't."

"Can't be true, Ian. That's bullshit. Someone's trying something on here, but whether the Vatican is interested or not, I have to assume that someone is, and that is far too close for comfort. I need to make some calls."

"I already tried Napoli but no luck." Burvill screwed up his face. He needed help, and De la Hora might as well pitch in.

"I have some numbers I can call anytime. Let me see what I can find out."

Burvill stomped out of De la Hora's office. *At least he doesn't seem to know what's happening,* he thought. *Maybe it's a hoax, but it sure is a serious one if it's true.* The door to Burvill's office slammed again as he dove onto his couch.

* * *

Bonafacio's call to Cardinal Alfonso was short. There was shock on the other end of the phone and total denial of any knowledge of Matthew Black or what Bonafacio was suggesting. Although there was some hesitation, which Bonafacio interpreted as the cardinal not being 100 percent sure of his footing. Cardinal Alfonso was one of only three in the Vatican who knew about the ties between the Mafia and the Nazi gold, although none of them had any idea of where it was. He was the principal keeper of the financial records that went back to WWII and had access to all the files.

"Is that all you know, Cardinal?"

"It is, Giuseppi, but I hesitate only because I cannot speak for everyone in the Vatican. There are many business dealings from many different departments, and we are not the clearing house for all of them. Perhaps..." He trailed off, lost in thought.

"Would you call me if you hear anything that even remotely sounds suspicious?"

"I will, Giuseppi, but for now I must think this through."

Their phones clicked off at virtually the same time, and Bonafacio headed down the hallway to Burvill's office to hear about his discussion with Napoli.

"Same as you, Giuseppi. Nothing. No word on the inside and no word in the pipeline. Just a blank. No one can figure out who Black is or what's going on, but you can be sure that Rome will get involved, and there's going to be a sit-down at the Vatican. Until then, all we can do is wait and lie low. No contact with Black and no word outside of this office. Let De la Hora make his contacts and get back to us before we do anything else—if there is anything else to do.

* * *

De la Hora made his connections in Sicily and New York. Nothing. No one knew Matthew Black, and no one had ever heard the word "Vatican" brought up in the same conversation as Toodoggone. *Niente*. Nothing. It had to be a hoax. But they were worried enough that the phones started to ring around the world.

De la Hora reported back to Burvill.

"OK, so what do we do about this whole thing with the Vatican apparently wanting to buy Toodoggone out?" Bonafacio asked as he sat on the edge of his chair and looked at the other two.

"We wait." Burvill had calmed down now that he knew that the Mob didn't appear to know anything about it. "Let's see where it goes. No way they can buy us out through stock. Toodoggone is too wrapped into Global and doesn't exist as a separate company with stock of its own. So it's safe where it is. We'll just wait and see if Black comes back."

De la Hora shrugged in agreement.

23
Trading Global

The next morning another trade went through for 50,000 Global Gold shares at $22 a piece, and the cages rattled. The following morning the same happened, then the day after and the day after that, a slight premium mounting with each transaction. All the buy orders went through.

Burvill and Bonafacio would look at each other each morning when the trades came through on the wire. Both were worried, and it showed on their faces.

"What the fuck?" was all Burvill could say, while his partner stayed silent wondering what the hell was going on. There was no way there could be a take-over, but the fact that someone was selling and buying out there was troublesome.

"Check out who's selling, Giuseppi! My guess is that it's that bastard Barnham this time! He left town pretty fast after the meeting with Black. It's just a gut feeling, but there was something wrong with him when he went. Just a gut feeling, but let's follow up. Get our guys onto it. Did he go back to Monaco or somewhere else? He must have been somewhere close to have executed the trades, but where?"

They were on the wrong track. Peter Barnham had left town after instructing his broker to sell as buy orders came in. His focus was on getting him and his wife out of Monaco and over to Guinea, where it would be difficult for others to follow. He was right. She had been freed but was scared and more than ready for a move as soon as he returned home.

Meanwhile, the buy orders for Global stock were posted each day until there were no more to buy. It would be impossible for ORB to become a majority shareholder, but at least they could keep Global occupied with anxiety as they made their physical play for the Toodoggone mine—if they could find it.

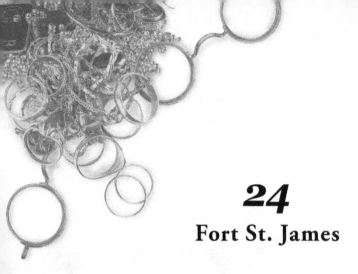

24

Fort St. James

Nestled on the southern tip of Stuart Lake, about 200 kms by air north of Prince George, and 550 kms by air north of Vancouver, British Columbia, lies Fort St. James at a latitude close to 55°N. Established in the early nineteenth century as one of the first fur-trading posts and now boasting a population of around 4,500, there is just enough income from tourism, hunting, timber, and mining to keep everyone at least partly employed to survive the extremes of the area's summers and winters.

In the mid-twentieth century, Fort St. James became a floatplane base, helping workers to access the area more easily. It was during that time that the first of the Nazi gold was hauled over from Prince Rupert by flatbed trucks and transferred onto tractor-trailers, then sledded into the mountains. That continued until all 2,000 tons had been moved and stockpiled in the underground adit in the Toodoggone range. Over two hundred tractor-hauled sled trains in groups of five, each one carrying two tons of gold ingots, and each train taking three weeks to get from the marshaling point just outside Fort St. James to the mine site. All in all, it took almost two years to get all the gold into storage, with one sled train leaving each week with a six-week turnaround to Fort St. James. It was Lucky Luciano and his small group of Mob professionals who had masterminded the plan and rounded up enough tractors and their local Native drivers and sleds with security and scouts to execute the expedition.

The drivers were never used to unload the freight or even saw it being unloaded. They had been confined to camp as soon as they arrived at the site until they were needed again to take the tractors and sleds back to Fort St. James. Some of the tractors were left up at the mine site with the sleds, for when they might eventually be needed, but over the years they had deteriorated and were scrapped and disposed of in pits off to the side of the property, buried with a covering of forest floor.

Now seventy-five years later, Matthew chartered a float plane out of Prince George to fly into Stuart Lake. ORB had rented a cabin on the lake, provided a robust four-by-four pickup with all the rough terrain gadgets he might ever need, a couple of snowmobiles, rifles, handguns, a satellite phone, and an assortment of other weapons as well as a pantry full of food to sustain him for up to a month.

Power was supplied by a diesel generator and the water via a submersible pump in a well somewhere on the lakeshore. There was a tile field for sewage water, a cell antenna on the roof of the cabin, and a shortwave radio setup for emergencies. The two Winchester rifles, Glock pistol, and ammunition were in a hidden compartment on the underside of the kitchen table, and a set of steel-tipped darts were on the table along with a dart gun and some paralysis formula.

Only the pilot of the charter chopper had seen Matthew go ashore and approach the cabin. There were no neighbors within sight, but that didn't mean a lot in that area of the country, and only when winter came and smoke spiraled from the chimneys would one ever know if there were other people around. But Matthew knew that Emma would be close, and he was comforted by that thought. She hadn't made contact yet, but he knew she needed her time to meet with her support team, get themselves settled, and test their equipment. They would get together when the time came and it was safe to do so. Meanwhile, he was on his own.

Matthew tossed his grip bag on the bed and got acquainted with his new surroundings and his gear. Then he took off in the pickup for his first visit to town. It was dusk, and he was thirsty. He thought about putting a sat call in to Emma but decided a beer might go down better at that point.

The Zoo was only one of three places to drink in the small town of Fort St. James. It was also a legacy of the town and the region. It used to be physically segregated between Whites and Natives. Now the physical barrier was gone, but culturally the groups still stayed divided as if the barrier were still there. Anyone who dropped in on a Saturday night could tell there wasn't a lot of mixing going on.

It was by no means a classy joint. One could easily get away with jogging pants, jeans, and a 1980s haircut and still be cool while dancing to the top-forty music from the 1970s and 80s under a dulling disco ball and strobes set to slow, with people wasted or passed out all around. There were pool tables and booths with old, ripped red faux-leather seats and the feeling of something icky stuck under the tables if one dared to venture a hand there. White to the south and Natives to the north with an uncomfortable grey zone between. Getting wild and crazy is what they did in their own way at the Zoo, and it was the best way to get a sense of life in that small town—if that's where one really wanted to go, though most didn't.

Matthew pushed one side of the swinging doors open and peered inside. It took a few moments for his eyes to adjust to the light. Then he made his way to the bar. One of Murray's people had checked the town out before he arrived, so he didn't need to waste time getting to know how things worked there or where the best place to meet the locals would be. He ordered an Okanagan light draft beer from the bar, then went back to sit in a booth somewhere in the grey zone. His strategy was to do this each day and stay for a few hours until someone asked who he was and what he wanted. Then the questions would come.

That first time Matthew had stayed in the bar for four hours. People came and went, and things got rowdy as time passed. He had a plate of pub food and a few more beers but didn't strike up any conversations. The second night was much the same, but by the third night he got a "How you doin'?" from the hairy, barrel-chested guy behind the bar and some questioning looks from a couple of Natives leaning against it, each one with a bottle in his hand.

By the fourth night, the bartender seemed almost friendly and asked "Same as usual?", and set Matthew up with a draft while he ordered him a plate of food. There was only one item on the menu, but it changed each evening.

Matthew cuddled a second beer.

"Howdy, stranger. What you up to in this part of the world?"

Matthew looked up at a wild but good-looking female who stood over him. Her long, black curly hair hung in a mess around her face, a once-white baseball cap with a fly-fishing motif on the front perched on the back of her head. Her hands pressed on his table while she waited for an answer. She wasn't getting one.

"Not from around 'ere, eh?" She pulled her baseball cap farther over her eyes, hitched up her form-fitting jeans, and tugged at the hem of her T-shirt.

Matthew took a sip of his beer and then rested the bottle on the table while he took in the woman before him. He wasn't sure if she was really attractive or whether it was all this mixing with F150s, being in the outback, and being around such an odd-looking bunch of drinkers that made her seem better than he had seen in a while, but something was working.

"Just taking a rest from the city, my friend. It's been a long drive up, and it's going to be a long drive back, but I needed a break, and this is as far as I wanted to come."

"Sounds fine by me. Jus' askin'. It's a great place if you wanna do a little fishin' or huntin'. I can show you where, and if you don' 'ave the 'quipment, I can get some fer you." She smiled, showing her white teeth and a crinkle in her eyes as they screwed up a little.

"I might take you up on that. What do I call you?"

She sat down opposite him. "Oh, I'm Sam. I do guidin' 'round these parts and have done for some ten years. Took it over from my father. He passed away a couple of years ago, God bless his soul, so it's just me now."

"Sorry to hear that, Sam. I'm Tom. Do you have a number?"

Sam reached into her vest pocket and pulled out a grubby business card that said, "Sam's Outdoor Sports—Fishing, Hunting, Trail Guide." Her telephone number and address were on the back, and a faded picture of a person wearing a hat and waders with a larger-than-life rainbow trout on the hook was pictured on the front as a backdrop to the details.

"Oh, you do fly fishing?"

"Nah, that was my dad, but I never changed it. Lotta good memories 'n' stuff. Everyone asks that. I guess I should get it changed, but both of us were called Sam—you know, Sam and Samantha—so it didn't seem logical to change anything," she said nonchalantly without showing any signs of discomfort about the situation. "Gotta go though." She stood up. "Call if you need some fun, and I can come get you."

"You know where I'm staying?"

"Of course. What kinda hunter do you think I'd be if I didn't know who or what was in my camp?"

"Why don't you come over and have a beer when you're in the area, Sam? We can talk about hunting and all that stuff."

Sam pushed her cap to the back of her head, winked at him, and sauntered out of the saloon doors. Boy, that was some view from behind.

Matthew pocketed the card and sipped his beer. Contact.

On the fifth night, he seemed to have become almost one of the regulars. Customers tipped their hats or raised their drinks to him when he entered. He sat in the same booth in the grey zone with the same beer and a plate of food as he had done on the previous four occasions.

This time a Native slipped into the seat next to him, his friend close behind. One was tall and skinny, the other short and stocky. Both were dressed in jeans and checkered shirts with a pack of cigarettes poking out of the top pocket.

"Lookin' fer some help, mister?" the tall, skinny Native asked. "We're pretty good at hunting an' trackin' if you lost somethin'."

"Oh, thanks. Yes, as it happens, I was thinking about going into the bush for a while and looking for something I lost a long time ago."

The Natives looked at each other and then back at him.

"Whatcha lost?"

"Well, actually, it was someone. My great-grandfather—they called him Black Mike—had a cabin out there in the forest. Any ideas?"

Their jaws dropped a little, and they frowned as the name hit them. They remembered the stories. They looked at each other and shuffled in their seats, then took a pull at their drinks and nodded grimly as they put their bottles on the table. The short, stocky one pulled out a cigarette, but the tall skinny one batted it away.

"No smoking, ijut. You wanna us kicked outta 'ere?"

"I weren't gonna smoke it, ijut yerself. I just wanna put it in my mouth. I ain't gonna light it."

120

The tall, skinny one looked back at Matthew. "Well, that's a name we ain't heard in a long while there, mister—Black Mike. An' you're his great-grandson? Well, I'll be. Who'd have thought the old buzzard had left anyone other than his missus around."

Matthew didn't flinch. "Well, I think I'm from before Mrs. Black Mike, as I understand it. I was an 'in-betweeny,' so to speak."

The Natives looked at each other and shook their heads, then looked back at him.

"In-betweeny?" Skinny looked perplexed.

"Yeah. I was conceived in between his wanderings. He was a gold hound, you know," as though they didn't. "He traveled all around these parts looking for the stuff. I don't know if he ever struck it lucky, but the story goes that he did find something before he died, but any information he may have had was lost. But I'm not looking for that." Matthew paused for effect. The Natives waited.

"Well, whatcha lookin' for then?" the short, stocky one asked.

"I'd just like to find his old shack and say a little prayer. I think I was his only survivor, and I want to let him know that his name has passed on. My name's Tom Black."

"OK, OK," Skinny mumbled and they both sat back and stared. Black Mike, Tom Black—maybe there was something there—could have been Mike Black, not Black Mike. OK. They had completely lost the memory of Black Mike really being Mike McClaire and that the Black part was just a nickname. But then again, his surname never was recorded. So it could have been Mike Black for all they knew, and it seemed to fit with this story.

"Well, I don't know if we can help any, but come tomorrow we'll get an answer for you and see what we can do. You gonna be around?" The Natives needed a little time to digest the information, check with their fellow tribe members, and get back to him.

"How about here, same time tomorrow?" Matthew asked.

They both knew it was their cue to disappear.

"Gotcha, Mike—I mean Tom. Whatever." Skinny tapped his baseball cap, and they left.

Matthew went back up to the bar for a refill.

Barrel-chest took the empty glass and started to pull a pint.

"Be careful with those Injuns, mister. They're a little loose in the head, if you know what I mean."

"Thanks," Matthew replied. "Do you know them?"

"Oh yeah. They been around fer years, those two. Part of the furniture of this town. Don't mean no harm, but you just have to be careful they don't skin ya." He looked at Matthew with his eyebrows raised. "They usually mean well, but they can get things kinda mixed up."

"Are they part of the band?"

"Oh yeah. If that's what yer looking fer, they're good fer that." Barrel-chest pushed the pint over to Matthew and moved on to the guys along the bar.

"That's what I need," Matthew said to himself. "A couple of loopy band members." He went back to his booth and sat for a while longer.

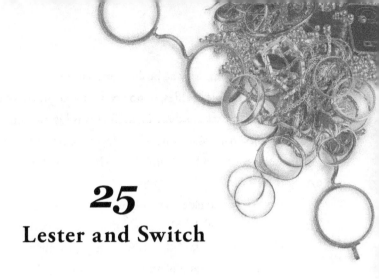

25

Lester and Switch

Skinny and his sidekick showed up the next evening at the same time as previously. They sat in the same booth as Matthew, in the grey zone, and sipped their beers.

"How much?"

There were no words of greeting, just the words squeezed out the side of Skinny's mouth as he sipped. He was a person of few words, but Matthew had little doubt as to their meaning.

"Five hundred dollars a day plus expenses. You bring the supplies and give me the receipts. Cash advance of two thousand dollars to buy vitals, with another advance after we've been in the bush for five days. After that, money gets transferred to you each week when I give the instructions over the sat phone to my bank. You need to let me know where you want the money delivered. If you want cash, I can arrange for someone to deliver it. Deal?"

"That for each of us?"

"Yes, for each of you. Deal?"

"When do we start?" Skinny had looked over to his pal for a nod of agreement.

"Soon. Sometime in the next few days, which will give you time to stock up. We'll use three ATVs to drag our gear and then head out on foot when you think we should."

Matthew counted out some advance money and laid it on the table. Skinny snapped it up and shoved it into his shirt pocket.

"Sounds good. Our guess is that this could be a four- to six-week turn-around trip, so travel light, warm clothes for the nights and solid steel-toed boots for getting through the bush. Gotta gun?"

"I'll bring a couple of rifles, so no need for you guys to be armed." Matthew deliberately held back on the Glock. That was his protection—just in case.

"Let's drink to it." Skinny held his beer in the air, and they all clinked glasses.

"I assume you two have some idea where we're headed?" Matthew asked, eyeing them both.

"We talked to the elders last night." Skinny was clearly the talkative one. "They know some of the Sikamni Tribe. They wuz the band that originally knew where Black Mike 'ad a cabin. They just about gone nowadays, but there's a few old uns hangin' aroun' in the bush still. They comes into town now and agin, so they all meet up and swap stories—usually the same ones over and over agin. They still tell the one 'bout Black Mike an' someone who tried to find his place way back. There was the story about this Italian-sounding guy, like a mobster or something, Loochiano or somethin' like that. Seems he had been sniffing around for Black Mike as well and then he kinda' stayed in the bush and was only seen now and then when he came into town." Skinny took a slug of beer and wiped his mouth on his cuff.

"There was a lot 'o commotion going on around those times, but no one's ever seen nor talked to anyone that wuz involved, so the story's kind of withered. But whatever it was, it stopped suddenly back in the forties. Then a number of years ago there wuz these guys in town looking for help to take some tractors into the bush. They rounded up a dozen or so of us and took off. They seemed to bypass the town after that, and when they would come out of the bush, they just headed to a place outside a town an' only came into town occasionally to get fueled up on liquor and gas. All pretty hush-hush stuff though."

"And Black Mike's place? Any ideas?" Matthew was anxious to move on.

"Yeah. It's over on the Toodoggone Ridge, near the big bend in the river. Just take a route to Baker Lake and then head north to the Fork."

"What's the Fork?" Matthew asked.

"It's like a jagged ridge line stickin' up from the mountains. Looks jus' like a fork. Can't miss it," Stocky answered nonchalantly as though everyone should know that.

"OK, and Baker Lake?"

"Due nor' east from 'ere. We can take the Skukum Trail for about forty clicks and then into the bush from there. Maybe them tractors that have been comin' and goin' from there 'ave worn some kinda path."

"OK, anything else?"

"Nope, that's all she wrote, but maybe we'll remember something else along the way."

"Well, you should know that there seems to be some dubious activity that I hope doesn't get in our way."

"What kinda activity?" Skinny asked.

"I'm not sure," Matthew lied. "It seems that I may not be the only person looking for Black Mike's cabin, as far as I can tell. Seems like some foreigners may be interested in it for some reason. Can't tell right now, but we need to be careful."

"Bit odd." Skinny looked over at his sidekick, who just stared back with no apparent interest.

"Look, it's probably nothing, but I know they're making runs into the bush in the same direction as we need to go. Who knows what they're doing—could be exploration or maybe something they don't want anyone to know about. In any event, I want us to be on guard. When we head in, we'll see where they're traveling, and maybe I'm just being super sensitive, but I want us to be careful. My senses say this isn't good, and maybe we'll find something that someone is interested in as well. So stay cool, and we'll find out.

"Let's meet at my place Thursday evening and set things up for a fast move out. Make sure you bring everything we need. I'll bring the ATVs, fuel, rifles, the sat phone, and my clothes. All clear?" Matthew looked at the two of them. Could he trust them? For five hundred bucks a day, he thought he could.

They nodded their understanding.

"I'm Lester, and this 'ere's Switch, by the way," Skinny said, introducing themselves.

"Switch? That's an odd name," Matthew remarked.

"He thinks he was switched at birth, but I think it's cuz he jus' seems to come and go," Lester offered.

"See you Thursday." They didn't ask where Matthew was staying, but then they would already know that.

With that, Lester and Switch sidled out of the bar.

Matthew could only hope they were up front and wouldn't end up in another bar somewhere spending the supply money. He figured the lure of some good money coming in over the next couple of months would be too much for them to resist, but that didn't always work. Sometimes the short-term gain was all that could be trusted in folks, and any longer-term potential just wasn't to be trusted because that's all it was ... potential.

He finished his drink and headed back to his cabin to put a call in to Murray. It would be coming up to six in the morning in London, where Murray had taken up some space near Covent Garden to coordinate things from. He would be up planning his day.

26
Found It—I Think

"Stockman." Murray's unmistakably deep, resonant voice answered the phone as clearly as though he and Matthew were in the same room. Sat phones had improved substantially over the years, and call costs had fallen dramatically. They still served a critical purpose in the outback. They were also secure, unlike cell phones and landlines, which could be tapped or traced.

"I had an interesting meeting at Global last week," Matthew said with no introduction. "It pretty much confirmed we're on the right track. It's pretty obvious where the gold is. And thanks, by the way, for the fast cash transfers. We need to keep that up until they really start to squirm."

"No problem. We picked up some dialogue from the Vatican that seems to corroborate their concerns, but they run a pretty tight ship, and one department rarely talks to the others without the pontiff involved. We got some very interesting stuff though, and I think our friend the pope is really in trouble."

"Good. I made contact with some local Native band members, and we're heading into the bush this week as soon as we know De la Hora has arrived and headed in. Any last-minute details I need to know?"

"Good to hear. We've got a line on the shipping company they use. Very exclusive and only private charters. Seems like they use the same one every time—routes to and from anywhere you want. Convenient. Comes in and out of Prince Rupert when needed. They use a specialized container maker. Some outfit in one of the Vancouver suburbs—Container Retro on Annacis Island, I think. Place fabricates all kinds of things but specializes in container retrofits for all kinds of uses—offices, remote camps, security, modular electrical substations, and all that. Anyway, we have one of our guys in there now poking around. He got a welding job with them, so we'll maybe get some more intel as we go along here. I don't know if we'll use them, but at least we know what they do.

"The legal beagles are still looking over the import rules for Turkey, if that's where we're going, and that has yet to be decided. We have to be extra careful because they don't let any used equipment into the country that's more than ten years old or it has to be turned around and leave within ten days—and that includes containers. And the manifest paperwork must be tight and right. Any deviation and your goods can get tied up forever in the quarantine yards—and they need advance warning of incoming shipments. So no amount of muscle is going to move those guys away from that unless we can use our friends in Ankara to help us. We just need to make sure the retrofits are carried out on new containers, if we need them, and get the paperwork through the system—although we're going to have to come up with an alternative and believable description of the contents than just 'gold.' But we do have a line on a reliable Turkish inland freight company, Savay Logistics, managed by a gal, Ebru Ozcelik, apparently a pretty dynamic individual who's well known to our Turkish friends. She runs a substantial fleet with offices all over, including Mersin, where we're thinking of coming through, although Istanbul may be a better location. She has the customs rules and regs down pat. Never breaks the rules but does get them bent a little, and that's all we need, and she has contacts in all the right places."

"Sounds good. Anything else?"

"If we decide to freight the gold out ourselves, we're still looking at shipping from Prince Rupert. Not the best of sites although they have started to receive cargo through a container terminal that was commissioned just four years ago—maybe by our friends at Global who are using it. Got great crane services these days, but their shipping points are limited to China and LA, apart from Vancouver and Seattle. So not much we can do about that unless we take things over completely.

"They would likely ship to Vancouver, then trans-ship to an intermodal line that goes through the Panama Canal and down to Brazil for the refinery.

After the processing, they would likely transfer to Argentina and ship from there to the Med. We still need to work out the details if we take things over at Fort St. James, but we would ship direct to Turkey through the Panama Canal. What we are sure of right now is that the northwest passage would be out of the picture. That would raise too many alarms that we don't need, although we'll still work on the potential, provided we find the right crew that has done it before."

"Sounds good, Murray. I'd better go. You won't be able to call me unless we fix a time, so I'll check in with you every three days—same time. I still have some planning to do, and I need to put in a call to Barnham. I'll talk to you later."

There was a knock on the door. Matthew jumped and grabbed a gun. It was nearly 2:00 a.m. Who could it be?

When he opened the door, he found Sam leaning against the doorjamb. She thumbed at the hat on her head.

"Need company?"

"A little late for a lady to be wandering through the woods, don't you think?"

"Yeah, if you're a lady." Sam sauntered into the cabin and headed to the fridge. "Been thinkin' about that huntin' I was talking about?"

"Yes, I was wondering where to start. Close by, I hope." Matthew watched as Sam pulled out a beer and opened it, taking a sip.

"Well, we could start right here. That's as close as it gets." She took off her cap and shook her hair out over her face. "You know, I was thinking about how we could put some kind of an easy payment plan in place, so you get your first hunting trip going soon."

"Sounds good." Matthew was mesmerized by Sam's confidence and extremely attracted to her physically. "Any thoughts take shape?"

"Well, for a start, I'll promise to keep my eye on my brothers and make sure they don't screw you." She wriggled out of her jeans, sat on the bed, winked at him, and pulled her T-shirt over her head.

Matthew's jaw hung open. It was one of those few times in his life he wasn't sure what to say.

"You mean Larry and Switch ... and you and them and family and things?"

"Didn't they tell you? Guess they didn't, but that's how they found you. I told them to get over to you and see what you needed. We're a close-knit family most times, and then sometimes I have to do some babysitting—of them, I mean."

"I'm lost for words, Sam."

"I can see you are there, Tom. But don't be. I jus' wanna tell you that those guys are good guys, and they'll be even better with me watchin' 'em, so why don't you come on over 'ere and let you and me do a little watchin' of our own?"

Matthew slipped off his own T-shirt and went over to the bed. It didn't take much effort for Sam to pull and Matthew to fall.

27
Get This Over With

"Peter, how are you doing? It's Matthew here, just checking in." Matthew put on a happy front for Peter Barnham, knowing he didn't need to use any threatening dialogue at this point. The man was already suitably agitated. He was back in Monaco with his wife trying to figure out what to do.

"Fuck, I don't know how long I can keep this up. After the meeting the other week, they were bloody livid. You really rattled them, and now they're looking for blood. I hope to God it isn't mine!" Peter was more than just agitated; he was scared.

"Take it easy, Peter. Nothing's going to happen. All I wanted to do was to get them agitated enough to start opening the communications with their associates. We'll take it from here."

Peter let out a long sigh.

"Anything else to report?"

"When is this going to be over for me? I've told you what I can, and I arranged the meeting. I've been selling the stock you called for, and I haven't heard anything from Global yet, but it's just a matter of time."

"You're almost finished with me, Peter, and then you can get away from all this. But my advice to you is to create a circumstance that will cause you to cut ties with Global and get as far away as you can from them. The lid is about to blow, and you really don't want to be standing too close when that happens. But make sure you still sell the shares. We need 50,000 at a time, and I'll be putting the orders through another company, so watch for them."

"What do you mean? What's going to happen, and why do I have to get away?"

"Peter, get out, that's all I've got to say. Now, what's new?"

There was another lengthy pause as Peter weighed his options, not liking any of them.

"De la Hora's on the move. He's heading up north. Something must have come up, and I would guess that's you. I have no idea what his plans are. I'm not in that loop. He comes and goes as he wants, and no one questions him. They don't even arrange his travel or where he stays. He does all that. No one ever knows how long he's going to be gone for, what he does, or why he's doing whatever it is he does—especially me."

"That's good, Peter. Anything else?"

"Sounds like Burvill is heading out in a couple of days. He got called back to his master—wherever he is. He's not in a good mood; that's for sure, but I don't know if that's a result of the meeting with you, or other company business. He's had some pretty crappy deals recently that are not helping the bottom line. Looks like he loaded Giuseppi with a bunch of Meridian stock in exchange for more Global stock that put them even further into the driver's seat. Meanwhile, the Meridian stock tanked after they discovered the operation was a bust on geology. What a mess."

"Isn't that par for the course though?" Matthew asked. "Lapa tucking crappy deals in Global's portfolio?"

"Yes, but this one was exchanged for a lot of stock that will dilute the shareholders even more. They're going to be really pissed."

"Does that matter if Lapa is in the driver's seat already? Who cares what the minority wants?"

"True." Peter paused as though he didn't want to say any more. "But the majority of the stock is held by Mob contacts outside of Russia, and that can only mean trouble."

"Got it," Matthew stated almost glibly.

"Anyway, I have to go. That's all I have. You need to let me go."

"OK, Peter, away you go. If I need you, I'll be in touch, but remember, I know where you live, and make sure you keep that cell phone on all the time, at least for the next few months."

Matthew didn't wait for a response, but he was pretty sure that Peter would be packed and headed to the airport within the hour to get on the first international flight out of town as long as it went east.

ORB kept close tabs on Peter and his wife and followed them from Monaco to Guinea, where they stayed in a small, discreet hotel while they looked for an apartment. They would likely need him again at some point if someone else didn't get to him first—which was a strong possibility. Not only was Peter selling his stock to Black, albeit through a broker, now he was on the run, and that was very suspicious to Global Gold—and, therefore, the Mafia.

28
Waiting for De la Hora

Matthew decided to wait the extra days in Fort St. James until De la Hora arrived in town. He passed the message on to Larry and Switch. They were happy to have the extra time to get things together and pack in a few more drinks while they could. There wasn't going to be much room on the trip for alcohol.

While he waited, Matthew scouted the area to the south of town that his newfound friends had suggested could be where anything coming out of the backcountry might arrive and anything going in might leave from.

On his first pass, Matthew didn't see any obvious gaps between the bushes along the east side of the highway that could have been made by motorized equipment. He slowed down and almost crawled along for his second run when he noticed a narrow, flattened corridor between some bushes that seemed to lead into the forest. He stopped to investigate. Sure enough, while the bushes had been pulled back over the entry point, the flattened ground cover remained. A narrow trail led farther into the forest. Matthew followed it on foot for about 150 feet before the trail widened into a manually cleared area where there were tractors, trailers, boxes of equipment, fuel drums, and various other paraphernalia lying around covered with camouflage canvas. Another narrow trail took off to the northeast, but Matthew didn't venture any farther and instead turned back toward the highway.

He had found the marshaling area.

Driving back to town, Matthew wondered what De la Hora was up to this time and whether it meant he would be bringing some more gold out or whether something had rattled him enough to come prepared to take it all. Matthew still had no solid idea of what was out there or even if he was really on the track of the Nazi gold, but he was going to find out soon, and without De la Hora knowing it, he was going to be helping him.

Matthew drove into the parking lot behind the Zoo and noticed a few vehicles he hadn't seen before. They were made for rough terrain, built more ruggedly than his, and caked in mud.

As he entered the bar, Barrel-chest raised his hand in greeting and signaled to the beer tap. Matthew nodded and then worked his way to the bar, keeping an eye on his usual booth while trying to spot the strangers. He saw a crew of guys huddled in a booth, three on each side of the table, with two pitchers of beer in the middle and two empty ones sitting on the side. They had been there for a while. If they came out of the bush where he had discovered the marshaling area, they must have been there for a while before he got there because no one had passed him on the highway.

Matthew sidled up to the bar and took his beer with a nod to Barrel-chest.

"Any ideas who they are?" he asked.

Barrel-chest shrugged. "They come in every now and again. I dunno where they're from, but they never create any trouble. They stay in rooms upstairs for a few days and then head out again. I guess they're from one of the logging camps up in the hills. They've been foresting up there for years and steadily moving south. This is their R and R, I reckon, tho' I woulda thought they coulda picked a better place than this." He shrugged and carried on wiping the bar, cleaning up some spilled beer.

"Same ones every time?" Matthew asked.

"They seem to rotate with others. Changes now and again, but I don't take no notice. Seems like nothing happens with them. Jus' come and go."

"Anyone meet with them? Maybe someone who doesn't come in from the bush?"

"Yeah. This kinda short guy with slicked-back greyish hair comes in after a day or so, and they all sit together talking low and drinkin'—but not so much as they do when they're by themselves. He leaves, and then a day later they all leave, and that's that." He thought for a moment. "Come to think of it, sometimes he leaves at the same time as them and gets in one of their trucks, so I guess they all go into the outback together. He's likely the boss. He acts like it, and they listen to him like he is."

"Any weapons that you know of?"

"Yeah. The cleaner said she noticed they all carried rifles, and she seen a couple of handguns lying around when she's been in their rooms when they been 'ere in the bar. But that ain't unusual in these parts. Guns are all a part of what folks do—you know that. You likely got some yerself, I s'pose."

He didn't linger, walking off to the end of the bar to serve one of the men from the table who had come up for another couple of pitchers.

Matthew made his way to his booth and shoved over to the wall side. The guys were in the booth behind him.

Matthew listened as closely as he could without seeming obvious. Clearly, they were foreign, but that wasn't unusual in those parts, what with the exploration and the forestry work. But where from? He couldn't place it. Could have been a foreign language bastardized by years of living in Canada or the US. There was nothing to learn there, but Matthew guessed it was De la Hora who would be meeting them—and likely the next day.

Matthew finished his meal, had another beer—he didn't want to disappoint Barrel-chest and ruin his habit—then headed out a little earlier than usual to the cabin.

It was dark, and the stars were out. Such a beautiful night with just the occasional sound of owls hooting their call signs to each other and looking for food.

Matthew got the sat phone out and dialed Murray's number.

"Hey, Murray—all good here."

"Good, Matthew. Things are going well here too. More information and plans being put in place. What have you got?"

"Looks like De la Hora's going to show up in town tomorrow. You can let Barnham off the hook for now, but keep the phone taps on him. I don't know how far we can trust him, although I think he's shit scared enough to get out of everything with Global. But he's done his job for now."

"That's good. I think we'll keep a tail on him just in case."

"I'm hoping De la Hora heads into the woods. That way he can lead us to the mine. All we have to do is keep a half a day or so behind him, but my guess is that they may have a four-by-four trail figured out, which would be good, but we'll still use the ATVs. See if you can get me a drone with some lasting power, would you? Everything is set with my guys."

"Sounds good. I'll get right on the drone and get it up to the cabin for your next trip in. It's too late now if you plan on leaving tomorrow or the next day. Anything else?"

"That's it for now. I'm going to head back into town and keep an eye open for De la Hora. Doubt he'll be here tonight, but you never know. Ciao for now."

"Talk later. Stay safe."

Matthew grabbed his wallet and keys and headed to the door, almost bowling Sam over as he headed toward his pickup.

"In a hurry there, Tom?" Sam smiled and held her hand in front of her to stop Matthew from smacking into her.

"Hey, Sam." Matthew pecked her on the cheek, and she seemed to blush, not being used to being treated like that. A peck on the cheek? What was that supposed to mean? But she caught on fast and recovered before her sudden expression could be interpreted as shyness. She wasn't that kind of girl.

"I was just heading into town to see if there are any new faces around." Matthew smiled back at her and they stood on the porch together, neither wanting to move first.

"There aren't."

Matthew gave Sam a puzzled look. "What do you mean? How do you know what I'm looking for?"

"You're lookin' for that little Italian-looking guy with the greased-back hair, ain't you?"

"Well, yes," Matthew replied in shock. "How did you know?"

"Bill, the bartender, mentioned it."

Not much got missed in that little backwater.

"May as well 'ave a beer, don't cha think, Tom?" There was a twinkle in Sam's eyes again. Matthew smiled, then erupted into a laugh.

"I really like you," he said as he pulled Sam through the door and then slammed it shut.

29
The Vatican Bank

The call from Bonafacio had rattled Cardinal Alfonso. He had no idea whether there was a tie between the Vatican and the Toodoggone land or not, but just because he didn't know didn't mean that another branch of the Vatican didn't either, and that troubled him.

He strode back and forth in the annex meeting room, clearly troubled, as he waited for the others to join him. Not only was there the call from Bonafacio, but he was also anxious and totally unprepared for the line of questioning he had been subjected to by a pair of anonymous men who had appeared earlier in the day with the blessing of His Holiness himself. Coincidence or not, he had to collect himself. They had shown no credentials to him but had immediately started to talk about the Vatican Bank and the financial mysteries surrounding the ways in which it conducted business. It was difficult to tell whether they were part of some independent financial "expert" group brought in by the pontiff to uncover more of the unsavory dealings, associates of the Italian banks that had been invited to help with the investigation, or some other nonpartisan group that, perhaps, had been brought in by an international financial oversight body. Regardless, it was troubling, and the signori needed to share the burden with his colleagues.

Cardinal Alfonso was one of five cardinals charged with overseeing the management of the Vatican Bank on behalf of the Catholic Church. He had been involved with the position in one way or another for over forty years and knew more than most about the troubles, the dealings, and the pains that the bank had gone through since the 1980s. He also knew some, but not all, of the history going back to its beginnings, and sometimes it was that history that really was hurting the Church now. But then, neither was he an innocent in the nefarious bank dealings that had maintained them as the bank of choice by international criminals.

The Vatican Bank, founded in 1942 and often referred to as "God's Bank" or, technically, the "Institute for the Works of Religion," was a private financial organization located within Vatican City and reporting to the pope and a commission of cardinals, of which Alfonso was now one. It was originally established to avoid the restrictions placed on bank accounts by the Allies during the war years so that records of transactions could be avoided if desired. It was exempt from wartime restrictions and became the world's best "offshore" bank.

Unfortunately, the power that the money brought to those who controlled the Vatican Bank, and the Church's insatiable need to meddle in world politics, resulted in skullduggery and scandals within the Vatican. Even before the Vatican Bank became a regular front for the transfer conduit of Nazi gold under the seal of a sovereign state, they had bundled together life insurance policies of Jewish refugees who had been sent to Auschwitz and other death camps and sold them at face value, only to hoard the payments themselves. Later, when the victims' children or grandchildren tried to collect on the insurance policies, they were refused on the basis that no death certificate could be produced.

The Vatican Bank's declaration of neutrality during WWII meant they could do business with everyone and, as author Gerald Posner proposed, "They abdicated their moral position as the head of the world's largest religion, especially at a time when they continued to make money with the people committing the murder."

At the time they were frozen by indecision and fear. They were afraid that if they spoke out, the Nazis might move against Catholics and take the pope back to Germany as a prisoner. They were desperate, greedy, and without conscience for what they needed for their own future.

Once Lansky had moved the gold through the Vatican, away from Europe, and over to Canada's west coast, where it found its resting place, the rumors surrounding the Vatican Bank, Swiss banks, and Nazi Germany subsided as the post-war initiatives overtook the thoughts of most. But some never gave up, and several interested groups, including Mossad, continued to try to trace the missing gold. Some of it turned up, but the majority vanished into thin air.

Then in 2013, Germany started to repatriate some of the gold back to Frankfurt and into the vaults of the Bundesbank. The German political story appeared clean insofar as the government explained that their gold stocks had been accumulating offshore over the years in anticipation of repatriating them when needed. But several NGOs and government groups associated with anti-Nazi doctrines doggedly pursued the German government and the Vatican, which had somehow managed to thwart the civil action brought against it in 2000. They didn't get very far, and the groups had to fall back on their Vatican Bank theories and their involvement in at least some of the gold transactions. Little did they know that the Vatican Bank was involved in almost all of them along with the Mafia and the German Nazis, who still held the reins of the German banks.

It wasn't until the first gold shipments returned to Germany that the pressure cooker blew its top, despite the story having not completely unfolded. But there was enough to show that the Vatican had become embroiled with the gold and that the Vatican Bank had taken a primary role in receiving it and, at the very least, keeping some of it—probably as a fee for services rendered. Some said the Vatican was the final repository of all the Nazi gold.

At one point, Italian prosecutors detained the former head of the Vatican Bank after searching his home and former office for suspected criminal behavior, including money laundering, although at the time he was not suspected of being tied to the missing gold—that was a stretch too far. He was sacked when the board passed a unanimous no-confidence vote against him. While the new pope promised to clean up the bank, little came out of the pressure cooker that could have led to the gold's whereabouts.

Cardinal Alfonso kept pacing until his colleagues started to show up. He shook each of their hands vigorously. They could tell there was something wrong, and they consoled their friend with words of comfort and religious anecdotes.

"What the bloody 'ell?" Signori Bertocelli yelled after they had seated themselves and Alfonso had summarized what he had just gone through. Bertocelli was not a man to be threatened. Normally, he did the threatening, so he was completely unprepared for this situation. "What the bloody 'ell is going on? Who are these people? Where they come from? What they want? I must see the pontiff. I must go now to tell him to stop these people. They have no right!"

"Wait, my friend." Dominici pleaded. "Wait, and let's talk before you go to see him. It's important that we know as much as we can before you approach him. We don't know where these people come from, but they may be from the pope himself, and if that's the case, it would be a mistake to raise his interest further by objecting to his methods. Perhaps we need to invite them rather than avoid them."

Signori Dominici was the thinker of the group. He never moved fast and never, ever impetuously. Steady, slow, and methodical. He was the brains behind the Vatican Bank when it came to dealing with those who might harm it. It took skill for high-ranking members of the Church to negotiate with the financial criminals of the world. The slightest error in judgement could expose them all, and they had survived over seventy years without exposing themselves beyond what they could repair. Their secret had always been silence. Beyond that, Vatican City's sovereignty protected them.

"Cardinal Alfonso, who are these people, and what did they ask of you?" Dominici had a peaceful, gentle voice that belayed the ferocity of the person within when it came to business. He could hold his own against any member of the Church or the Mob.

Cardinal Bertocelli slumped in his chair with an air of having been scolded. He cupped the side of his face with his hand and hid the angry quiver of his lips with one finger. "Well, the pontiff called me into his office this morning and introduced these two men to me as financial experts who were going to provide a second opinion on the way we allow the Vatican Bank to do its business. It seems they have some good thoughts about cyber-security, simplifying record keeping, and transparency, all in the name of our survival in the future.

"He said we must be sure that we are seen to be conducting business in a rigorously moral way, and to do that we have no choice but to become more transparent. I told His Excellency that we could not. There is too much to consider, too much they cannot know, too much at stake!"

He told them of how the pope had put a hand out and touched him on the shoulder.

"He told me that the sins of our history are our sins, and we must protect ourselves from the light, but from here on in we must also work with the outside world and not behind it."

Cardinal Alfonso told them he was a little relieved by the words but that he was having a mental block as to how to deliver on the promises to the pope. How to answer the questions while at the same time not saying too much, and certainly not about those parts of history that would certainly be destructive to the Church.

"But how?" Alfonso had asked the pontiff. "How do we accomplish that? How can we be transparent but opaque at the same time? The gold, the insurances, the Mafioso, what do we do about the land, the artifacts—all those things we have collected over the years or sold or bartered with or used to our advantage?" They all knew the problems to which Alfonso referred.

"You will find a way, my son," Germane had reassured him.

"He told me it would become clear, but first we have to get rid of all records that might implicate us. Everything must have a murky trail with little or no historical substance. Transactions must be reinvented or even destroyed. Our clients must work with us since they are accomplices, and they will need our protection as much as we will need theirs."

Cardinal Alfonso relaxed as he told the story and shared the words the pontiff had uttered. It would take a substantial effort to change the records, to lay false trails, contact their clients, and work with them to ensure they cooperated and understood the magnitude of the problems.

Now he was here with the commission to start the process. There were so few of them that it would take years to undo the records that had been established. But the records could be their ruin, so they needed to be destroyed and replaced by a trail of simplified but modified transactions, instructions, and descriptions. They would need a group of trusted clerical and financial people from within the Church to do the work once they laid out their plan, but first they needed to computerize and encrypt the files, get rid of all hard copies, and hide the computer files. They would be much easier to store away from prying eyes than the binders of bank records that filled two bookcases from floor to ceiling. It was a monumental task that needed professionals.

"Leave it to me," Cardinal Dominici offered. "We can use the computer group we've been using for the archiving of much of the Vatican Library where the words have become much more important than the documents and where we have been making room for more documents as the scientific world becomes more and more verbose on subjects that must be archived for our survival."

As Dominici left the room, the others wrung their hands and whispered amongst themselves as they considered the activities they had been involved with over the years that were clearly illegal, all the while trying to convince themselves that it was all for the good of God and humankind and that without them there would be no Church. That was likely true, but the past was catching up to them, and it was not a pleasant feeling.

30
The Vatican Archives

Dominici reached his own offices and called for Carlo, who was responsible for overseeing the recording of the archives. He brought with him the senior tech from the team.

"We have an urgent matter that requires your attention, Carlo," Dominici said, looking at both of them.

"Si, Signori. As you wish."

"I want you to pause your work on the archives. We need you to scan other records that are taking up some room where we're planning a special placement. I will have others bring you the documents in the order they are to be catalogued. Do not deviate; that is very important. Once catalogued, the papers will be sealed in a secure vault, so it is imperative that you follow my instructions and work continuously until the work is complete. Only then will you go back to the archives. Do you understand?"

"Si, Signori," Carlo replied. "Should we work in the same place or move to another location? And how large should the computer files be? Do you want them on the same size hard drives as we are currently using for the archives?"

"We will take over one of the smaller conference rooms at the end of the Great Hall," Dominici said. "The binders will be taken there ten at a time. Each group of ten binders is to be put onto one hard drive. Each drive will contain no more than ten binders and be delivered to me personally as the work is completed."

"Si, Signori. We will start immediately if you assign the room we are to use."

So it was that the task of scanning the documents started in earnest under the guidance of Carlo Mancetti, an ORB operative placed in the Vatican some twelve months earlier for other reasons on another case. There were over 400 binders, each containing over 150 files, or some 60,000 files altogether, with each file containing on the order of 30 pages—1.8 million pages in total. They had four high-speed scanners, but it would still take a month to scan all the pages even if they worked twenty-four hours each day—and they would.

*   *   *

"Tom, it's Carlo in Rome. Game on. We're moving over to the Vatican Bank records. Something's happened to scare Dominici, and he's the talking head to us for the Bank Commission. Don't know yet, but I would guess that we'll start scanning the banking documents tomorrow and run twenty-four hours a day. We think it could take a month or so, and we don't know what order the records will come in, but I'll let you know as I identify information. There are four high-speed scanning machines to come in, so I'm not sure what I'll see and what the others will see, but I'll try to work something out."

"Good, Carlo," Tom replied. "Things are starting to move here, so whatever you can feed me, do it as fast as you can, and make sure you use the secure link. Those guys are going to do whatever they have to do to keep this thing hushed up. Any idea if they've shared any information?"

"Not yet, and we may never know. That's not where we are in the communications loop. Just computer techs, you know. They keep their eyes on us all the time when we're scanning to make sure we're not reading what we're copying. But I think I have a way of avoiding that and getting what we need through a wireless transfer to other sticks. Should work. Never saw the need to use it for the archives, but this may be what we're looking for—a direct and irrefutable link."

"Make it so, Carlo." Tom put the phone down and contacted Murray to pass on the news.

*   *   *

"OK, OK," Murray said. "Let's see if we can pin down the gold transactions primarily, but pick up any other knowledge that could be useful as well.

This could be the mother lode of information. The exposure not of just the Vatican Bank but also some of the worst financial criminals, and others, in the world. Good work, Tom. Keep me in the loop."

"Of course, boss." Tom clicked off and went back to his work on the Bundesbank investigations involving the archives until he was ready for the Vatican Bank project.

31
Scanning the Files

Carlo had installed a wireless transmitter to each of the scanner units that could be accessed remotely when scanning was in operation. Each transmitter was uniquely encrypted to be recognizable on the receiving drive. The wireless information automatically transmitted whatever was being scanned. That meant all the documents would be scanned, but the information might not all run serially on just one of the receiving hard drives, since four scanners could all be in use at the same time on various parts of the same document. But sorting them out would be a task for others with more sophisticated equipment.

Carlo had his work cut out for him just making sure he could bring in a sufficient number of drives to provide the original for the cardinal and a copy for himself. His tactic was to double up on each drive needed for the cardinal on the pretense of needing a spare unit in the event the first one failed. While the security was tight in terms of oversight and searching, they would never question the number of hard drives being taken into the Vatican, and since the drives were collected at the end of each day and stored in a safe, Carlo simply had to identify the originals from copies when they were secured for the night.

Taking the copies out from the Vatican posed a problem, but Carlo would use a mule for that purpose and found the nuns that visited each day ideally suited to the task of taking the copies off site for him to pick up later on the pretext of the hard drives being the "tools of the trade." The nuns didn't ask questions and were only too happy to help Carlo, who, they were sure, was helping the pope.

It took over a month to download the information onto the hard drives and steal them out to a courier via the nuns. From there they were flown to London for analysis and collation so that a "story" could be pieced together, primarily for the transactions associated with the gold. The rest of the information was put on other hard drives and transferred to government security services in London and New York, where they would comb the information for other dubious or incriminating information.

Carlo's work was done, so he returned to the Vatican Library to continue his work there.

Meanwhile, the cardinals considered their next step. It would be laborious work, but with the help of auto search-and-replace functions, they could access the information they needed relatively quickly and replace words and actions at the tap of a finger. "Gold" was retitled "artifact." "Swiss" was revised to "benefactor." "German" was changed to a variety of dioceses from around the world. Each cardinal had their own selection to pick from. In some cases, short paragraphs were altered to hide the truth, entries were blanked out, or more elaborate descriptions were reduced to more mystifying short entries where the passage of time would help to hide the facts. These became the files that were transferred to the Vatican Bank investigators while the original documents that were copied were sent to the Vatican vault, where they were labeled with nondescript names and buried behind dusty boxes and metal cases that never saw daylight. The vault was located in a chamber well away from reach and never discussed other than between a select few who held more of the Vatican's secrets. Even the pontiff was ignorant of its existence, or so it was thought.

And so it was that when the time came for the forensic search to begin by the pope's financial investigators, all they were given were the hard drives and told that the hard copies were no longer in existence. Who could challenge them? Not even the holy father.

But it was too late. The information was in the hands of ORB, who doggedly combed the copied hard drives and searched for any references to the Nazi gold. There were many, and they all indicated transactions made by the governing cardinals at the time during the war years and some shortly afterwards that were made with the Cosa Nostra, who had channeled the ill-gotten plunder from Swiss banks controlled by Germans through the Vatican. The gold all flowed through the Vatican's hands, but little stayed. It seemed that only a percentage remained with the Catholics as they advanced the gold shipments on to a variety of European ports under the Vatican seal to avoid inspection by customs. From there the records weren't clear, but they didn't need to be since the destination had become clearer as ORB dug further.

Fort St. James, a small, old mining and forestry community in the interior of Canada's westernmost province, would be the receiving point, and from there on into the mountains to rest a while, until it was needed. The exact location was unknown to the Vatican, the Swiss banks, or the German hierarchy. Only the Mafia knew; they had inherited the task of transporting and hiding the gold.

32
The Mine

Matthew, Lester, and Switch met at Matthew's cabin just as dawn approached on a crisp late August morning. They arranged their supplies onto three skids, each of which would be towed into the outback by a four-wheel Polaris Sportsman 500 ATV equipped with extra-wide snow tires and a liquid-cooled 500 cc high-output, overhead-valve, single-cylinder engine. Easy to maintain, reasonable haul capacity, and reliable. Each could carry spares and two people if needed, and each had a haul capacity of 1,225 pounds on a hitch. That would be enough as they prepared for their foray into the forest.

They needed to wait for De la Hora to show up in town before they made their move and left their supplies at the cabin while they waited.

De la Hora had blown into town a day later and rounded up his men early the next day, after a night at the Zoo. Matthew had decided not to go there that evening, but at 5:00 a.m. the next morning he went to the Zoo parking lot to watch for their departure. They had set off in two powerful pickup trucks and headed out the way that Matthew had assumed they would. There were six of them, all foreign looking, loaded with supplies and rifles.

The next day it was Matthew's turn to head into the bush with Lester and Switch. De la Hora would be one full day ahead of them, and they needed to keep their distance. Better to lag farther behind than to catch up. The evening before, Matthew had checked the entry point into the forest and located the two pickup trucks in the clearing, well covered with brush. Some of the tractors had gone with their trailers.

It was a crisp beginning as the three of them set off with maps and compasses for the Toodoggone property. They were keeping as close as they dared to the fresh tracks made by De la Hora's crews while at the same time being as careful as they could to parallel, where it was possible, rather than religiously follow the trails left by the tractors. There was no room for them to leave evidence that they had been on the same trail, and certainly any out-coming traffic would not bother to look for parallel tracks, but they would be extremely suspicious of tracks that covered their own.

Loaded with fuel, supplies, firearms, and optimism, it was still like looking for a needle in a haystack for Matthew, but with the guidance of the local Natives, he hoped that their search would narrow to Black Mike's cabin and from there the gold. Lester and Switch didn't seem to need the maps or the compass, but every now and again they would stop to confer, cast their eyes over the landscape, sniff the air, and think awhile before setting out again without discussion or comment to Matthew. They were focused and intent.

The forest was thick with fallen trees, bush, marshes that were just start-ing to freeze over, and the occasional but non-intrusive bears and shy moose that skirted them rather than them having to skirt the moose. There were occasional pastures, but the marshy soil hid the dangers of trusting those serene-looking areas, and Lester and Switch earned their keep by knowing how to circumvent them and not being lured by their placid invitation.

They camped in clearings surrounded by the majesty of the forest without being smothered by it and allowing them to fire their wood pits without posing a danger to the surroundings. There were no signs ahead of campfires from others. Lester and Switch knew how to survive in the outback with a style over and above what Matthew had expected, but it was still rough. Their tents were not impenetrable, other than to rain, and the cold of the late-August nights had to be accommodated, together with the thought that a marauding bear could easily tear their tents apart in an instant. But Switch and Lester knew how to keep the night fire smoldering sufficiently to keep lurking intruders from investigating too closely, the smoke disorienting their senses.

Each morning at the crack of dawn, the trio moved onwards after the rejuvenation of coffee and hot cakes cooked over the remnants of the night fire. They covered their ashes and returned the forest floor to as pristine a state as it could be before they left. There was no room there to be intrusive. It was Native instinct, a sign of respect.

There were creeks to cross, steep hills, marshes, and thick forests to navigate, and small mountain ranges to trek through. All the while, Matthew consulted his compass, but the Natives just seemed to smell the air and know which way they needed to go. Now and again Lester or Switch would venture out to check the trail that De la Hora's crews had made. They would return with renewed energy and spur the little group forward.

"What are you looking at, Lester?"

"The sky, the birds, the way the trees bend."

"What does all that tell you?"

"Not a lot, but it all gets blended into the mix. In the end it's a feeling, and feelings are usually right. Don't ask me how." Switch seemed to agree with a small shrug of his shoulders as he looked down at the ground and fingered his beard.

"You say that every day, Lester. Are you sure you know which way we're going?"

"No, but I trust my feelings, and you should too. You ain't got any better ones."

"That's right." Switch actually said something, but it was meaningful enough for Matthew to believe it was all true.

It took ten days to reach a point where Lester and Switch halted and made it known that they were close enough to their quarry that they needed to rest awhile and consider their strategy.

Matthew wanted to press forward. There was nothing he could see that indicated there to be a sign of others. Lester put a finger to his lips that told Matthew to keep quiet, listen, and follow. Lester and Switch inched forward to a small hillock where they dropped to their stomachs and peered over the edge. Matthew followed and did the same.

Over the hill they saw a fenced compound, a couple of guards with fire-arms, and tractors sitting idle next to a couple of cabins. The cabins were simple wood structures with canvas roofs. A stovepipe exited each, and smoke spiraled into the air, along with the smell of burning cedar.

There wasn't a lot of movement. An occasional figure would emerge from one of the cabins and head over to another or up the adjacent hill into a portal of some kind.

Matthew used his binoculars, but he didn't recognize anyone or anything. They waited where they were and then eventually retreated to a safer area to discuss their strategy.

Lester and Switch were becoming nervous now that they had reached their quarry. Perhaps it was time for them to be paid off, and they would return to Fort St. James. Matthew coaxed them to stay with the promise of more money.

They stayed and watched for two days, looking for anything that would help them strategize.

"What now, boss?" Lester asked now that he knew what Matthew was looking for. Black Mike's cabin was just a short distance away from where they were, yet Matthew had not ventured there.

Matthew didn't expect any more help from his guides. They had done their job, and there was no reason for them to stay around or know his real intent. He needed to get closer to the activity and figure out if this was really the place he had been looking for.

"Lester, you and Switch can head out. I'm going to stay awhile to see what these guys are up to. I'll catch up to you in town, and we'll square up. Meanwhile, don't go blabbing about what you've been up to, and lie low, low, low."

"Roger that," Lester answered with a tap of fingers to the side of his nose. Switch stayed silent but touched the peak of his cap by way of a primitive salute. They walked down to the clearing below and over to their ATVs. They pushed them another two hundred feet before firing up and heading back the way they had come.

Matthew was left to ponder. He checked his GPS, confident that he knew the way back to town, but then, there was the trail if he chose not to take the high ground. He decided to lie low for another day or so to see if there was any indication of what was going on with De la Hora's camp, although he was already 99 percent sure of what that was. He would contact Murray to double check the situation and strategize his next move.

* * *

"Are you there?" Matthew asked—no names.

"Come in."

"I'm up at their storage area. Took us over a week to get in here, but so far so good. I'm going to stay a few days to confirm things, but it looks like we may have hit the jackpot. I'll send the GPS coordinates in case we need to get some help in here. I think this is all there is, but who knows if there's more to this camp, maybe some outposts. I'm going to follow the fence line and see what's out there. It's that time of year, and the nights get pretty cold, so there could be some fire smoke that gives things away."

"Good job, Matthew. Keep in touch, and call me at the same time in two days. If I don't hear from you by then I'm going to assume something's happened to you, and I may have to send the troops in.

"Oh, by the way, it seems there's some activity within the Vatican, and his lordship is involved, according to the calls in and out. Something's rattled them. Maybe a call from Global about the gold or from our friends in the Mafia in Rome. Whatever it is, they're cleaning up fast, but it's a little late; we're already on it. I don't think they know that, but whatever they're up to, it has his lordship's blessing."

"My guess is they're suspicious after I told them about the claims we had staked around their property and our interest in buying their claims out."

"I should think so," Murray replied. "I can see the robes flying from here. They must be beside themselves trying to figure out what to do, especially if they think you've been masquerading as their representatives. Not to worry. Your tracks are covered. No way they'll ever figure out who you are or who you really represent. This has really set the cat amongst the pigeons!

"Take care, my friend. The only thing you have on your side right now is to act fast and take advantage of them having been so lax all these years. Now that the gold has started to flow, they're going to have to be more vigilant with, or without, you on their tail."

"You're right. No way they've seen this kind of a threat before. This place is almost quarantined in terms of exploration. Toodoggone is completely tied up and hasn't been threatened by potential neighbors for years. Now suddenly, here we are."

"That's right, my lad. But at the same time, their complacency over the years will slow their reaction time. It's not exactly a place where they can come in guns blazing, but nevertheless, you need to be extra careful. We have no idea what resources they have or what they may send. We're going to continue to monitor the chatter and stay one step ahead."

Matthew unconsciously touched the Glock in the holster on his belt as though he needed the comfort.

"I've got it, Murray—I think! I'm just staying around long enough to get some photos and check the place out. Then I'm out of here, and we can figure out our next move."

"Good. The safer the better. No need to go in with guns blazing at this point. Maybe we should let them bring some gold out and then take it and shut them down, but let's talk about it after you do your initial recce."

"Over and out, but see if you can get that drone to me sooner rather than later."

He returned the phone to his case and then checked his watch. It was midday, a good time to do a little exploring around the edges of the De la Hora camp, although dusk came early, around 3:30. He would go on foot and be well hidden by the forest. He needed to know the extent of the occupied area and plan how he was going to get closer. Were there cameras, more sentries, more fencing?

Matthew had already realized that he needed to get closer to the portal and had loaded up with a camera, metal detector, scope, rope, and other necessities that he might need. They were all lightweight and easily accessible. He even took some rations and some water. The portal was the busiest location at the moment, but perhaps as dusk fell that would change, especially around chow time.

From a distance, he could see that people were not only going into the hole in the ground, they were also coming out with something. Their walk was labored and slow. They almost staggered to the tractor trailers, and someone on the rear end of the trailer was taking the loads from them and moving it farther along the flatbed. It seemed obvious to Matthew what the loads were, but it was imperative that he confirm it.

Matthew started to skirt the property through the bush, his rifle slung over his back, and the Glock at his side. For additional safety he was armed with a dart pistol with six 1,800 mg Ketamine darts with a range of 100 feet. They would immobilize immediately on contact but not kill.

He stopped frequently to take in the forest sounds and listen for anything that seemed alien. He was sure they must have guards around the perimeter. They would be camouflaged and blend in with the forest. His steps were slow, soft, and careful. His head turned continuously, and he lifted the rifle scope to his right eye almost continually. It was equipped with a heat sensor that could detect any warm-blooded animal or human.

A sudden movement to his left froze him, and he fell as silently as he could to the ground. He wasn't in camouflage, other than the charcoal around his face to absorb the light, but he blended well with the forest. Not daring to breathe, Matthew pulled out the Glock and fitted the silencer. As he screwed it into place, he spotted a silhouette passing just fifty feet ahead in a direction that would have crossed his. He focused all his attention on the figure as it moved stealthily across his vision. The figure bent and seemed to be examining something on the ground. Matthew couldn't make out what it was but guessed that it was likely a trip wire of some sort. Maybe electrical or maybe just a wire—or perhaps an occasional bear trap just for luck. This was going to be a more difficult exercise than he had anticipated, yet he wasn't surprised.

The figure stood up and moved slowly forward, a flashlight leading the way, although it wasn't yet dark. Matthew decided to follow, maintaining his distance and feeling the ground as he went. He pulled out the small metal detector from his backpack and checked the battery condition. It was still maintaining almost 100 percent power. He used it to poke his way forward. If it detected anything, the needle would swing toward the red on the dial, but no noise would be made. It was difficult going. While the sky was heavy with grey clouds, he could still see his way. As he drew up in the wake of the figure, the metal detector showed signs of a find. Matthew bent low enough to spot a wire that traveled in the same direction as the figure. It probably surrounded the property, and the figure was checking to make sure it was still intact.

Matthew cautiously stepped over the wire, making sure he stayed on the same side as the figure, following in the same tracks. The figure would bend to the ground every one hundred feet or so and tug gently at the line. This went on for a mile or so. They had moved in a semicircle some 150 feet from the De la Hora camp. The figure detached itself from the path of the wire and started to head down the hill toward the cabins. When he reached the six-foot-high barbed-wire fence, he unlocked a padlock on the gate, let himself through, and locked it behind him. He hadn't looked up to check his surroundings and had probably done this exercise in the late afternoon every day just in case an animal had snagged the wire and exposed it.

Dusk started to settle as Matthew waited for the figure to disappear into one of the cabins. If he wasn't careful, he would get caught there in the dark. While he had the GPS coordinates to lead his way back to his own camp, it would be doubly difficult if he couldn't see his way forward.

Regardless, Matthew decided to get through the gate and cross the compound to the cabins.

It all seemed quiet, likely supper time for the De la Hora people. Matthew made his way to the gate, took out a multi-purpose lockpick from his backpack, and needled his way into the keyhole. It took him less than twenty seconds to feel the lock release, and then he slipped inside, locking the gate behind him. He crept forward, watchful for any movement beyond or behind or above in the hills. There was none, but he couldn't trust just his sight. There could easily have been a sentry higher up with a view of the encampment. He scoped the area with his heat seeker and confirmed what he had felt. No one was around.

Matthew stood inside the gate and turned his head as he searched the land around him. Then, keeping low, he made his way to the nearest cabin, pushed himself upright against a wall with a window and peeked inside. No one, no movement, and no sound. The logs in the furnace were burning, but no one was watching it. He made his way over to the larger cabin, and this time he used his flexible scope to lift over the sill rather than show the top of his head. This time he saw movement as the group inside ate supper. There was little conversation, and what there was seemed to be in Italian. There were nods and serious looks passing from one to the other as they focused on the speaker and the meal. Beyond was the cook, still busy at the stove preparing more food and concentrating on his task.

As he was about to move away, a movement caught his eye as a figure headed toward the same cabin—a sentry looking for food, perhaps. Matthew froze and closed his eyes enough that the whites wouldn't stand out, but the sentry seemed more engrossed in thinking about food than intruders as he pushed his way through the cabin door that banged closed behind him.

Matthew wondered if there were more. There likely were, but now that he was inside the compound and it was supper time, perhaps another sentry might believe him to be one of theirs as the light faded fast.

He almost crawled over to the tractor-trailers. Whatever they had loaded was covered by a heavy tarpaulin, tightly ratcheted to the undercarriage. Matthew loosened one of the straps on the side of the trailer facing away from the cabins and close to the tractor where he would be able to hide if needed. The tarpaulin lifted several feet above the trailer bed, and he shone his flashlight underneath. Neatly stacked and strapped separately to the trailer bed were bundles of gold ingots. The trailer was only partially loaded. Whether this was the extent of the current haul or not was questionable, but if Global had got the word out to De la Hora about neighbors in the Toodoggone area, they may be trying to move as much as possible out of the area.

Matthew took photos with his cell phone and then headed up to where he thought the portal was. By then it was dark, and he had to pick his way with surefootedness, all the while glancing back at the cabin for any sign of De la Hora's people coming out, but all was quiet.

Matthew climbed up the side of the well-worn path to the portal under cover of darkness but with his metal detector helping him in the event any traplines had been connected while the portal was shut down for the night. When he reached the portal entrance, he glanced back, sideways, and up into the forest above for any signs of life. All seemed quiet.

He crept into the portal and saw that the tunnel curved almost immediately to the left. On the tunnel floor were boot marks and skid marks from something that had been dragged to the mine entrance. One of the skids was just around the first bend—a simple contraption with four sturdy steel-rimmed wheels and an articulated handle. Matthew followed the tracks farther down the shallow dipping adit and noted the pockets that had been blown out of the sides for waste rock to be stored. The waste was piled and pushed back as far it could go. There were more excavations in the walls for generators, fans, and safety gear, as well as an explosives bunker made of steel and rock-breaking tools. A string of unlit lights hung from the roof parallel to two flexible tubes that probably transported fresh air to the adit.

Matthew moved on and finally reached a point where the gold was stored in ingots, sacks, and boxes. Each package was sized for a person to be able to lift, so perhaps each would be in the order of 18–20 pounds, or 300 ounces. Two thousand tons translated to around two million ounces. That was a lot of tonnage to move, and each trailer would only hold about fifteen to twenty tons at a time—if that, given it had to be hauled out through the bush. It would more than likely be taken in ten-ton loads at the most. That would mean about 200 trailer trips.

Matthew took more photos as he pressed himself against the adit walls to see if he could see the end of the stash. He could, and he snapped a few more shots.

It was time to move out. Matthew scrambled down the waste that had been left on the side of the adit around the gold containers. He made his way to the entrance in the dark, alert for any noise.

As he reached the portal entrance, two figures ambled toward him, talking and not really focusing on where they were headed. Matthew scrambled back into the adit, not knowing if the guys were coming in or just checking around.

He leaned against the adit wall and peered out. The two figures were heading straight toward him. One of them switched on the lights, and the whole tunnel came alive. Matthew dodged farther back into the adit until he reached one of the waste rock repositories. He scrambled over the top and ducked down against the far wall, his head barely below the top of the pile in front of him. He pressed himself as close as he could against the waste rock, his ears tuned for voices.

There were no voices, just the sound of scuffling feet, followed by the overhead lights being inside of the tunnel. Their searchlights augmented the overhead lights and flashed over his head slowly and then returned to the adit.

"Tutti chiaro qui," a gruff voice said.

"Anche qui. Andiamo." They both headed back toward the entrance.

Matthew peered over the top of the waste pile when he saw their flash-lights receding. He watched as the two men, perhaps the short one being De la Hora, went back out, switching off the lights as they went. He waited a few minutes, his ears straining for any sound other than his own breathing. Everything was silent.

Matthew crept over the mound of waste and down to the adit floor. He worked his way around the bend and put his flexible scope out around the corner. There was no movement. Again, he waited, his senses heightened. Everything was quiet, no shadows. He made his way toward the entrance.

As he approached, the flash of spotlights caught him off guard. Searchlights had been activated and glared at the entrance. There was no way he could exit without being silhouetted against the mountain. A guard had been posted down the slope, his back to the portal. He packed a serious-looking rifle and slouched against a rock as he peered out across the camp. He wasn't interested in the portal.

Matthew reached for his stun gun, set a dart, and moved forward. The last thing he needed was for an alarm to be sounded. He crept behind a rock outcrop at the portal. He needed to get as close as he could to his quarry. Matthew edged down the slope until he was in range, bent down on one knee, aimed, and fired. The shot was silent and accurate, and the guard slumped to the ground without a sound. He would be out for several hours and unsteady for a couple more once he regained consciousness. It would give Matthew time to get back through the fence, hide his tracks, and beat it back to his camp, but before he did, he removed the dart from his quarry and packed it into his pocket.

Matthew followed the rock face around and upwards, hiding his form in the shadows of outcrops. He dodged the last few yards from the perimeter of light to the darkness and stayed low, watching and waiting. He decided to get to the fence and follow it around to the gate. His path forward would be in darkness, but he couldn't take a chance on using his flashlight.

The going was slow and his footing unsteady as he navigated his way across to the fence line. He had estimated that from the nearest point of the fence to which he was moving, it would take him less than fifteen minutes to reach the gate. He looked over at the cabins, but there was still no movement, although he guessed that someone would come out for a smoke soon.

He reached the fence and started toward the gate. By then a couple of De la Hora's people were outside the cabin lighting up, but they had no reason to be looking in his direction. Now and again, they would look up at the portal, and Matthew wondered if they were wondering where the guard was.

Regardless, they didn't act on it if they were and went back to smoking and talking. Matthew stopped each time he glanced over at the cabins.

When he reached the gate, he made short work of the lock and slipped into the darkness of the forest. As soon as he felt it was safe enough to do so, he opened his GPS and set a route back to his camp.

Suddenly, he heard a yell from inside the De la Hora camp. Someone had just discovered the unconscious guard. A voice called for help, and two more people came running. They carried the man back to the cabin. Minutes later, all hell broke loose as four men, including De la Hora, came thundering out with their rifles cocked and ready.

Matthew moved swiftly despite the blackness around him. He expected a barrage of flashlights, but they would have no idea where he was unless they had night-vision scopes, and he was certain they did.

A few minutes later, the night sky lit up with flares in every direction around the gate area, although it wouldn't be clear which way the intruder had gone. Matthew sought the cover of tree trunks at every opportunity, in the event night-vision scopes were being used. He tried to make a path back to his cabin by reaching tree cover between him and anyone who might be following.

He heard shouts in the distance, but it didn't seem as though they were concentrated in any one place but spread out. And at the rate Matthew was going, he would reach his camp soon. Then he would need to get out of there without giving his position away. After that, his pursuers would need to get back to their cabins and mobilize what vehicles they had for a night chase. That seemed highly unlikely, although Matthew realized they probably assumed that their quarry would be heading back to Fort St. James by roughly the same trail they had used.

They would be gunning for him as fast as they could go. He had to decide fast. Make the run to town—but then what?—or let them pass him in the night. His logic told him to make the run and head straight back to his cabin on the lake, where he could lie low for a few days. He had no idea what types of vehicles they had or how fast they could go, but one could only move so fast through the forest at night, and it would take eight days at a push to make it all the way back. He decided to run for it. De la Hora's people had no provisions on them to make the long trip back without first stocking up at their camp, and that would cost them at least two hours.

At his camp, Matthew threw all he had into his bags and pushed the ATV a couple of hundred feet before starting the engine. The noise of the shouts behind him had receded as his pursuers had fanned out and followed at a slower pace than he had been moving. They didn't want to miss a clue as to his tracks, but he hadn't left any.

Matthew punched through the undergrowth, his headlights on as he ducked under low-hanging branches. He pushed through the creeks and stayed away from the marshy areas, as the Natives had taught him. He was moving at a faster rate than when he and his companions had gone in to Toodoggone. At some point he was going to have to rest up and eat, but for the moment he increased the pace as much as the forest and the darkness would allow. His headlights picked up the trail, and Matthew kept to it rather than try paralleling it. There was no point.

After a ways, he stopped and turned off his engine, focusing on the sounds around him. There was nothing other than the occasional scrabble of some animal in the bush or an owl looking for prey. He guessed that De la Hora's people had gone back to their camp. Then he heard an ATV engine in the distance. It was coming toward him, and it was moving fast. Maybe an hour or so behind, but who could tell? Sound carried so far at night that it wasn't easy to be specific. Matthew listened a little longer and decided that his tracker had probably assumed he would be following the same path that they had taken into the area. Was he alone? It sounded like it. Maybe they had taken the chance that they might catch their intruder sooner rather than later, in which case they wouldn't need supplies badly, and perhaps the others would follow and replenish. They undoubtedly were equipped with sat phones, so they always knew where each other was.

Matthew decided to set a trap, stringing a wire between the trees across the trail, set about four feet above the ground, the approximate height of the chest of an ATV rider. It took him almost thirty minutes to complete the job before he returned to his own ATV and pushed it into some bushes. He turned his lights on to dim and listened to the sound of the approaching engine. He heard an extra rev as his pursuer picked up the lights of Matthew's

ATV. They were dim, as if Matthew was taking a break and had stopped on the trail. Then he turned them off and ducked into the undergrowth where he had covered his ATV with a tarpaulin to hide any reflection.

The pursuer's ATV roared forward as it reached the point where the lights had been. There was an almighty thud as the rider hit the wire. He was thrown backwards, where he lay dormant in the undergrowth. Matthew moved as silently as he could toward the body. The clothing was ripped, and the man lay in a crouched position. His head was flung back, his arms sprawled and a line of blood across the chest. Matthew took no chances and fired a tranquilizing dart into his neck.

Then he stood up stock still, focusing on the night air and listening for any other sounds that would be alien to the forest. There were none.

Matthew clambered back to his ATV and fired it up, deciding to keep going until daylight at least. Then he would rest for a few hours, hydrate, eat, and call Murray before moving on, so his friend could alert the troops to storm De la Hora's camp. He may even make it to town in six days at this rate. At least he could follow the trail back and not have to worry about the marsh.

33
After the Mine Discovery

Following a brief rest after driving all night, Matthew called Murray.

"I was starting to worry, old boy. Everything OK?"

"So far so good. I got up to the mine, saw the gold for myself, and have photos. It was one hell of a ride back out of there, and they knew there was an intruder, but it couldn't be helped. Too much security, and I had to put a couple out of action."

"Great," Murray replied. "We picked up some activity via the satellite, but it's a bit of a stretch to understand the detail. I'll bet it was one hell of a chase."

"It was. But I'm here to tell the story so far. I still have a ways to go before I can claim to be safe though. Hopefully they have no tricks up their sleeves. I figure another four to five days with the fuel reserve I still have, and I should be back at the lake. Any thoughts about getting me out?"

"We should have a chopper up there when you arrive. Clear the cabin, stow the supplies under the barn floor, and come on out. I'll meet you in London a couple of days after that, and we'll go over our strategy for the next step."

"OK. Anything else I should know?"

"Well, we know the Vatican top brass have been in touch with our Mafia friends as well as Global. We think they believe you were a plant but have no idea by whom or why. We know they're scrambling to make sense of it. De la Hora was sent up to Toodoggone to figure out how to get the whole stash out of there into another hiding place as well as to bring a small haul out.

We don't know where they might store the gold or how long his operation will take, but we can be sure they're on it thick and fast. Watch out in town in case reinforcements have been called. They'll be watching the entry point into the forest."

It had been a grueling twenty days in all as Matthew finally sprang out of the forest and onto the road on the other side of Fort St. James from De la Hora's entry point. The exit he used was at the suggestion of Lester, who thought there could be a better way to come and go and to avoid confrontations. Matthew gunned the ATV toward his cabin on the lake. By then a helicopter had arrived and was waiting on the shoreline. Matthew wasted no time packing his things, destroying any evidence of his stay, and parking his ATV in the old wooden garage. He had stripped it of supplies and thrown them through the hatch in the floor.

The helicopter fired up as soon as the pilot saw him. He was ready to lift off the moment Matthew hoisted himself into the passenger seat, clamped the door shut, and belted himself in. As they flew over Fort St. James, Matthew saw a small group gathered close to De la Hora's entry point into the forest, leaning against their 4x4s and staring intently ahead, as if waiting for Matthew to come through. It would be a long wait. None of them looked up at the helicopter, which had already climbed to 1,000 feet above them. Clearly, De la Hora had more people on the ground in Fort St. James that Matthew hadn't been aware of.

34
Crescent Beach

Matthew landed on the tarmac in Vancouver and took a limousine to his home on Crescent Beach, a fifty-kilometer trip from the city. He loved the fresh air that Vancouver always offered as he stepped off the plane and inhaled a deep draft of it.

The forty-five-minute drive to his home went quickly. They took the off-ramp to the beach area, with Matthew giving directions. He clicked the remote, and the gates to his property swung open. The limousine slid through and took him to the steps that led up to the front door. He paid the driver and watched him disappear through the gates before stepping up to the front door and closing the gates behind him.

Matthew unlocked the double wrought-iron front doors and stepped through. A single Lutron switch lit the entire house in a soft glow.

He saw immediately the chaos of his overturned dining table, emptied cabinets, chairs, and sofa pushed over onto their sides with the seating crudely ripped, drawers pulled out and emptied onto the floor, and even rugs that had been pulled back.

He walked up the stairs, only to find the bedrooms completely ransacked. Mattresses overturned and torn, coverings strewn about the place, and tables overturned. Lamps were knocked over, and everything from the dressing room areas had been tossed to one side. But there had been nothing for anyone to find. The place was clean, and this was likely just a warning.

Matthew considered calling in a clean-up team but quickly concluded that it wouldn't really help. Any prints would not be on the Interpol records.

It would be better to leave things as they were and hightail it away from the property. He would likely have to sell and move on, but that was not his immediate concern. He had no high-value items in the house that were irreplaceable, and what he did have was insured. But that would all be dealt with later.

He called Emma.

"Hi, Emma. You home?"

"Yeah. Arrived back a few hours ago. Just waiting for you."

"Can I come over? Bit of a problem over here, and I need a little TLC."

"You know where I am but make sure you park on the street before you come into the complex."

"Right. See you in twenty."

Matthew didn't bother putting anything back in place. It wasn't worth it. ORB would take care of the details, but this would be the last time he would be there. He didn't think his cover had been totally blown, but he realized that this personal invasion of his privacy was going to seriously compromise his activities for the future.

Matthew fired up the Range Rover in the garage and drove through the motion-activated gates onto the secondary road out of the beach area.

He vaguely knew the way over to Emma's place but always lost himself in the labyrinth of the townhouse complex she had buried herself in. It took him forever to locate the place. Then he reversed out onto the road and parallel parked between two cars. He walked down to Emma's place and rang the bell.

Emma appeared at the door in a black cocktail dress, beautiful and totally inviting with a glass of white wine held out to him. She threw her arm around his and drew him in, closing the door behind. She led him up the stairs to her living area and pushed him onto the couch before handing him the wine.

"You like it?" Emma asked as she circled the room with her arm. "This is what I've been working on for the last two years."

"I love it, Emma." Matthew looked around at the antiques and back at Emma as she glowed with confidence and pride. "Everything's so perfect. I love it." Matthew was temporarily comforted by the homeliness of what Emma had created.

Emma swung in a circular motion around her living space. "I love it too, and it's all for you."

Matthew looked perplexed.

"I mean, what I think you want, Matthew, nothing more intended." Emma swung to a stop in front of him and reached out for his hand. "Want to come upstairs?" she asked with a come-hither look, a glass of Chablis managing to stay upright in her hand.

How could one resist that kind of offer? Matthew took his glass of Chablis and followed her up the steep stairs to the bedroom. It was a mass of plush cushions, flowery accessories, and a sweet smell of lavender that permeated with everything female. Emma had disappeared into the bathroom.

Matthew removed his clothes and stretched out on the bed. He wanted to get under the comforter and just go to sleep, but he resisted and waited for Emma.

Emma announced herself wearing only a red sable fur jacket. Clearly, it was the only thing separating her from thin air. She came slowly over toward him as though she had rehearsed this a thousand times, opening the jacket slightly and shutting it tight around her, then opening it again and repeating the move. She was really enjoying herself, and Matthew was mesmerized.

"Like it?" she asked as she smoothed the fur and closed her eyes. "It's real."

"Love it," was all Matthew could respond. He reached out to feel the soft fur, running his hands over it. She opened it just far enough for him to slide his hands inside and feel the warm silkiness of her skin. The two sensations were similar. As he smoothed the fur, it fell away over her shoulders, and he felt her body. The soft hair between her legs. The small but firm breasts. The chest bone and over the same body again and again. The fur jacket had fallen to the floor. Matthew looked down at it as though he had lost something precious, but he soon came back to the main event. They entwined and rolled. Onto her back and onto his. Back onto hers before she submitted and allowed him to enter her. It was all consuming, and everything he had gone through over the last month was forgotten in that moment of passion.

Afterwards, they lay side by side, her head under his curled arm and resting on his chest, his arm protecting her from who knew what. He stared blankly at the ceiling. It was pure bliss. But gradually his thoughts returned to the present, his few moments with Emma unable to eradicate them.

Matthew wanted to sleep through the night with Emma as she cuddled up closer to his naked body. She was still and innocent, but he felt the urge to move on and extricated himself from the blissful moment.

Emma didn't stir as he slipped his clothes on at dawn and stole downstairs. She would be leaving to go back up north in a couple of days. Her team was on a one-week-in/one-week-out schedule unless things heated up, and they had to schedule themselves accordingly. But all they could do right now was watch and report. He left a loving note against the almost-empty bottle of Chablis and then made his way down to the front door and out to his Range Rover. He got the call thirty minutes later.

"Say hi to Sam for me." It was Emma.

Matthew laughed. "Is there anything you don't know?"

"Not much. Happy travels." She hung up.

He wondered whether Sam knew about Emma and what her group was up to. He guessed she did. They were like two peas in a pod.

He made his way down Highway 99 to the city and sought out breakfast at the Moose, a below-street-level place where the early morning crowd gathered for breakfast. He stole into a booth and ordered scrambled eggs, tomatoes on the side, a round of whole-grain wheat toast, and coffee. While he waited, he scrolled through his messages and caught up on the news from around the world. There was nothing from Murray, but he hadn't expected anything unless there was a problem.

Focused on his day ahead, he typed an email to Burvill. "Suggest we meet up today and consider where we are," was all he said. He received a response less than a minute later.

"See you at nine."

That was it; it was all Matthew wanted.

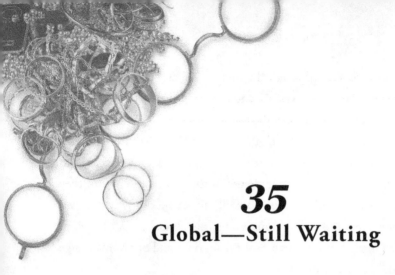

35
Global—Still Waiting

Matthew sat in the Global Gold lobby staring at the same robotic, stereotypical narrow-waisted, perky-nosed blonde receptionist he had previously encountered.

All she had said when he entered was "He'll be with you shortly." She had already cautioned that she was only in attendance at the desk three days a week, so she didn't really know what the inner workings of the company were—although she hadn't expressed it quite like that, more like "They don't tell me what the fuck's going on around here, so this is the best I can do!" Then she had gone back to whatever she had been doing, which was likely no more than exchanging mindless chitchat with someone unassociated with her employer and who more than likely wanted to know more about the color of her nail polish. Matthew knew he was jaded, but he had come through his fair share of experiences with the opposite sex, many of them a little egocentric and lonely in their perspective of the world around them, just looking for a TGIF once a week. That was human nature, and while he appreciated it, it was also difficult to absorb within his lifestyle. Or perhaps he was just getting old.

A blip sounded on her switchboard. "You can go in," she said without looking up. She pointed to the same room where Matthew's previous meeting had taken place.

Matthew tossed his jacket onto the back of a chair and plonked himself down while staring at his cell phone, a habit that everyone had seemed to have developed rather than just stare at nothing. There were no messages, but he kept staring at it as though he was busy.

Burvill almost pounced into the room. He pulled out a chair, slapped himself into it, and looked up at Matthew. "Well, you've been a busy boy, Mr. Black."

Matthew stared at Burvill, giving nothing away through his facial expressions, just put his palms on the table in front of him.

"Listen, we're not stupid, Black. We know you're interested in Toodoggone. We're pretty sure you were up at the property last week, and we're also pretty sure you stumbled onto our property and trespassed inside the fence. We can't prove it, but... " Burvill set his hands on the table and waited for Matthew to respond.

"Sorry, old boy. Don't know what you are talking about. The only thing that interests me is whether you've thought over my introduction to an offer for the property and what your thoughts are."

The corner of Burvill's lip curled up in a sneer, but he was trapped. Clearly, he couldn't prove that Matthew had visited the site, although his people were talking to folks in Fort St. James to verify if he had been in town.

Matthew pre-empted their investigations though. It would be easy for them to find out just from Barrel-chest whether Matthew had been in town. He doubted the Natives would be cooperative—they knew there was likely more money to come from him.

"Well, I did make a trip up there—took a chopper and stayed a few nights just to get familiar with the place. I don't have anything that could support me in the outback though, neither am I a forest type of guy. My guess is that there are some avid explorers out there who are interested in what you have and what it may do for them in the surrounding areas. Maybe they're staking as we speak. Who knows? It's all fair game, and there seemed to be some talk about the Toodoggone area while I was there."

Burvill squinted, the corner of his mouth remaining curled. "Listen, if we do catch you or anyone else who shouldn't be there, and you end up on the wrong side of the fence, we'll consider that trespassing, and you can be sure we'll take aggressive action."

"Are you threatening me, Ian?" Matthew allowed himself a slight smile.

"You bet I am." Burvill was indignant and still uptight, but he let his lip uncurl, his eyes relax a little, and his hands drop to his side.

"Let's get down to the matter at hand," Matthew said, trying to de-escalate the discussion, although his subject matter didn't help, but he did maintain a modicum of decorum and refused to be taunted.

"Listen, we think this whole business with the Vatican is bullshit and put out there to get us rattled for some reason," Burvill said. "We know you aren't working for them, but we don't know what your motive is or if you're even employed by anyone who matters. We have no idea why you're buying up stock in Global, but clearly you can't get anywhere close to a controlling interest, so why are you doing it? Trying to get control of the Toodoggone mine is pointless. It's a part of the Global Gold portfolio, and I told you there's no way we'll part with it." Burvill sat back in his chair and put his hands together in front of him on the table. "Is it possible for you to come clean?"

Matthew was quiet for a moment. He had anticipated this kind of reaction. "Well, Ian, first of all, you are mistaken about my representation of the Vatican. I don't know who your contacts are over there, but I suspect they're not the same as mine, and I also suspect they don't know what the other hand is doing. The fact is, a number of separate groups are all vying for power and control. It isn't a recent occurrence; it's always been part of the makeup of the Catholic Church. There's the religious side, the financial side, the archival side, the legal side, and several others. There's no way the pontiff can keep control of all the balls in the air. I would guess he doesn't know all the groups either—let alone what they're up to. It just so happens that a part, just a part, of the financial side has me on their payroll."

He waited for a reaction, but there wasn't, although it was clear by the lack of reaction that part of Burvill believed him. The Lord knew he found it difficult to keep tabs on who was who and who yielded the power one day but wouldn't the next.

"Now, let's talk about the Global Gold stock purchases," Matthew said, watching as Burvill's mind shifted in a different direction. "You have to admit that our purchases caught your attention enough to get me in to present a case. Would you have done that if I had not made such a fuss? I doubt it. But it also shows serious intent, does it not?"

"I don't know what it shows. As I've said, Toodoggone isn't a separate company, and it's staying as part of our portfolio. I don't care how much you push or who you claim to represent; nothing will change that."

"Listen, Ian," Matthew said, leaning forward, "the Vatican group that I represent are interested, and I suspect they will pursue it whether you're willing participants or not. I would suggest you split the mine at Toodoggone out from the Global portfolio, wrap a bona fide incorporated company around it, package it, and sell it. In exchange, we will pay you handsomely for the property, as well as sell the Global shares back to you at our cost."

Burvill shook his head. "No fucking way, Black. I told you it isn't up for sale, nor will it ever be. I don't care what you offer, who's employing you, or how much stock you buy in Global. It will never be enough for you or your employer to become influential enough to separate Toodoggone out of Global and put it on the block." Burvill was getting worked up again, and his face and eyes told the story.

"You know something, Ian? You're playing the short game, and I don't think you have any pull to do anything about what you're describing. That tells me there's a force above you that holds the cards, and you're going to have to excuse me if I go away and find out who they are. If Toodoggone really does not add anything precious to Global's bottom line, it makes no sense to keep it on the books, and I don't think it has anything to do with sentimental value. That's your bullshit."

Matthew got up, picked up his jacket, and made toward the door.

Burvill shot to his feet, his temper was starting to overflow, and came at Matthew with his fists raised. He tried to grab Matthew's coat lapels but missed as Matthew ducked past him and casually made it out of the door, past the receptionist, who was still glued to her phone, and down the stairs, waving behind him.

Burvill gave an exasperated gasp as he disappeared into Bonafacio's office.

"Bastard is making things really difficult. I don't know who, if anyone, in the Vatican is running him, but I think someone is seriously onto Toodoggone enough to make a play. Problem is, can we hold them back?"

Bonafacio was unable to come back with anything constructive, so he stayed silent.

"Where's De la Hora?"

"Still up north I think," Bonafacio replied.

"Get a hold of him and ask him to call as soon as he can.

Bonafacio picked up the phone and put a call in to De la Hora. He didn't answer, so Bonafacio left a message.

* * *

"What's up?" De la Hora asked, having called back a couple of hours later.

"Hold on. Let me get Ian in here." Bonafacio went to the office next door and motioned for Burvill to come into his office.

"OK, Marino," Burvill began, "what have you been up to over the last few days?"

"Why? What's up?" De la Hora wasn't about to give any details about his activities without some compelling reason.

"Listen, that guy Black has been in here again talking about how he wants to get his hands on Toodoggone. Claims he's working for some branch of the Vatican. He wants us to separate Toodoggone out from the Global Gold portfolio, turn it into an incorporated company, and sell it to him—or should I say sell it to whoever he's actually working for."

"Wow, you guys have sure been busy with Black, and here I thought I was having enough trouble with him."

"What do you mean? Black says he visited Fort St. James but never went to the property, just did a bit of a recce around town."

"Bullshit! That guy was into our site; I swear it. He led us on one hell of a dance getting back to town. I got one guy down with a tipped dart and the other just about sliced in half chasing Black on his ATV through the bush. Bullshiiiiiiiit! He's gotta go."

"I can't argue with that, but we're not the ones who can do that. We gave his place a going over just to ruffle his feathers, but you guys know where he lives and hangs out and what to do. You need a couple of heavies to get in there and see to him."

Burvill was agitated and unprepared to go the distance to get rid of Black. All he had done so far was rough his place up as a warning. But that wasn't the same, and it wasn't going to go any further than that just on Burvill's say-so.

"I'll take care of it. I'll let you know when he's out of the picture," De la Hora said, already thinking about his next move.

"Look, even if we get rid of Black—"

"You mean *when* we get rid of Black," De la Hora said, already getting worked up.

"Yes, *when* we get rid of Black, there's likely going to be someone else we'll have to deal with." Burvill was in fast-forward thinking mode.

"Yeah, yeah, but I'm going to get Toodoggone cleaned up, and then we'll see who's interested. Maybe we'll split the property and get rid of it, but only after we do what we have to do. It's going to take me some time though. That's a lot of stuff to move out."

"OK, one step at a time," Burvill agreed. "Meanwhile, I need to get back to the Vatican while you get to your people. Can you get down here and stay in town for a couple of days while we work out what we're all doing?"

"Yeah sure. OK, but let's keep close. I want to get back up here ASAP."

36
The Bundesbank

In 2013, the German finance minister announced, "The Bundesbank has completed the transfer of some of its gold reserves from New York and Paris to Frankfurt and Munich three years ahead of schedule."

Carl-Ludwig Thiele, member of the executive board of the Deutsche Bundesbank, stood by and looked impressed with himself as he stared at the journalists around him. This was an important day, one that would fill the shareholders with confidence that their country was not about to suffer the same kind of fate that many countries in the European Union were suffering from: economic failure. Germany had been on the brink of the same.

What journalists missed, and the bank had not known, was that the repatriated gold was part of the Nazi gold that had been looted during WWII, some sixty-eight years earlier, and hidden in northern British Columbia until it was needed.

During the war, the Reichsbank, the national central bank at the time, was greatly affected by the Nazis' consolidation of power during the years of the Third Reich. The bank was intended as a guarantee to redeem promises to pay depositors, note holders (e.g., paper money), or trading peers during the eras of the gold standard and also as a store of value, or to support the value of the national currency.

A 1937 law re-established the Reich Government's control of the Reichsbank, and in 1939, it was renamed the Deutsche Reichsbank and placed under the direct control of Adolf Hitler, which lasted until 1945.

The bank knowingly benefited from the theft of the property of numerous governments invaded by the Germans, especially their gold reserves, and much personal property of the Third Reich's many victims, especially the Jews. Personal possessions, such as gold wedding rings, were confiscated from prisoners, and gold teeth were torn from dead bodies. After cleaning, they were deposited in the bank under accounts with false names, with some of it melted down as bullion and shipped out to Swiss banks and others controlled by Germans in Turkey. The Hitler regime desperately needed the gold to boost its reserves as Germany headed into bankruptcy and could no longer pay its debts from WWI.

The defeat of Nazi Germany in May 1945 eventually resulted in the dissolution of the Reichsbank after the economy was reorganized by the Allies. The explanation for the disappearance of the Reichsbank reserves by 1945 was discovered by Bill Stanley Moss and Andrew Kennedy in post-war Germany.

Moss and Kennedy had traveled back and forth across Germany and into Switzerland and corresponded with fugitives in Argentina to research what had happened. They talked to many witnesses before finally establishing what they thought had become of the treasure trove. What Moss and Kennedy uncovered, and the conclusions they reached on the various people responsible for the disappearances, have not been disputed to this day, but neither is it considered that they had accounted for the vast amount of hidden gold.

In 1948, German monetary policy was taken over by the Deutsche Bundesbank, and the Reichsbank ceased to exist, but the records remained, as did some of the administration staff. The president did not, and he was brought to trial for war crimes.

The Bundesbank was now expecting to receive a third tranche of gold and had been communicating with the Swiss banks which, in turn, were in communication with the Vatican and, consequently, the Mafia.

The Mafia set the timeline based on logistics. They were responsible to get the requisite amount of gold out from hiding and over to Prince Rupert for shipping to a port near Lima, Peru, where it would be transported by road to the refinery in Brasilia. Following the refining process, the gold would then be transported to the Argentinian coast for trans-shipment to Naples. From there it would travel under papal protection by road up to Zurn and on to Frankfurt, where it would be deposited in the Bundesbank vault for safekeeping by the government.

It was Tom, stationed in the Vatican and working on the archives, and then the scanning of the banking records, who had discovered the extent to which the Bundesbank had been involved in the gold transfers. Their records went back to the beginning, and there was nothing altered or left out as far as he could tell. There was no reason for the Bundesbank to adjust entries in their books at that time. It was clear when Nazi gold was originally put through their accounts, when it was shipped out to the German-controlled banks in Turkey through Swiss banks, and when gold was received back in 2013 and 2017. Clearly, this part of the story was well recorded and confirmed what ORB had put together.

The Bundesbank records also implicated the Vatican, and their records were currently being examined by ORB in London to verify the movements of gold.

So far Tom could confirm that the Bundesbank had retained a percentage of the gold value it managed, as did the Vatican. Any fee payable to the Mafia appeared to be "off the books" and likely came directly from the other two players.

37
The Heist

Matthew and Murray met in the Club Quarters, just around the corner from Trafalgar Square on Northumberland Street in London, three days after Matthew had come out from the Canadian bush. They needed to meet with the Canadian consulate in Trafalgar Square to lay out their concerns and what they were doing. They particularly needed their help with the immigration people at the US-Canadian borders.

The hotel was an unassuming establishment that offered reasonably sized rooms, a restaurant, and a number of meeting rooms. It was a short walk to the Houses of Parliament, MI6, Scotland Yard, and a number of government-run offices, including the Foreign Office. It was in the middle of the theater district and offered everything a tourist would want as well as being a quietly clean and private environment for business talk.

Murray had reserved a small meeting room down the hall from the front desk for them to talk over their business in private. He had also organized coffee and pastries. Matthew had arrived in London that morning, and it was imperative that they talk as soon as they could. His flight was due to leave for Vancouver at 2:30 that same day unless there was some compelling reason why he should delay.

They met in the breakfast bar near the entrance, and then Murray led Matthew into the meeting room where four leather club chairs were set out with a small coffee table between. The coffee and pastries had already arrived.

"What now?" Matthew asked as they both settled into their chairs and went for the coffee.

"Well," Murray began, "we know our friends are still at their campsite in the backwoods. Our satellite imagery tells us they are continuing to load their trailers, and it looks as though they're getting ready to move the first batch out in what could be just a few days. It also looks as though they're a little short on equipment, but from what we can tell they have more en route."

"Wow, quite a move," Matthew said. "By my calculations they'll need to take out some two hundred or so trailers if they want to move it all. They're not going to be able to move it all in one run—too much equipment needed and too much manpower, let alone the loading logistics involved. My guess is they're going to take some time, probably weeks, if not months, before they get everything out, if that's what they're up to."

Murray nodded. "I think that's their plan, and that's what the radio chatter is telling us—get it out of there and store it somewhere else, or get it down to the ship and move it offshore again." Murray paused to grab one of the pastries, licked his thumb and forefinger, then settled back in his chair.

"But where would they store it if they don't ship it out?" Matthew asked. "That's the question. The answer will determine when and how we strike."

"I guess we need to talk about the options," Murray suggested.

Matthew nodded. "I've been thinking about that. One thing we haven't considered is the distance from Fort St. James down to Prince Rupert. That's quite a haul and maybe not practical for us."

"How far?"

"About four hundred and twenty miles, about an eight-hour drive. That's OK until you think about the logistics of how you get that many loads on the road, down to the shoreline, and then loaded onto the ship without De la Hora and company catching up at some point. It'll be a fight from beginning to end." Matthew flicked his eyebrows at Murray and pursed his lips. "So here's what I've been thinking. There's no easy way for us to get all the gold down to Prince Rupert without bringing on a whole lot of trouble with De la Hora and his cronies. We have some options to consider, and this may not be all of them.

"We could get rid of De la Hora and his people at the camp, but then we'd be left with having to get the gold out of there. Or we could take the first load when they get it to port, take out the guards, and send the ship off as a distraction while we take out the rest of the group and then get the gold to a safe spot somewhere around town once they get it out of the bus. Or we could let De la Hora get all the gold out of there and onto the ship and *then* take them out."

"What about using a helicopter to transport the gold out to the ship?"

Matthew shook his head. "Too heavy and too many trips even for something like the Sikorsky Heavy-Lift helicopter, which is limited to carrying twenty-two tons. Regular US army equipment transfer choppers only operate in the range of ten tons. Can you imagine that kind of a campaign?"

"Planes?"

"Better, but there's nothing in the area that has a runway of at least nine thousand feet long, which would be needed for something like an Antonov 225. Too bad because it has a payload up to two hundred and seventy-five tons. At least that would cut it to eight flights to get it all to Europe."

"What if we lengthen the runway at Prince Rupert?"

"Wow, there's a thought, but it won't happen overnight, and it will cost a small fortune."

"Listen, I doubt the money would be a problem, but we would need to store the gold until we were ready to ship it out."

"I think we could do that," Matthew agreed. "We can get it to the Native lands just outside Fort St. James until we need to get it out of there. My guess is they would be OK with the idea of storing our freight for a while—provided the price was right. We could just tell them it was mineralized rock we were taking offshore for processing. It's been done before, in Greenland. And if we use their land, no one is going to mess with them."

"OK, my friend. That would leave us with figuring out how to grab the gold."

"Yes, I've been thinking about that as well." Matthew reached for another pastry and a refill of his coffee. "We know where they come out onto the highway from the forest after they transfer their loads to tractors that will latch on to the trailers. We also know they're going to have to take the only highway there is down to Prince Rupert—there's no choice." Matthew paused again, carefully considering the next step.

"We let the first four trucks through and on their way to the ship. At the ship they load the gold and make the turnaround to come back. My guess is that all the truckers are Natives, not Mafia, and we should have no fight with them. Let them go back to camp for a refill."

"OK." Murray nodded, a thoughtful look on his face. "What about the rest of the haul? And don't forget De la Hora."

"My guess is that De la Hora won't come out of the camp until after the first load is out and they call him to let him know they arrived at the ship. He'll leave the rest of his team at the site and come out to head down to the ship. We get him before he has a chance to get there. After that, we leave his guys to do the same thing over again."

"How many men do you think they need for the job, and where do you think they'll recruit from?" Murray asked.

"Well, let's assume the truckers do the return trip to camp in something like fourteen days at best. They will certainly work on the camp access to get things moving in and out faster, and my guess is they've already started, so you should get the satellites searching the area to confirm. So a turnaround time in fourteen days, a week to get another five trailers ready, which means they probably need about fifteen trailers minimum with fifteen truckers and a few loaders at the camp with some security. So let's say ten on the road at all times, with two per truck, and about twelve at the site loading and waiting to drive out. They keep going like that and it would take something like eight to ten weeks to get the whole amount out of there if they load the trailers to fifteen tons a piece instead of ten. At the outside it may take twice that amount of time, but I don't think that matters much as long as we get De la Hora out of the way."

Murray raised his eyebrows. "Possible?"

"I think so, provided we have the bodies. Frankly, I doubt if we have to kill off any more than De la Hora, his two security guys at the port, and the two at the camp once they finish up. The rest will be Natives and they'll scurry off at the first sign of trouble, so we may as well let them do all the work, put a little money in their pockets, and then wave goodbye."

"Are we coming around to taking the ship when it's full instead of storing it?" Murray asked. "And what happens if they figure out something has happened to De la Hora when he goes AWOL after the first five trailer loads are on the ship?

"Maybe we let De la Hora take care of the whole load and then take it after he's done," Matthew suggested, thinking on the fly. "But to answer your first question, yes, I think getting the ship when it's full would be the better way to go. We kill off De la Hora and the last two Mafia guys when they turn up at the end and let the Natives go on their way. They can have all the trailers, tractors, and equipment, and we make it out of there."

"Sounds like a plan, Matthew. I'll keep checking on progress through Emma and let you know when the trucks are heading to port and what's going on at the camp."

They were both silent for a minute as they absorbed and rehashed the plan in their minds.

"Anything more from the others—Global Gold, the Vatican, or the Mafia?" Matthew asked.

"On Global, nothing. The same with the Mafia. Shut tight. The Vatican is breaking out in warts though. Seems as though they have a little war on their hands with the Mafia that is likely propagated from Global. We don't know that, but we do know they're looking for Peter Barnham. They must suspect him of being the weak link, but he seems to have gone to ground with his wife. We haven't tried to pin him down precisely, but we know roughly where he is. Regardless, I don't think he could tell them anything of value. We've been buying his Global stock now for two weeks, so I suspect they're extremely anxious about his motives."

"And the Vatican?"

"Nothing of any great importance there, other than panic. We have all of their financial records and, clearly, they are totally implicated all the way back to 1944. They were funneling the gold out and taking their cut. But then entries stopped until ten or so years ago when the gold was coming back. There were a few small amounts coming through the system before that but nothing that raised the interest of the press. We assume they stopped in forty-six because the move was complete. After that it all went quiet on the financial side of things until when the gold was on the move again. This time it was coming back. The records indicate the Vatican took a 10 percent cut for stockpiling the gold coming out from the Swiss banks and then funneling it out through various ports under the Vatican seal.

"We're still tracking things, but it looks like the gold was taken to a port south of Lima and then trucked over to Brasilia for refining before being taken to the Argentine coast for trans-shipment to Marseille or Naples, maybe both. That's where the freight got its Vatican seals and it was pushed on to Zurich before it ended up in the Bundesbank in Frankfurt and Berlin.

"Nothing startling there, but the secret has been heavily guarded for some seventy-five years, and the Vatican still remains a conduit for the Mafia on quite a number of other transactions, apart from the gold. They're also on the hook for some dubious international financing transactions that also don't pass the smell test. It seems that Vatican officials were planning on investing hundreds of millions of dollars in Angolan oil fields instead of supporting papal charities, for which the money was intended. There's also lots of evidence of embezzlement, fraud, abuse of office, and money-laundering among the Vatican's upper echelon of managers. We've been leaking our findings to the world press—everything except the information on the gold, that is. That can wait until we complete our mission.

"I'm going to have to face the pope with all this pretty soon, so we should see some fireworks after that. He'll have to go, I'm afraid. Too much going against him. He's the one who has to answer for the Vatican's past."

Matthew nodded. "OK, but the Mafia worries me. They're the real controllers."

"True, but we don't want to stir up their nest just yet. Let them get their exodus organized, and then we'll swoop in. Western Canada isn't exactly a major center for Mafia activity, so they're going to be scarce on the ground and unlikely to want to make too much of a fuss.

"I think we should keep a sharp eye on their movements, let them load the ship, and then make our move. We'll cut them off in Prince Rupert and then go in and clean them out. That way nothing gets back to their handlers, and they'll be left guessing what happened to their stash." Murray paused and took a sip of coffee and a bit of pastry, wiping his mouth with his napkin. "You're going to have to go back, my boy, and get things organized. We've been looking for a ship to take the haul, but it seems as though the better way is to use theirs. Don't you think?"

"What about their crew?" Matthew asked. "They're not going to stand by and watch."

"Already arranged, my friend," Murray said smugly. "The captain had to leave suddenly on personal family business and the rest of the crew, well, they got healthy severance packages and were sent home. We replaced everyone, including the captain and the chief navigator, with our own. All this has been going on over the past couple of weeks as we rationalized the plan. Let's face it, none of them really had any inside information, and for all they knew, they were only enlisted to take the cargo as far as Lima. They had no idea what it was or who was paying for it, so the whole arrangement went a lot more smoothly before the fireworks started to fly. At this point we have a ship, a crew, and a destination. All we need now is the gold." Murray sat back and enjoyed the last of his pastry and coffee.

"You don't think De la Hora will be suspicious about the crew change?"

"I doubt he knows them at all, Matthew. They were likely organized through Italy, are not Mafia, and were just a crew that was available. They know nothing other than what they were told."

Matthew nodded his agreement. "Once we talk to the Canadians over at the consulate, I'd better get back and pay a visit to Burvill and the boys at Global. See if they've changed their minds about selling Toodoggone." Matthew took a sip of his coffee. "Anyone I need to liaise with up north?"

"I think it would be best to start by liaising with the captain over at the port. He's one of ours and has been involved in a couple of our missions, so he understands our 'culture,' shall we call it, but not the details of this story. All he knows is that he must coordinate with De la Hora, get the ship loaded, secured, and wait until he's told to leave. Winter is fast approaching in those parts, but I think there could still be time for them to make a move. If they don't, and they get trapped at Toodoggone, they're going to have to spend almost six months there before the snow starts to melt, and I don't think they want to do that, so be prepared for a lot of movement going on around Fort St. James, and keep out of their way. We'll be sending reinforcements over, and they're going to be positioned around the area in some of the cabins we've leased. I'll let you know the lead man shortly.

"My guess is De la Hora will call for reinforcements, so we need to prepare for having to deal with more than what we currently know about. And they're going to be armed to the teeth.

"They may also be camped out on the ship, so you'll need to stay in touch with Leif, the captain, in terms of their numbers and whereabouts. I think there are only two right now. Maybe you're going to have to pick them off one by one, but you'd better not leave them in the open. Find a place to dispose of the bodies on the ship, and make sure your tracks are well covered." Murray paused for another sip of coffee and a bite out of his croissant.

"Any thoughts on Global?" Matthew asked.

"Just keep pressing them, and keep your ties with the Vatican out there. I'm sure Global is on the edge of believing what you've told them. At the same time, I'm sure they know that the Vatican is a complex institution to deal with, so they'll be wondering about whether there's a group working with you that they don't know about. They're going to be extremely suspicious after your last venture up to Toodoggone." Murray took a last sip of coffee and brushed his lap of crumbs.

"OK, I'd better be off," Matthew said. "But keep the satellite imagery coming in, and get that drone to me. We'll stay in touch every two days at 8:00 a.m. my time starting in three days' time. I don't know where you're going to be, but that should at least find you somewhere still awake." He grinned.

"We have a 10:00 a.m. meeting with the ambassador over at the Canadian high commission in the morning," Murray said, standing up. "I've already briefed him, but let's lay the plan on the table in more detail and ask for his help with the Canadian Immigration boys on the borders. We're going to need it."

They shook hands and then left the meeting room thirty minutes apart, Matthew first. Murray had placed some spotters around the hotel, but all was quiet. He needed to get with Daryl on the legalities of their plan, including importation of the gold into Turkey. He felt the time was getting close, although he was still looking for final confirmation from Matthew, which could only happen when he actually saw some of the artifacts that had been snatched from the fingers, faces, necks, and teeth of the Holocaust victims. That would confirm that the rest of the gold was also stolen.

Murray and Matthew sat with the Canadian ambassador and his team in the beautiful British Columbia Room located on the first floor of Canada House in Trafalgar Square. Clearly, Murray was an important visitor for them, and he was treated with the respect usually afforded a foreign dignitary. His missions were always rated top tier, highly classified, and brought together the best minds that governments could provide for the cause. The ambassador understood the situation well, having been briefed by Murray beforehand as well as having already contacted his own informants, who briefed him further on what was happening with the Nazi gold. The Canadian immigration people would be brought into the project immediately, and all international borders with Canada would be under surveillance from that point forward and until further notice that Murray was satisfied that the caper was concluded.

Matthew made his way to Heathrow to get the 2:30 flight back to Vancouver. He had the names of the local Canadian Immigration managers who would be his contacts for whatever he needed, and he was looking forward to getting back up north to execute the next part of the plan.

38

The Opus

Matthew arrived back in Vancouver nine and a half hours after leaving Heathrow. It was only 3 p.m. on the same day as he had left London. He rented a limousine and headed into the city to stay at a boutique hotel away from the crowds. He needed some down time.

The Opus was a small, friendly, laid-back, hotel in the Yaletown area, down by one of the marinas. It had a well-stocked bar and beautiful people relaxing in a smooth off-high-street lounge where the music was blues or jazz. He always reserved a high-end top-floor suite with a fireplace and a wrap-around balcony that looked out over the city to the west and Granville Island to the south. He loved their rooms with incredibly plush beds and a sofa, work area, ultra-modern everything. One could live there for a week without wanting to leave. It was so comfortable and convenient, and it had great service away from the mainstream of regular tourists, with a nightly price tag above most.

He made it there in time to join the Scotch Club in the bar, sampling the latest imported whiskeys from around the world. The place was buzzing with wealthy would-be's—crisp, firm people with body sculptures that needed to be shown off while they could—and a plethora of older types in the shark tank looking for easy pickings, and there were a lot: bald, old, fat, wrinkled men with tans; cougars with hard, well-maintained faces; and younger ladies with softly lined faces only just getting into the Botox scene, with their pixie cuts or curly hair and strategically applied makeup. They all felt comfortable in the company of each other as they shared their common passion for whiskey

Everyone was kissing cheeks, tapping shoulders, laughing at anything, and generally reveling in the event. Talking art and music and travel and the extraordinary experiences they had had in Venice or Morocco, Barcelona or Splitz. It was all exciting and added to the color. Whiskey was like that. It wasn't a downer; it was a socializer, if you could get by the first three tastings and still make sense.

Matthew was about to join in, but a little voice told him he needed to be fresh in the morning, and he had yet to make his appointment with Global, so caution was the word. He wasn't entirely convinced he should refrain while in the company of such high-quality whiskey though. It was still early by Canadian time, so he paid his cover charge of $150, which gave him entry to the sampling room, and waltzed up to the bar.

"Caol Isla nine-year-old on a single block," he said to the bartender. "I'll do that one first and then go on to the tasters." He smiled at the bartender, who shrugged back with eyebrows lifted as he reached beneath the cabinet with liquor bottles on show.

"Great choice, Mr. Black. Good to see you here again." He smiled dryly as he brought the bottle up and reached for a glass. "Not many call for this one. Maybe a little too rich? The fifteen unpeated is still the favorite, and, of course, it's less pricey. This one deserves a special glass though." He placed a Glencairn on the bar and poured an ounce.

"Yes, but I like that slight pass of the whiskey through the peat smoke. Just enough to scorch it. Make those two ounces, would you, Pete?"

Matthew was salivating as the scotch was placed in front of him, and he took in the aroma.

"Enjoy your Artful Dodger, sir. I'm afraid it isn't included in the cover."

"I'm sure it's not," Matthew replied as he sipped his reward. Charge it to my room, would you, Pete? Room 950."

"You got it, Mr. Black. Have you been to the island?"

"Aw, naw," Matthew replied in the best Scottish accent he could muster. "But I feel as though I was born there. Gradually working my way through all their distilleries though. Once I've done that maybe I'll go and visit."

They laughed, and Matthew took a sip. Deliciously fresh with an aftertaste of the cask it had matured in as well as that fine nuance of peat. It was casked in 2009 and bottled nine years later.

The whiskey subdued him. Feeling relaxed, he decided to see what the crowd was doing, which turned out to be everything they could. There was a lot of laughing and snorting sounds with one-liners flying in all directions.

Matthew caught sight of a brunette sitting on her own at the end of the bar with a few samplers in front of her. He sauntered over as she turned toward him.

"Rebecca, for god's sake."

The brunette smiled as her corn-blue eyes lit up. "This is great, isn't it? My first time here, but I'll be back." She raised her tumbler to him and smiled. "Laphroaig." She saluted him with her glass and then got up and threw her arms around his neck, hugging him. He kissed her on the cheek and held her waist. She felt good. She smelled good. He had missed her.

"What on earth are you doing here?" Matthew was still stunned to find her there.

"Murray mentioned you would probably be here, so I thought I'd drop by and say hi. He said you were on assignment, and I'm in town for a couple of days, so I thought..."

Matthew wasn't shocked, just a little stunned. It was not unusual for Murray to organize a little surprise for him during his down time, and it often had something to do with another assignment in the future, or in this case an assignment in the past. But for now, he would just enjoy it.

It had been a year or so since she had helped him with an ORB project in the Pacific Northwest. She had a tough time and a near-death experience but did a great job. Completely fearless and great in bed.

"Enough said, sweetie. We may as well take advantage of each other now that we're both here, don't you think? You're like a member of the family."

"I hope it's not too close a family member." They laughed and sipped their whiskeys.

Matthew let Rebecca out of the room at 2:00 a.m. after he had called the front desk to have them bring the hotel car around to take her to her own hotel across town near Stanley Park.

They kissed, said goodnight, and promised to get together again as soon as they could. One never knew with ORB; they could be on another venture together.

*   *   *

It was 8:30 before Matthew opened one eye and stared at the window blinds. There was daylight outside, and it signaled him to get in motion.

He showered, shaved, and downed a coffee that had been delivered.

At 9:30 he made the call to Global.

"Good morning. Global Gold. How may I direct your call?" The receptionist's response caught Matthew off guard. He would never have guessed she could have been so professional sounding—and polite.

"Ian Burvill, if you would," Matthew said, smiling. "Ian Burvill," he repeated in case she still wasn't with it.

"Mr. Burvill is in a conference. Can I leave a message for him?"

"Tell him Matthew Black called, and I need to talk to him urgently."

"OK," she replied, and then the line went dead. She hadn't asked for his number, so perhaps it had shown up on her computer. She was back to her old self.

Within five minutes, Matthew's phone rang.

"I'm listening, Black," a voice said.

"Thought I'd check in on my investments, Mr. Burvill. Want to meet?"

"Not really, but we likely should—10:30 at our place."

The phone clicked off, and Matthew had got the message. They were pissed but ready to talk.

He needed to talk to Murray first though to find out what was going on with the Vatican.

"Murray, I have a meeting with the Global guys at ten-thirty this morning. Do they know anything?"

"Put if off until tomorrow morning, old boy. They'll know what's happening by then," Murray responded without a pause. He was in Rome and just finishing off organizing his meeting with the pope.

"OK, but keep in touch. I really need to know where we are with things. Otherwise, they might make some move we haven't accounted for."

"Got it, Matthew, but lie low for twenty-four hours, and by then we should have it organized."

"OK, but keep me in the loop. These guys are skittish at best."

After he hung up, Matthew got back on the phone to his favorite receptionist. "Tell Mr. Burvill that I can't meet until tomorrow and that I'll be there at eleven. Got that?"

"OK. Is there somewhere he can reach you?"

"No," Matthew replied, then hung up.

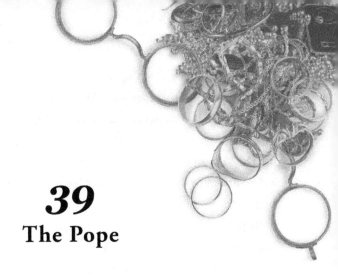

39
The Pope

Pope Germane sat with Cardinal Alfonso, his confidante, Cardinal Dominici, representing the Vatican Bank, and two other cardinals behind locked doors.

"What do we know?" Pope Germane asked. Behind closed doors, the members of the Church hierarchy were casual with each other and disregarded the mannerisms they maintained in public. Even their titles were laid aside for the sake of simple talk. They had known each other for many years and often as far back as priesthood.

"Our friends at Global Gold in Vancouver tell us their stock is being purchased by someone representing the Vatican and that we're interested in purchasing the site where the gold seems to be stored," Alfonso replied.

"Perhaps it's a coincidence," Dominici said, "but as you know, Germane, we've been cleaning up the bank records in accordance with your instructions and on the understanding that there was to be an outside audit of our records. That work is complete, and our books are now open to scrutiny. However, given the information that Alfonso has now provided, I have to wonder whether these things are linked in some way."

Germane stroked his chin and took a sip of water, deep in thought. "We need to get in touch with Capelli and have him come over."

Capelli was the local representative of the Mancuso family, a powerful section of the Ndrangheta Mafia, based in Sicily. Unfortunately for them, there were currently 355 suspected mobsters and corrupt officials charged and more than 900 witnesses expected to give evidence on charges including murder, drug trafficking, extortion, and money laundering. It was the largest court case involving a Mafia group since the 1980s, and it drew on almost all of their managerial resources, slowing down the activities of Mafia groups worldwide as they watched the case unfold, wondering who may be next. Their minds were preoccupied, making it difficult to focus on the problems that the Vatican was trying to manage. As for De la Hora, his concerns were at the bottom of the priority list and likely to stay there for the next two years as the trial continued.

Regardless, the relationship between the local Mob representative in Rome and the Vatican was still strong, although any problems that required the attention of Sicily were likely to be lost in the mess of the court case. The upside to the court case for the Vatican was that it could be an appropriate time for them to break the Mafia shackles that had gripped them since the 1920s. Germane was anxious to take advantage while at the same time being faced with legal challenges himself with the Vatican Bank and now the Global Gold problems.

Capelli joined the group within an hour of the call. His access to the Vatican chambers was unfettered, and he entered the meeting with no announcement or greetings. Clearly, they needed his attention at the earliest.

Germane waved Capelli to a chair and pointed to the coffee table. No words were spoken, but the look on the cardinals' faces told Capelli that something serious was amiss.

"It seems we have a problem with our friends in Vancouver," Germane began.

"Yeah, I guessed so. De la Hora has been calling me about some nut over there asking questions about our business and claiming to be acting on behalf of the Vatican." Capelli grabbed a cup of coffee and made a show of the three spoons of sugar he stirred into it. "I guess we need to do something about it, so I'm thinking of sending some more guys over there."

"We may need to do more," Germane said. "We think they've been sniffing around our records here at the Vatican Bank. We don't know for sure, but if they have copies of the records there's going to be real trouble for all of us—you guys included." He fixed his eyes on Capelli and then Dominici.

"We know that this outside group copied the Vatican archives," Dominici said. "We don't think the operation was compromised, and we were never suspicious given the circumstances of the arrangement, but we don't know for sure. When we came to archive the bank records—"

"What you do that for?" Capelli raised his eyebrows and pushed forward in his chair, clearly taken aback.

"We were about to be audited by the Ministry of Finance, and we needed to, let's say, adjust our manual records to avoid prying eyes. Unfortunately, it was my error," Germane explained. "I should have pushed back based on our being a sovereign state, but I didn't. I had promised transparency after the last financial problem we had, combined with the bad press on a number of other issues over the past ten years, and it was, to me at least, a matter of 'coming clean,' as they say."

"Well, things may have backfired on you and maybe us, Your Holiness," Capelli said with a touch of sarcasm. "I gotta get back to the guys and see what needs to be done. But with all this legal stuff goin' on, I don' know what we're gonna do. In the meantime, you need to let the auditors do their stuff, and we'll have to wait and see what else may happen. Maybe nuthin', but you guys need to get some lawyers to surround the place. If someone's digging in your books, it's gonna be a tough place to dig outta. I gotta go. Gino's gonna shit himself."

Capelli stood up and headed for the door. "Stay in touch," he said as he let himself out, muttering all the way.

The pope and his three cardinals sat in silence, deep in thought.

"Listen," Germane said finally, "it sounds as though more gold is coming our way. I'm not sure of the timeline or the amount. De la Hora is getting all the gold out from storage and storing it elsewhere as well as sending some over here. It will take a while, but we need to be prepared. Dominici, I'll leave this to you, but Alfonso is here to help. No records, Dom, nothing that can be copied or passed on. You'll have to be extremely cautious. This won't be the last load, but I'd like it to be the last time we deal with the Mafia, so start closing the doors to them. Blame it on the audit."

"How shall he handle the Vancouver man who's been pestering Global Gold?" one of the other cardinals asked.

"Let Global handle it. They may lean on De la Hora to help, but the problem is in their territory, and they would be the best to manage it. They know he's not ours, so ..." Germane got up from his chair, letting the impli-cation hang. "I think we're finished here."

The cardinals nodded and then headed for the door behind the pontiff.

Germane Aloisius Meyer was born in 1926 at 5:00 a.m. in his parents' home in Fussen, a small town in Bavaria, in the district of Ostallgau, three miles from the Austrian border and located on the banks of the Lech River. It was a farming community and a center for violin making.

Meyer's family, especially his father, bitterly resented the Nazis, and his father's opposition to Nazism resulted in demotions and harassment of the family. In his early teens, Germane was conscripted into the Hitler Youth—membership was required by law at the age of fourteen. During his time there, he thrived and made friends for life. Some of them went on to become prominent members of the Nazi movement, but Germane was more of a quiet academic with a bent toward religion, even at that age.

During Germane's early years, it so happened that the Vatican became destitute despite having accumulated substantial reserves up to the end of the nineteenth century. They had real estate holdings, gold, works of art, and other treasures that exceeded the value held by most countries. Some have suggested that they had over $50 billion dollars in securities by the end of the century. By 1929 though, the pope was living in a damaged, leaky, pigeon-infested Lateran Palace, and he worried about how he would pay for even basic repairs.

Things had to change, so the pope focused on creating and signing the Lateran Treaty between the Vatican and Mussolini's government. It came with a $90 million payment to the Vatican, sovereign status for the Vatican, tax-free property rights, and guaranteed salaries for all priests throughout Italy. All this in exchange for the support of Mussolini by Italy's Catholic population.

With the stroke of a pen, the pope had solved the Vatican's budgetary woes practically overnight, but he had also thrust the Catholic Church into league with some of the darkest forces of the twentieth century, including the Mafia.

When war broke out, Germane was drafted into the German anti-aircraft corps as a Luftwaffenhelfer and made friends with not only his peers but also some of his superiors. He was highly regarded, trustworthy, and devoted to the Nazi cause, so much so that he moved upwards faster than most.

Eventually, however, he stopped his rapid advance through the ranks as his religious calling became stronger, but he achieved the rank of wehrmachts-dekan, or chaplain, by 1944.

Germane was ordained as a priest and went on to become a theologian and advisor to cardinals on religious history and culture before he himself went on to become a bishop and then a cardinal. His connections included a litany of powerful names, and he was often called upon for guidance or favors. Some he resisted, but many of his close friends became embroiled with the Cosa Nostra as they became more and more embroiled with the Vatican because of those financially difficult early days. The Mafia considered Germane a close ally in the Vatican. He had the ear of the pope, and became a close confidante. It was difficult for Germane to resist their pleas, for fear of reprisals from other cardinals who lusted for wealth and power. The pope was not immune to the Mafia either and knew only too well that the status of the Vatican, amongst Italian Catholics in particular, was closely tied to them.

Germane's power reached to the top of not only the Church but also to the highest political circles in a number of countries. Few knew about his background with the Nazis or his connections to the Mafia.

When the war ended, Germane helped many Nazis escape offshore and used his connections in the Vatican to help them in exchange for the promise of gold. That exchange came in the way of the creation of a conduit that allowed gold to enter the Vatican from Swiss-controlled banks and then move on to various Mediterranean ports for shipment offshore, all under the protection of Vatican seal, which authenticated its status as a sovereign state, immune to customs and excise control and inspection.

It was the Vatican Bank itself, under the guidance of cardinals, that presided over the control of the arrangements made between the Mafia and the Vatican. This was the pivotal point for the Vatican's involvement in colluding with the Nazis, although they had been engaged with them in many nefarious banking activities before and during the war, all of it undertaken under the pretense of protecting the Church from invasion by the Germans. After the war, it simply carried on.

Germane was elected pope in 2010 at the age of seventy-seven with the help of the 220 members of the College of Cardinals in a single round of voting.

There were a number of attempts on his life as he traveled from country to country as well as in his adopted home in the Vatican. At one point while he was about to celebrate Christmas Eve Mass at St. Peter's Basilica, a woman later identified as twenty-five-year-old Maria Goldstein, an Italian Jew, jumped the barrier and grabbed the pope by his vestments and pulled him to the ground, shouting, "What about my family? Who cares for them?" before she was restrained and forcefully removed. No one heard from her again, but she was not the only one to challenge the pope. Others, all bearing the same ethnic identity as Maria, tried to injure or kill Germane. They were all repelled before they reached their goal, but the message was becoming clear. There were serious issues between the Italian Jewish community, and this pope had yet to address them.

Germane knew he had inherited major problems when he became pope. His relationship with the Mafia continually came back to haunt him as they pushed for more and more power using the guise of the Catholic Church to funnel their money offshore. Some of his problems were the product of events that had occurred many years previous, during the reign of other popes, but Germane had always maintained a central position as advisor to the popes who came after the war, and every pope carried the same burdens through their papacy. Most problems were never resolved and likely never would be. Some of the issues were associated with the history of the Catholic Church over the previous hundreds of years and beyond and their involvement with international politics, clerical celibacy, opulence, laxity toward religious critiques, financial corruption, and pedophilia. Some of these problems were associated with the twentieth century, particularly those regarding their financial situation.

Germane was a central figure in the Vatican's financial issues, but he managed to avoid suspicion, despite evidence coming to light that showed that the Church had had substantial and morally questionable dealings with sinister organizations since the end of WWII. It seemed to prove that the Vatican had accrued enormous wealth during the Great Depression by investing in Mussolini's government and was connected to the Nazi gold. Interpol and the FBI also uncovered a billion-dollar counterfeit stock fraud known as the "Ambrosiano Affair." Finally, there was the pope's appointment of Mafia chieftain Michele Sindona as the Vatican banker.

In fact, the Vatican's problems became exponentially more complex at the close of WWII as a secret alliance was forged by the CIA, the Sicilian and US Mafias, and the Vatican to thwart the possibility of a communist invasion of Europe. This added to the complexities that had already caused headaches at the Vatican by their earlier association with Mussolini and, consequently, the Mafia. It seemed the Mafia was playing all sides.

As a consequence of the secret alliances, governments were toppled, genocide occurred on a wholesale basis, death squads were created, financial scandals erupted on a grand scale, the mujahideen were created, an international narcotics network was established, and selected cardinals were prepared for their rise to the Holy See.

Germane had not only inherited all these problems, he was also directly involved in them and had even caused some of them. While he had been a very successful right-hand cardinal to the popes before him, his failure of leadership as pope opened the more recent pedophilia scandals, the ongoing financial corruption, a gay prostitution ring inside the Vatican, and criminal investigations of connections between the Holy See and organized crime. It seemed an impossible task for Germane to restore his church to what he envisaged as a religious leader of morals and influence.

As pope, Germane was weak when faced with the robust inner circles of the cardinals, bishops, and priests who surrounded him and who essentially controlled the Vatican's inner workings. Despite all these problems, his mandate was to protect the Church at all costs.

40
Tronetto Hall

Tronetto Hall was usually reserved for business leaders meeting the pope, but in this instance, Murray was led to a small annex to the pope's library area adjacent to the hall—a slightly less formal setting and one that was reserved for more intimate discussions. The library was located inside the Vatican Palace, with the papyrus room and a storage area for manuscripts just on the other side of the main doors.

The library itself had some twenty-six miles of shelving, but the annex was a simple thirty-by-forty-foot sitting area with comfortable couches, armchairs, coffee tables, and tapestries depicting ancient religious stories adorning the walls, dim lighting, and books everywhere. There was no desk and no indication of formality.

Murray settled into one of the club chairs and reached out for the glass of mineral water that had been placed on the side table next to him. He had brought no one else. The pope entered the room by himself, closed the doors behind him, then walked over to shake Murray's hand. All manner of papal piety was gone. They had met several times before on other business. In fact, one of the ORB's projects had been executed successfully on behalf of the pope.

"Many thanks for sharing this moment with you." Murray wasn't into titles, especially when he was bringing formidable news.

"My secretariat tells me you seek some particular information and want to impart some information that is essential to us, Murray," Germane stated in a somewhat formidable manner tinged with the informality of calling Murray by his Christian name.

"Well, let me say the information I need to discuss is not for all ears, not for governments, and not for political gain," Murray replied without hesitation. "In fact, I believe you're the only one who needs to know this, and it's imperative that we understand each other."

"Intriguing, Mr. Stockman," Germane said, returning to formality. "I can't imagine what you want to imbibe, but I am, as they say, 'all ears.'" The pope smiled sardonically, as though he had heard such things a million times before.

"Signori—may I call you that?"

"Of course, Mr. Stockman. May I call you Murray?" Germane asked, returning to informality.

"If you like," Murray replied, his guard up.

"Good, then let's continue—Signori, Murray." The pontiff smiled, but it was one that hid an age of secrets that belied his suspicion of Murray.

"Good. Let me start somewhere near the beginning, Signori." Murray paused and stared at his hands. "Of course, we know your history—everyone does—but it seems as though some of it is somewhat, shall we say, murky?"

"Murky? What does this mean, 'murky'?"

"Unexplainable, unclear," Murray replied. He looked up at the pope, who was staring back with a smug smile.

"Oh? Please explain, Mr. Stockman. This is quite intriguing, but," he looked at his watch, "I have limited time to give you, so perhaps you can be clear."

"Yes, yes, of course." Murray paused to mentally prepare himself. "It seems as though you have some dubious financial connections that have led us to a central theme."

"What might that be?" The pontiff still looked relaxed and ready for anything. The audit was nearing completion, and nothing had been identified as suspicious.

"Well," Murray paused and caught his breath, "we believe you're directly linked to the gold that was moved from Germany during World War II to a secret site overseas."

Germane sought to restrain himself as his entire body tensed. His holy garments hid the reaction, and his face remained passive. "What gold? And when are you talking about? Seventy-five years ago? I was so young, so what do you mean?" He tried to look amused.

"Signori, please don't play coy. We know you were recruited by the Nazis in the forties. We know your history, and we know you were the conduit for the transfer of the gold through the Vatican. We also know who your contacts were at the time and the deal you brokered for the Vatican. Now here you are, the head of the Catholic Church and back to your old roots, helping the Cosa Nostra and moving the gold again," Murray added for effect.

"You are mistaken, Mr. Stockman. I know nothing of the gold that you talk about, and I take exception to your suggestion that the Vatican is in any way connected to the Cosa Nostra. It is a despicable criminal group that has committed great injustices against our people. There is nothing that connects us and nothing that we would want to be connected by."

Murray sighed. "Signori, you must excuse my directness on these matters, but you have only allocated thirty minutes for this meeting. The fact is that you were not only implicated in the 1940s, but you are also involved now, as we speak."

There was a slight change in Germane's disposition. He stared down at his palms. "Mr. Stockman, you're talking to St. Peter's primary disciple. To God's chosen representative here on Earth. To a divine entity who has the power to condemn or condone. Who are you to shake the ground of divinity? To doubt my word? Who are you to come here with these accusations and suggest that the Holy See had anything to do with meddling in such despicable things?"

"Well, the facts are clear, and you are truly the culprit we seek. You are culpable and very much involved. I want you to listen to this recording."

The pontiff gave Murray a nonchalant wave of his hand. "If you must, Mr. Stockman." The friendliness had vanished.

Murry took out his phone and turned up the volume, then placed it on the table between them, his eyes on the pontiff. "This is a recording of a call made between you and Cardinal Alfonso nearly three weeks ago—and there are more." He clicked the "play" button.

"Your Holiness," the cardinal began, "it seems we have a problem with our friends."

"Which ones, Alfonso? We have many, and many of those problems have problems."

"It seems there is an intruder in our midst who has presented himself to Global Gold. You recall Theodore Munch many years ago when you were a priest?"

"Yes, I do, Alfonso, but he has long been dead, my friend."

"Of course, Your Holiness, but he was the one together with Lansky."

Murray paused the recording, waiting for a signal of name recognition. He saw one and continued.

"You remember he was the one who inherited the transactions that our Holy Church was, let's say, embroiled with regarding the pass-through of the gold coming out of Nazi Germany, and you were the Vatican contact at the time?"

"Yes, I do, but it was all done to protect us and His Eminence at the time from becoming another victim of the Nazis. There was no choice."

"Well, it seems the Vatican is being investigated and misrepresented to our friends. An individual, Matthew Black, has been propositioning Global Gold into selling their property in Canada."

"What has that got to do with us, Alfonso?"

"That is the property where the gold was moved to after the war. It also appears that our financial archives have been passed on to those who I fear could be a major threat to us."

"But I thought you dealt with that and changed the entries. How could anyone else have access to our documents?"

"We believe that during the computer archiving, the documents were copied and transmitted to others outside the Vatican walls."

There was a pause.

"How could you, Alfonso?"

Another pause.

"But what can we do now? There must be something." The pontiff sounded anxious and out of his depth.

Murray stopped the playback and let the information sit for a few moments. The pontiff slumped back in his chair, his fingers arched and pointed at his forehead. "What do you want, Mr. Stockman?"

"To start with, you need to cooperate with us." Murray stared the pope in the eyes.

"And if I do?"

"You will be removed from office with no blemishes on your record, and after such an illustrious career I imagine you would welcome that." Murray searched for a response on the pontiff's face.

"It would seem you have all the cards, Mr. Stockman. Where do we go from here?"

"First, I want you to contact your Mafia friends and let them know you have an agent negotiating with Global Gold for the Toodoggone property. Second, we want you to resign as pope."

"I cannot resign my position." Germane was shocked by the demand. "No pope has ever resigned. It would have to be an extremely compelling reason such as a dramatic failure of health. One can't just walk away from such a position." The pontiff leaned forward in his chair, his eyes protruding and the sides of his mouth sagging.

"You have a compelling reason, sir. Unless you resign, you will bring the entire Catholic Church down." Murray was being blunt. He had no time to bargain.

Germane sagged further, deep in thought. "All that I've worked for, all that I've achieved, and all the struggles I've endured, now this is what it's all come to."

"You are a criminal, Signori, no better than your Mafia friends and probably far worse. You may have initiated things for good, but you knew, even at that time, that the gold was coming from murdered Jews and many others who suffered at the hands of the Nazis. Why you did it, I can't say, but I can tell you that it was criminal, and for what? Gold, just gold. Now you're trying to help those that profited to retain it for the benefit of who, the Germans?"

The pontiff sat quite still, his hands wringing and the medallion around his neck resting on his knees.

"Doing so much good in your life doesn't make up for the atrocities that were carried out," Murray continued, "and while you were not involved with the extermination, you profited from it." Murray stopped again. Germane was clearly considering his position.

"I will help wherever I can," he replied, his voice nearly a whisper. "Let me know how to proceed."

"Let's start with you having Alfonso call Global Gold and let them know you've discovered who in the Vatican has engaged an agent. Let them know that the person has been dealt with and that Matthew Black has been called off. Let them also know that the Vatican is aware of where the gold is, but it is of no concern of yours."

"I can't do that. I've already met with my inner circle on the matter, and they have their instructions. The Mafia know what's happening, and they need to do whatever they have to do. They all know we did not engage an agent to infiltrate Global Gold, and we all know that the gold is being removed from storage. I can't stop these things at this point."

Murray pursed his lips in frustration and was about to say something but then stopped. "OK. You know what you have to do."

The pontiff nodded solemnly, then stood up to leave.

Murray also stood, touching Germane's arm. "Once Alfonso has made the call, let him know that his bungling of the financial archives means he'll have to take an early retirement and move out of public sight. Then he needs to be closely watched and monitored. I don't want him talking. Do you understand?"

Germane nodded and then moved toward the door. "And when do you want me to resign?"

"When I tell you."

Murray made his way out of the library, across the square, and into a waiting car. He wasn't going to linger while the news was hot, and he didn't trust the Vatican. His private jet would be taking off for London as soon as he arrived at Ciampino Airport, to the south of the city.

Murray dialed Matthew on the sat phone from the limo.

"You're on, Matthew. My guess is that the Vatican is talking to Global as we speak, so be prepared for some interesting discussions. You'll need to hotfoot it back up to Fort St. James and get the place ready for action.

"The pope is going to resign, and the Mafia are going through a bit of hell here in Rome. Seems the government has thrown a wide enough net to capture over 350 members of the Mafia and haul them into court for a whole bunch of problems. None of it has anything to do with the gold though. That news has only just come onto their radar. Seems the pope had a talk with the local Mafia hood and let him know what he knew of Global's problems. My guess is that this is going to be the perfect time to get that gold out of there with the least amount of fight from the Mafia. As for the Vatican, they're going to be scrambling to keep their heads above water, especially with their boss gone."

"Interesting times, Murray. I'll let you know what happens after my meeting with Burvill."

41
Global Gold Revisited

Matthew pushed the doors to Global Gold's office open at exactly 11:00 a.m. He was greeted by the same sullen and distracted receptionist who suggested he take a seat, and she would find out where Mr. Burvill was. No offer of coffee, tea, or water, but he sat with one of the international newspapers and skimmed the headlines. One headline caught his attention: "Hundreds of alleged members of Italy's most powerful Mafia group are set to face justice in the country's biggest organized crime trial in decades."

Matthew did not read the whole article, but it reinforced what Murray had mentioned earlier. It seemed that the defendants included politicians, police officers, civil servants, and alleged members and accomplices of the Mob.

It was fifteen minutes before Burvill and Bonafacio rounded the corner to meet him. Again, no handshakes and no smiles, just business. Burvill waved Matthew into the same small, unadorned office they had met in previously.

"Thought I would check in to see how your thinking is going on the proposed transaction," Matthew said. "So where are you at with that?"

"We don't know what's going on here," Burvill replied, "but it would appear that your client has absconded from the Vatican, or perhaps was never there and left you somewhat high and dry."

Matthew smiled. "Now why would you say that, Ian?"

"Because no one there knows you. I think that should suffice, don't you?"

"Oh, that's odd," Matthew said. "Maybe I misunderstood."

Burvill and Bonafacio didn't quite know how to react.

"What the fuck are you talking about?" It was Burvill.

"All I know is that my instructions were clear."

"From whom?" Burvill almost spit the question out.

"Come to think of it, I think it was a third party. So I don't know other than I get paid, and I guess the point is that whoever hired me, they wanted Toodoggone, so the question for you is, have you thought about it?"

By then Burvill was almost apoplectic, and Bonafacio was coming on fast behind.

"Go fuck yourself," were the only words that Burvill could come back with.

"Was it you who went up to our camp?" Bonafacio asked.

"Not that I know of, why?"

"Like we told you the last time, we had an intruder in our camp. Someone tranquilized one of our guards and then seriously injured another as he was pursued. Do you know anything about that?"

"Strange." Matthew put on his most worrisome look. "Hope they haven't messed with our stakes."

"This is a very dangerous game, Mr. Black," Burvill said. "I hope we don't discover that you were involved."

"I hope you don't either. There's nothing that I'm aware of."

"Call it all coincidental, Mr. Black, but we remain very suspicious of you and your activities, but at this point we will still buy the shares back at exactly what you paid for them, when the time comes—whenever that is."

"Very good. I'll have my broker draw up the papers once I'm through with them."

With that, Matthew got up and walked toward the door, then turned back. "Oh, by the way, how is Peter Barnham these days? When you see him, please give him my thanks."

"Thanks for what?" Bonafacio asked.

"For giving us a little help when we needed it. I suggest you don't pursue him though. He really is an innocent in all this, and I would hate to see anything happen to him."

"What do you mean?" Burvill spat, his eyes wild. "What the fuck do you think you're doing messing with us?" He pushed his chair back against the wall and stood up. "What the fuck are you up to, Black? And who the fuck are you to tangle with us?" He was clearly in a state of psychosis and ready to pounce at the slightest hint of defense from Matthew.

"My job is almost complete," Matthew replied. "Thought you might want to know."

Burvill looked like he was about to froth at the mouth. "You come in here with your ludicrous story, claim not to be involved with the attack on our property, buy our stock by intimidating our shareholders, and then suddenly it all stops? I don't think so. You have to pay a price for what you've done." Burvill's eyes were completely psychotic, and he was looking for blood.

"Take it easy. You're overreacting," Matthew said. He remained cool and calm, not at all intimidated by Burvill's antics.

"You ... you have to tell us what's really going on, Black, and no bullshit. No bullshit!" Burvill was almost apoplectic

"You need to settle down, my friend, or you're going to burst a blood vessel. Nothing going on here that you don't know about if you really think about it, so save your anger for another day."

Burvill couldn't seem to control himself. "There's something very wrong with this, and we want to know what the fuck is going on!" he yelled.

Matthew took up the challenge. "The truth is that we know all about Toodoggone, and it's all going to come apart no matter what you do. Global Gold has been involved in one of the greatest heists of all time, and now the truth is out. I'm just a pawn in the game, and I'm backing away, but count on others to follow up."

Bonafacio and Burvill were stunned. Burvill collapsed back into his seat. "What the fuck are you talking about?"

"You'll find out soon enough, but for now you need to control yourself and go back to Australia where you came from. Maybe they don't know about you and your shenanigans."

Burvill went quiet as the color of his face started to return to normal.

"If I ever meet you in the street, Burvill, you can be sure you won't leave without some serious damage," Matthew warned. With that, he went out, gave the uninterested receptionist a wave, and then disappeared into the elevator.

"Christ, I knew Peter was into something. Have we figured out where he is yet?" Bonafacio asked. He looked worried.

"No," Burvill said impatiently, "but it really doesn't matter now. The cunt."

42
Burvill and the Mob

"Burvill, this is Carlioni in Chicago."

Burvill was struck dumb for a moment after answering his cell phone. He couldn't think who this Carlioni guy on the other end was. And what was with Chicago? He didn't know anyone from there.

"Hello." Burvill was stuck for words for one of the first times in his life.

"Alfonso called me from the Vatican. Seems you got a problem. Wants us to help. His associates are too far away. I told him we would see what we could do."

A shiver went down Burvill's spine. He had never talked directly to Carlioni, who was as close to the top of the Mob ladder as one could get without being a don. Burvill was dumbstruck. Carlioni continued, as though he really didn't care if Burvill was listening or not.

"I don' like dis ting, Burvill. What the fock's happenin', and what you doin' about it?"

"Well, sir, I mean Mr. Carlioni, it seems as though we have a breach in protocol—"

"What the fock you mean 'breach in protocol'? There ain't none, just a focking problem to get rid of, so what's a goin' on?"

Burvill explained about the purchase of the shares, the intruder at the Toodoggone site, the attempt to buy the property, and the Vatican involvement.

"So dey know?" Carlioni interjected before Burvill could finish.

"You mean the Vatican?"

"Nah, I mean dis intruder guy! Who else d'ya think I'm talkin' about?"

"Looks as though they do," Burvill said, "but we have De la Hora cleaning things out. It's going to take him a while though. Maybe a couple of months even."

"What about dis intruder guy? Whatcha doin' about im?"

"Well, De la Hora—"

"Listen, De la Hora ain't gonna be able to look after everythin', you know. He's gonna need help. We'll send some guys up to handle the intruder and let De la Hora handle the gold. How'd they know anyway?" Carlioni asked.

"Like I said, we're pretty sure someone in the Vatican spilled the beans, and here we are." There was no way Burvill was going to pin any blame on himself or Global Gold.

"Spilled the beans? What you mean?"

"I guess they discovered where the gold was and decided they wanted it and cut the rest of us out. I can't say any more than that. I just don't know. We're doing what we can to contain the situation, and I think by the end of the month we'll have control back."

"I think you're wrong about the Vatican. No way they would cut us out. There's something else goin' on, but we ain't gonna waste time thinkin' 'bout dat. We need action. So you need what I said?"

"Definitely. Absolutely. You need to get some people up there to help not just with the intruder but with the operation as well. De la Hora's going to need trailers, drivers, security—the whole works. We have no idea how big a problem we have or whether it's just restricted to the Vatican, if they are part of the problem, and this intruder. We're pretty sure the intruder has backup, but we have no idea who or what or how big a problem he presents."

"OK, OK. Listen, Alfonso wouldn't be asking for our help if the Vatican was involved on the bad side of this situation, capiche? Send me what you have on this intruder, and we'll try to figure it out. In the meantime, I'll get some boys up there from Chicago to help out. How many you think?"

Carlioni was struggling to get a handle on the magnitude of the problem. All he knew was that the issue was worth billions, and it was extremely high on his list of priorities. He just wasn't so sure of how to deal with such a remote location on the Canadian side of the forty-ninth parallel. He did know, however, that Mob help in that part of the world was scarce, and there was no point in counting on any help west of Montreal and Toronto. He wasn't going to go to one of the gangs in that part of the world either. They were too untrustworthy and always fighting amongst themselves over their little part of the drug trade.

"Better watch where your guys cross into Canada."

Burvill was getting his courage back and realized that, as big as this man on the other end of the line was, he was lost in Canada. He probably didn't even know where Vancouver was, let alone Fort St. James.

"If this intruder has any kind of substantial group behind him, and I think he does, they would have put the word out to the Canadian feds to watch the borders. They're not going to let anyone in if they're the least bit suspicious, so you need guys with no rap sheets. You may need to take the long way around. Not through Vancouver."

"I'm on it, but you gotta make sure my boys know what to do when they get there, so I'm relyin' on you to point them in the right direction. You got that, Burvill?"

"Just let me know who they are and when and where they're coming in."

"You got it. And send me that stuff on the intruder."

Carlioni hung up, leaving Burvill to wonder what the hell he was involved in. The Mob—how did this happen? His world had gone from a placid pool of the good life to a stormy ocean in a matter of weeks. For years everything had gone so smoothly. He was never really involved with Toodoggone; it was just a blip on his radar of ignorance, and now suddenly it was on the center of the map in front of him.

"What the fuck?" was all Burvill could say. "Giuseppi," he said, calling out to him in the next office, "get hold of De la Hora and let him know help is on the way from Chicago. They should be here in a matter of days. See if you can find out where Black is and then put a tail on him, so that we have a target for Carlioni and his boys."

43
Back at the Cabin

Mathew arrived back at his cabin near Fort St. James in the same Bell helicopter he had used when he had left a couple of weeks earlier. The chopper made a low circuit around the property sufficient for him to take a good look around to make sure there were no stakeouts, and then it landed on a shallow bank as close to the cabin as the pilot dared. The chopper tilted back on its tail sufficient for Matthew to get out. He gave the pilot a thumbs-up before the chopper got airborne again. It flew toward the lake, climbing steadily as it headed south.

Matthew edged toward the cabin but checked out the garage area first. There were no signs of tampering, so he creaked open the doors and peaked inside. The ATV was still there, and the trapdoor in the floor was still covered by the boxes he had placed over it before he left.

He made his way over to the cabin and examined the door and windows. No signs of forced entry. Once inside, Matthew examined everything, but there was no indication that anything had been compromised. He tossed his baggage onto the bed, set the equipment bag on the floor, and then went over to get a fire going in the potbelly stove.

His whole body was on alert, but nothing out of the ordinary attracted his attention. Gradually he settled down, poured a coffee, turned on a light, and started to sort out his pack.

He had brought a RMUS remote surveillance drone that the police often used for local operations. It had a thirty-zoom camera, six motors, and six batteries with twelve spares and a whole bunch of spare propellers. Matthew had spent some quality time practicing with a qualified operator and was quite proficient. The unit needed to be packed on the sled with a small diesel generator that could recharge the batteries. With a drone flight time of only thirty minutes, it was important that Matthew keep the other batteries charged at all times. That way he could have the drone keep a check on his surroundings and the way forward. The drone was fitted with a thermal 4K camera that could be used for daytime and night operations.

The sat phone rang, and Matthew started with uncharacteristic edginess, his senses on high alert.

"Thought I'd give you a call and let you know you're not alone," Murray said.

"Thanks. I think I have everything I need. Just feeling a little lonely not knowing who's out there to help if needed."

"I know. I've been there. Remember, we're as close as you want us to be. Our guys are in the three valleys over to the west of Fort St. James as well as the two to the south. All of them are on high alert. Remember that! The call sign for help on frequency 13.6 MZ is 'Emma.' Don't forget that, but don't use it unless you really need it. Otherwise, there will be hell to pay! Emma is your main contact. If we must, we can send our guys in by chopper."

"Got it!" Matthew replied.

"OK, talk in two days." Murray terminated the connection.

Matthew sat at the table and put a list together of supplies he would need, trying to prepare for any eventuality. He may be gone for just the time it took to travel into the camp and back out again, which was most likely. He was anxious to take an upfront look at what De la Hora was up to and how far he had gotten with his plans—that is, if his plans were what Matthew thought they were. There was always a possibility that De la Hora was playing a different game, but Matthew didn't think so, judging by the radio chatter that had been picked up and the discussion between Murray and the pope. De la Hora was under orders to move everything out, whether that meant all to the ship or split up between the ship and alternative storage. It was likely De la Hora was the one who would make that decision. If he could find a convenient, secure alternative location for the loot to sit for a while he may go for that, but at this point it was all up in the air.

A sudden knock on the door made Matthew go for his Glock. A second knock was followed by a raspy voice. "It's me, I mean us—Lester and Switch—'member us?"

Matthew looked out of the side window and saw the shadows of two people. He unlocked the door and invited the two forlorn characters in.

"Gotta beer, Matt?" Lester really meant two beers, one for him and one for Switch.

Matthew smiled and then went to grab a couple of a Molson out of the fridge. The boys settled back in some chairs next to the potbelly stove but didn't speak, just glugged their beer.

"OK, boys, what brings you here—not just the beers, I assume?"

"Sounds like you got some troubles, Matt. Want some help?" Lester asked as he took another slug of his beer.

"What kind of trouble do you think I'm in, Lester?"

Lester looked thoughtful for a moment. "Well, me thinks there's some trouble in them thar hills. My friend and I, we," Lester pointed a thumb at Switch, who nodded, "are thinking we may be able to help you some."

"Now how would you do that, Lester—and Switch?" Matthew gave the latter a passing glance.

"Seems to us that your friends up there at Toodoggone are planning a major exodus kinda thing. Don't know what that really means, but we think yer involved and need some help. Seems to us that we could do some scouting and help you out of this dilemma. What d'ya think, Matt?" Lester offered the empty bottle and received a full one in return.

"What is it you think you know, Lester?" Matthew looked from one to the other.

"Well, we knows that those folks up at the mine don't care a tinker's arse 'bout Black Mike or 'is cabin, and we don't think you do neither. That means skullduggery, and we think you could do with a little of our help 'cause we likes you, and we think we trusts you."

Lester paused and watched Matthew, calculating his thoughts.

"OK, what if I bite on your offer? What do you propose?"

Lester pulled his cap even lower over his eyes. "Seems to me, us, that we could track those guys all the way outta the bush just in case they comes out in places other than you think. And what if they places folks ahead to secure the trail? And what if they's armed with all manner of things and you need to know? And what if they—"

"I get it, Lester—what ifs."

Matthew sat back in his chair. He liked the idea of local guides helping out. It wouldn't be easy with or without them, but at least this would improve his chances. Even though he would have the benefit of a drone overhead any time he needed to get one into the air, he could still do with some other eyes on the ground, and these two in front of him were likely the best.

"OK, fellas, 500 a day plus expenses on the same terms as before. This time you need to make your way slowly back up to their camp, keeping a watchful eye on your surroundings in case they post guards along the route, and keep me updated on their movements and their route—or perhaps I should say routes."

Lester and Switch held out their hands, and Matthew shook both.

"You might as well start as soon as you can. Scout around for other possible exit sites to the highway, and check out the camp and where the security folks are stationed. Remember they'll likely have stretched out farther than they usually do. When I was there, they only secured the fence perimeter and the mine portal. I think they're going to double the guard on the portal, including from above, and cover twice the area. If it was me, I would radiate out in two more circles, but I don't know if they have the manpower to cover everything to that extent.

"Take these two walkie-talkies and keep in touch. I'll give you the frequency, and you need to call me and let me know where they are, when anything leaves, and who's staying behind. Got that?"

"Gotcha," Lester replied, tipping his cap. Switch did the same.

"And listen, if you do get caught, get rid of the walkie-talkies. They're a dead giveaway that you're up to no good. Without them you can just claim you're on your own and doing some scouting for a hunt."

"Gotcha again." Lester gave a thumbs-up.

They sidled out of the door, tipping their caps again. "We'll be in the bush next time we talk. Oh, and the money, just put something in our accounts. We know yer good fer it. Thanks fer the beers."

Matthew was happy with the arrangement, and he started to feel better about the project. Having on-site and off-site eyes was going to help a lot.

Matthew relayed the news of Lester and Switch to his people, so there would be no surprises. The only response he received over the radio was "Received, Emma." That was all he needed.

*   *   *

Early the next morning, Matthew headed into town to pick up the supplies he needed. He had already brought the additional firepower, radios, and the like with him. He didn't want to pick up anything in town that might raise suspicions and start people talking. He assumed that De la Hora's manpower was all at the camp or on route. He had no idea whether De la Hora had called for or received reinforcements, but that would be on the agenda for his next call with Murray.

Meanwhile, Matthew made contact with two of his ground crew, or perhaps a better way to put it was that they made contact with him. They "accidentally" bumped into Matthew as he was loading his truck at the store. They offered to help, and before long they had made sufficient eye contact and innuendo that Matthew knew who they were without asking. They followed him out of town and back to his cabin, where they sat and talked over a coffee. There were no formal introductions, but they all knew they were working for the ORB on a project and not to go into detail. Matthew sketched out what he would be doing for the next couple of weeks and what he needed them to do. Essentially, he wanted them to watch his back when he returned. They were to stake out an exit point from the forest that Matthew would radio to Emma.

The guys confirmed what Murray had told him about the main support being located on each side of town. They were in constant communication with Emma, and Murray was the one who would be giving the instructions based on his communication with Matthew. The circle seemed tight and efficient. The only other person involved with Matthew would be Murray, and he would update him unless something went wrong, in which case Emma would be Murray's contact. Matthew told the two guys about Lester and Switch and let them know they might appear on the scene at any time, so they needed to be aware and careful.

Their business complete, Matthew's two support people left the cabin, hopped into their SUV, and headed out to the main road.

Matthew spent the rest of the day retrieving his gear from the barn and packing his sled. He was taking the same kind of ammunition that he had taken the last time, although he wasn't intending to breach the camp security fence this time. But he wasn't so sure what might happen with all the extra security that De la Hora could have stationed around the place.

Matthew's focus was on trying to establish, with some certainty, what De la Hora was up to next and what his schedule would most likely be. He also knew there was no guarantee of what De la Hora would eventually do or whether he would be able to capture him alive or kill him. It all depended on the circumstance, but Matthew was counting on being a step ahead all the time.

Lester and Switch had left earlier in the day but would still be in the area as they scouted the potential highway access points from the forest. Matthew wasn't sure when they would head out into the forest, but he guessed they would leave first thing in the morning, just before dawn. There was no need to communicate with them for a while.

*   *   *

The sky was overcast and grey when Matthew left his cabin and headed out to the forest entry point and into the clearing where De la Hora had his equipment staged. Most of it was gone, likely at the camp. Only a few remnants remained together with old engine parts, oil cans, some empty fuel containers, and trash to tell the story of what the site had been. Matthew snapped a photo and then took off into the bush armed with his GPS, his supplies, and the comfort that somewhere out there were Lester and Switch. They would be out in front of him most of the time, and while they would always know Matthew's approximate location, he wouldn't be so certain of theirs.

It would take Matthew approximately eight days to reach De la Hora's camp by ATV. His fuel reserve, stacked on the back of the sled, would be enough for twenty days. He decided to keep to the main track for the first six days. He hoped he wouldn't meet up with De la Hora's load coming out of the bush. If he did, he would have to do some quick maneuvering. After that he would use a parallel route. Based on his estimated distance from the camp by the sixth day, he would slow down and watch for any signs of De la Hora's extended security perimeter, unless he heard otherwise from Lester and Switch.

He would make contact with Lester and Switch on day five to check in, test communications, and hear if they had had any encounters with De la Hora's security forces. He would follow up with them on the sixth and seventh day at the same time if he hadn't heard from them first. He fully expected they would come across a sentry sometime during the sixth or seventh day at the latest. Hopefully, Lester and Switch, having established "contact" with the first security operative, would stay around to figure out how spread out around the perimeter before heading farther in toward the camp.

Matthew ran at almost full throttle whenever he could on the tracks that De la Hora's equipment had made, then plunged into the denser bush on the seventh day. By then he had started a slow climb out of the muskeg areas and into an area of small streams that merged farther down in the valley. He felt more comfortable in the forest than he had previously. Lester and Switch had taught him a lot on that first trek into the camp.

*   *   *

It took Lester and Switch twenty-four hours to spot the first security detail. They had decided to travel the last forty miles on foot and left their ATVs in a well-hidden spot off the main trail up in the hills. That allowed them to travel on higher ground above the trail and look down over the forest and clearings rather than risk making contact face to face. There was also less brush up higher, which meant they could move along quite fast.

The lone security guard was sitting against a tree, sheltered from the misty rain that was saturating everything. He didn't appear to be particularly alert, although, to be fair, he was looking for any movement at all, whether it be an animal, a bird, or a human. The sudden movement of animals and birds were a good sign of an intruder, and it would put the guard on notice.

Lester and Switch made no movement that would alert the wildlife, seeing as they had no intention of inviting the guard to interact. All they wanted was to establish whether any other guards were in proximity on the perimeter. It seemed there weren't any, but Lester and Switch waited for an hour, watching for any signs that might give away the position of more guards.

Once they started moving again, Lester glanced back and spotted the guard they first saw amble along one hundred feet or so to the west. He bent over, touched something close to the ground, and then headed back to his tree. But he didn't stop there. Instead, he headed east for about one hundred feet and again reached down and then kicked at something.

"Whatcha think, Lester?"

"Well, if I wuz to guess, I would say there's a trip wire of some kind on both sides of 'im. An' if that's the case, my guess would be there ain't any other guards on the perimeter, so we may as well make contact with Matthew an' let 'im know what we found."

Lester didn't need to wait for Switch to agree. He had already made up his mind, and he also knew that his buddy wouldn't have any other ideas that would count for anything.

Lester sat on a nearby rock and punched in the frequency Matthew had given him for the walkie-talkie.

"Ay there, Matthew. It's me, Lester. Oh, and Switch is 'ere too."

Fortunately, Matthew had just stopped his ATV to grab a drink of water when he heard the walkie-talkie chatter.

"Hey, Lester. Everything OK?"

"Sure is, Matthew, but I gotta give you an update on them other folk. Seems like they set a guy out on the six-day perimeter. By my calculations that puts us about thirty-five miles from the camp. The guy is set by a tree all on his own right smack dab in the middle of the trail."

"OK, now we know. Any others on the perimeter that you can tell?"

"I don' think there's no one, Matthew."

"You mean you can't see anyone or what?"

"Well, I suspect they has a trip wire set up on each side of this guy for about a hundred feet in each direction. That tells me it's likely there's no one else but 'im on the perimeter. Also, we been 'ere for about an hour lookin' for signs in each direction, but we ain't seen nuthin'."

"Great. Thanks. I'm making good time, but I'm not sure I'll get to the camp as quickly as I wanted. It's a bit slow going off the track."

"No worries, Matthew. Switch and me are on foot 'cuz we didn't want any guards hearin' us. You better be careful as you come through 'ere unless you take a wide circle to the west or east with the ATV, if you're gonna keep it."

"Good advice, Lester. Thanks. Call me at the same time tomorrow unless you come across anything interesting before that."

"Roger that. Over 'n' out."

44
Eyes on De la Hora

Matthew's ground support crew was covering the exit point from De la Hora's camp to the forest. Their mission was to confirm the direction the trailers were taking when they headed out of the forest, north or south. South would likely mean they were headed for the port. North would mean they were heading to another hiding spot.

At that point it was unlikely that any of De la Hora's people would emerge from the forest for at least the next seven or eight days. Matthew was quite sure he would have heard them pass him if they were on their way out.

He released the drone for a thirty-minute flight. It hovered up at the 400-foot limit and gave him a view of about 1,600 feet in every direction. The thermal-imaging camera picked up a few warm bodies that could easily have been bears or moose—or Lester and Switch, although they were likely farther ahead than the drone could see. He landed the drone, packed it up, and moved on. He would recharge the batteries that night when he settled down for some rest.

It took Matthew another day to get close enough to the six-day perimeter to put the drone back up to search for the guard that Lester had called him about. The drone's thermal camera picked the body out as well as the small heat signal emanating from the trip line on either side. It had been electrified to provide a mild but halting shock to anybody who crossed it. The power source would be the extra hot spot detected by the drone, close to the guard.

Matthew figured his best course lay to the east, about a half mile from the guard. He would travel during the day to limit the noise that would alert the guard to an intruder moving along his eastern flank.

Lester and Switch called again just before the prescribed time.

"Got another one, Matthew," Lester announced, as though he had just caught a fish. He and Switch were keeping to the higher levels above the trail and looking down.

"What you got?" Matthew asked.

"Same as before. Some guy resting against a tree on the trail. Likely has the same setup as the last guy. Don't see anyone else within range, so can't tell you if they 'ave anyone else out on the twenty-mile perimeter. We're jus' headin' out. Should be at the camp this time tomorra. Call you then."

"Thanks. Keep your eyes open, and stay safe."

Matthew moved on. It had taken him seven days to get to the twenty-mile perimeter line. Lester and Switch were a full day ahead of him.

Again he used the drone to locate the guard. Once he found him, he brought the drone down to just above tree-top level to establish the easiest route around him. He decided to go west and curve back to the trail a mile or so farther on from the guard.

Eight days into his trek, he reached the high point where he had originally camped with Lester and Switch. He had sent the drone up several times over the last twenty miles to look at the trail ahead. He confirmed what Lester had told him about the lack of guards along the route.

There had been no intrusion into his camp, and what he had left there was still in place, well hidden by the undergrowth—tent, lights, fuel, food, and some tools.

He made contact with Emma with a quick message: "Arrived at camp. Guards out to thirty-five-mile limit. No interaction. Will call again same time tomorrow."

"Understood." Emma replied.

Matthew rested up before he made the move toward De la Hora's camp. It was dawn as he popped his head over the ridge and focused his scope on the area below. There was a lot of movement, and he saw loads being stacked at the portal entrance and down at the camp as they prepared to move out. Tarps partially covered the loads as they rested on pallets waiting for the forklift to do its job.

It looked as though De la Hora had almost five trailers loaded and ready to move out within twenty-four hours. Matthew spotted De la Hora, coffee in hand, waving furiously at his team, driving them on. It looked as though they were loading about fifteen tons onto each trailer and were finishing off the fifth. The other four were already tarped. It certainly seemed as though they would send the first five off to the ship while they loaded the next five trailers, which were standing by.

Lester and Switch had arrived a day before Matthew. They had taken advantage of the cold and crossed marshy areas that were unpassable when they first traveled in with Matthew. They had set up camp on the west side of the De la Hora camp to watch for any alternative routes that could be used. Their viewpoint was vastly superior to Matthew's.

Matthew decided to contact them. "Where are you guys?"

"We're up above the camp, on the west side. Nuthin' to do but wait. We scouted the guards, and there are four of 'em that we can see. Two at the portal—one above and one on the side—and two others out at the fence line. So far it looks like they're on a twenty-four-hour watch."

"OK. Stay in place, and wait for my word if we have to move. I reckon they'll move out once they fill the fifth trailer, but I need you to stay with me in case I need help. If De la Hora leaves, as I think he will, I'll probably follow him, and you can both follow me, just in case. By the way, see if you can confirm whether the drivers are local. We only want to take out the Mob boys—no one else."

"Sounds good."

Matthew kept his eyes glued to the camp as everyone went about their business. When daylight turned to dusk, Matthew thought it was time to get back to his camp and settle down for the night. He would be back up on the ridge at dawn to watch as De la Hora made his final preparations for sending out the first set of trailers. Would De la Hora travel with them, go his separate way, or stay at the camp?

45
Get out of the Mine

By 6:00 a.m. the next morning, Matthew was on the ridge with his binoculars focused on the camp. The weather was clear, and it looked as though it would be a cloud-free day, although the cold had started to set in.

De la Hora's people spilled out of the kitchen trailer and headed to the portal. All of them, including the drivers, would be moving the gold down from the portal to the skids waiting at the trailers. One of the group headed to the forklift and fired it up. Black smoke belched from the exhaust. It was a slow haul down the hill to the trailers, but within a few hours the last of the skids had been loaded onto the fifth trailer and the tarp thrown over the freight and lashed to the cleats bolted to the trailer's sides. The tractors were started, belching and coughing as their mighty engines rumbled to life.

Matthew spotted De la Hora over by the portal but then lost him as he entered the tunnel. There was no rest for the group remaining at the portal as they started to bring the next load down to be loaded onto the next trailer— the first in the second group to head out. This time some wooden crates were being manhandled to the portal entrance and stacked to wait for the next person to take them down to the trailer. As one of the men reached up to take one of the boxes from the second row, he stumbled, and the crate he was holding fell with him to the ground. He managed to stop himself from rolling down the hill, but the crate went flying and bounced three times. It broke open, spilling most of its contents. Matthew studied the contents as best as he could through the binoculars. The crate had contained small, loose gold articles. While he couldn't identify the details, he could see they were not ingots. This was an important piece of the puzzle that he knew Murray needed desperately before giving the approval for the final part of the mission.

The first of the initial five loads moved out, followed closely by the other four. Matthew could hear the roar of the engines from up on the ridge. Each tractor was hauling fifteen tons of gold. Two drivers were in each tractor, one for daylight and one for night driving. It was an eighteen- to twenty-four-hour per day campaign that could take five to seven days and nights. Their fuel was stacked and strapped down on the sled behind them.

"Hey, Lester, Switch, are you there?" Matthew asked over the walkie-talkie.

"Yeah, boss, we're 'ere. What's up?"

"It's all go here, boys. The first batch of trailers has left the camp. Each looks as though they have two drivers, so it's going to be almost a twenty-four-hour-per-day show. By my reckoning, that will put them onto the highway in, say, five days if they push it, and I'm sure they will."

"OK, boss. We'll wait up here fer you to let us know when we should leave. We figured all the drivers are injuns. So are the camp staff and laborers. It seems the Mob boys ain't gettin' their hands dirty, so that makes 'em jus' security."

"That's what I thought," Matthew replied. "Listen, I'm going to wait for De la Hora to make his move and then decide what I have to do."

"Sounds good. Talk again soon."

By the time Matthew picked up his binoculars again, De la Hora had disappeared.

About twenty minutes later, De la Hora appeared from the kitchen and headed over to the bunkhouse. Another twenty minutes passed before he came out with a bag in his hand and headed over to an ATV.

"I guess he's made his decision," Matthew mumbled as he realized that De la Hora was heading out sooner than later. He got as close as he dared to the gate and set his bionic ear device directly on De la Hora.

The ATV stopped at the security gate for about fifteen minutes for De la Hora to repeat his final instructions to the guard. Everything at the camp had to be destroyed using the dozer and forklifts. Those two pieces of equipment would remain at the site.

The portal was to be sealed by two blasts that would bring part of the mountain above it down to block the entrance. The pathway to the portal was to be scarified and disfigured enough to cause confusion if anyone came snooping around. There was, after all, still gold in them thar hills, albeit gold that had to be mined, but it was still valued at one ounce per ton—better than most gold discoveries these days. It would be crazy to just abandon a resource of such value without saving it for another day, even if it was for someone else. That would be De la Hora's secret... he hoped.

The gates opened, and De la Hora disappeared through them. The second group of tractors would follow in about two hours.

With those trucks driving eighteen hours a day, I doubt De la Hora will beat them to the ship, Matthew thought as he got up from the ridge and headed back to his camp, planning to keep about a four-hour gap between him and De la Hora.

He called the boys to let them know he was on his way and that they should follow as soon as possible. They had a forty-mile hike before they could pick up their ATVs, but they didn't seem to be worried about that.

"See ya later," was all Lester had said as he signed off. They had no plans to contact each other on the journey back unless there was trouble.

Matthew picked up the sat phone and called Emma.

"Five trailers en route. Should take five days minimum to reach the highway. De la Hora is following, but he'll take more like seven days to get to the highway. Local Native drivers, two to a truck. Will keep you updated. Let me know which way they turn when they get to the highway."

"Message received," Emma replied.

It took Matthew almost an hour to get his stuff together, pack the skid, clear out all his supplies, and fire up his ATV. He planned on contacting Murray at his first overnight stop. Once he had confirmed that everything was rolling along as expected, or not, he would make his way out of the forest.

* * *

The first trailer came roaring out of the forest just over five days after Matthew had first reported them starting out from De la Hora's camp. It was quickly followed by the other four. They wasted no time turning south onto the asphalt toward Prince Rupert, an eight-hour drive away.

Matthew called Emma after he had been driving through the forest for five days. Emma confirmed that the trucks had reached the highway and turned south toward the port. Matthew needed to know when and which way De la Hora was heading.

"Haven't seen him yet," Emma said. "Likely be another two days, but we're watching and will let you know."

*   *   *

The trailers drew up against the dock, and the shore crane started unloading their payload and putting it into the ship's hold. The unloading took less than three hours. The ORB captain was on hand to supervise.

Emma's team had followed the trucks to the ports. The only stops they had made had been for gas, cigarettes, refreshments, and the restroom.

"All safe and secure. Trucks on their way back for the next load," Emma reported to Matthew.

"Thanks. Better leave a couple of your guys with the ship and send the others to follow the trucks back to the forest entrance. We don't want any of them slipping away. Any word on recruits for De la Hora?"

"Seems as though some were caught trying to cross the border over at Sumas, east of Vancouver. I guess they didn't try to hide themselves much. Stood out from the crowd, so to speak, but Murray was on it and had a lot of the border crossings on high alert."

"Do we think that was all De la Hora was going to get?"

"Don't know. There may be others coming in through Alaska, but the boys up there know what to look for as well, so let's hope they get the job done. Of course, there's always the potential for some to come in by sea."

"Well, I guess there's no point in worrying about it right now. Keep your eyes and ears open, and keep scanning the frequencies."

"Got it. Take care."

*   *   *

The next call Matthew made was to Murray. No names were used, but the first part of the message was clear.

"All confirmed by sight. Let's go."

"Understood. Mission on," Murray replied. "Immigration also apprehended a couple of men trying to cross the border by coming in from Blaine, Washington, by boat into the north arm of the Fraser River near the Vancouver airport where there's no customs post, just a phone. Radar picked them up coming in fast on a route not normally used. Their suspicions paid off, and the boat was met on arrival at a small marina south of Vancouver.

"Other than that, it seems all's quiet with the Mafia as well as the Vatican, although the pope is still waiting for my call before he resigns. Clearly, he's giving his minions instructions for when he's no longer at the top. Oh, and Alfonso has slipped away from the Vatican, back to some small town in southern Italy where he can blend in with the local population. He's divested himself of his religious garments and gone back to being a banker.

"So far, from what I can tell, Dominici and his cardinal friends seem intent on maintaining their positions of authority with the Vatican Bank. They're just hanging on thinking they'll avoid prosecution and carry on doing what they've always done. They're using the same playbook as in 2000 when they were under fire by the Italian legal system for issues related to the missing gold. At that time, they foiled their accusers by claiming their sovereign status. If it worked then, they think it should work again."

"Thanks for the update, Murray. I'd better get out of here though. I need to stay close behind De la Hora. I'm not sure yet which way he's going to turn once he gets to the highway—north to Alaska or south to Prince Rupert."

"Good work, Matthew. Stay safe, and keep in touch."

Murray had no intention of pursuing the cardinals unless he was asked to do so. Now that the ORB had exposed the Vatican's wrongdoings, he wanted to concentrate on getting the gold back home and letting the legal authorities handle those implicated as they saw fit.

* * *

Matthew pushed on through the forest. He used the trail created for De la Hora's fleet for the first five days, but after that it was time to find an alternative. The first trailers would be on their way back from the port and coming into the forest any time now.

Matthew sent the drone up to search the trail ahead of him. He picked up the first set of returning trailers coming in fast about twenty minutes from his location. He estimated that the second load would already be on its way from the camp. He had calculated that the entire campaign would take about thirteen weeks if all went well with the trucks. It was over a 1,200-mile round trip from the camp to Prince Rupert, including some 350 miles through the bush, which would mean a lot of work for each truck engine.

Mathew watched from a hidden vantage point as the first five trucks passed his position on their way back to the mine. At about the same time, he watched De la Hora speed up to the front of the trucks from the opposite direction and stop them and talk to the lead driver. He would be out onto the highway later that day. Matthew would stay a discreet distance behind him and stay on the same track. But first he called Emma and alerted her to De la Hora's progress.

Six hours later, De la Hora burst into the clearing where he had left his truck near the highway. He wasted no time heading south to Prince Rupert, leaving the ATV under some cover, though it didn't really matter anymore what happened to it. He wouldn't need it again.

Two hours later, Matthew appeared at the highway and raced back to his cabin. He found Sam was waiting for him.

"Hey, Tom, or should I say Matthew?" she asked, smiling at him.

"Well, now we know each other a little better, you can call me Matthew." He smiled and grabbed her by the waist, pulling her close to him.

"Boy, you sure do smell like forest and shit."

"You don't hold back, do you? Want me to shower?"

"Not really. Reminds me of my roots. But maybe a bit of a cleanup would be appropriate. After all, we are adults."

Matthew showered, wrapped a towel around himself, and then joined Sam for a beer on the porch. They looked out over the lake.

"I'm gonna miss you. Will I see you again?" Sam looked sad as she sipped her beer and slid a hand over to undo his towel.

There wasn't a soft spot on the porch other than for the two bodies that stretched out on the towel. Sam slid her clothes off, and they made love as the sun went down.

"I'm going to miss you too, Sam. It's been a wild ride but a good one. Unfortunately, this is the end of the road for me, though, and who knows when I'll get back here? Do you ever to down to Vancouver now and again?"

"Well, I have been known to wander, and I clean up real well, so who knows?"

"Come visit anytime."

He kissed her as he got up. The time had come, and he needed to move on. Sam stayed on the porch, naked in the setting sun, and waited until Matthew got dressed and then came out and threw his things into the pickup. Sam stood up and waved goodbye as Matthew set off for Prince Rupert. He was an hour behind schedule.

Emma called Matthew to confirm that De la Hora was traveling south toward the port. Everything seemed to be going the way Murray and Matthew had hoped.

Matthew arrived in Prince Rupert and contacted the ship captain by sat phone from a coffee shop on the outskirts of town.

"Yes, De la Hora arrived here about three hours ago. We talked a little. He didn't appear to be suspicious. Then he took off, but I don't know where. He left me a cell phone number in case I needed to call him. He has two people here. I think they have guns, but I'm not sure. They keep to themselves and stay up at a local hotel. One of them is always here. They park themselves at the entrance to the port just a hundred yards or so from here, so I can see them well enough."

"Thanks, Lief. You know how to contact me. Let's keep using the sat phone. It's the most secure, and I prefer not to use cell phones just yet."

Matthew hung up and then sat down in one of the booths and picked up a menu. He was starving.

* * *

After he ate, Matthew called Lester and Switch.

"Hey, how you doin', boss?" Lester was his usual chirpy self.

"Where are you guys?"

"Well, we're followin' that guy, De la Hora. Where are you at?"

"I'm in the coffee shop outside town. Where is he?"

"Looks like he's headin' down to the ferry terminal."

"What?" Matthew asked incredulously. "What do you think he's up to?"

"Our guess is he's gonna take a ferry ride to Skidegate, on the island. Probably take the plane from Masset, just up the coast, to Vancouver. Not much else you can do from here if you ain't going by plane direct from Prince Rupert. Too long to go anywhere by car. An' there's no ferry from Haida Gwaii to Vancouver."

"Does that make sense?" Matthew asked, immediately realizing he had asked the wrong question of the wrong people.

"Dunno, boss. Just seems to be what he's doin' an' all. I guess he don't need to be 'ere anymore and don't need no one following 'im. That's an eight-hour ferry ride to the island, then an hour by cab to the airstrip at Masset and a couple of hours by air down to Vancouver. Business has been taken care of, and he's outta here."

"You're probably right. My guess is he's going to Vancouver to check in before he heads out to wherever home is."

"Could be right, boss. Wan' us to stay put and keep our eyes on 'im?"

"Yeah, that would be great. See if he boards the ferry, then let me know. After that I'd like you to stay around the port until all the loading is done and the ship leaves."

"How long d'ya think that will be, boss?"

"Likely a few months before they pull anchor and set sail. Think you can last that long?"

"Is the money still goin' in the bank?"

"You bet."

"Then we're staying, boss, no problem."

"Great."

Matthew decided to stay until the ferry left and then get a flight to Vancouver. He needed to pay a visit to Burvill at Global Gold after he had met with De la Hora. He also needed to get someone to follow De la Hora from when he arrived in Vancouver until he left. He didn't want to lose him before he got out of the country and went to warn his friends.

He picked up the sat phone and dialed. "Hey, Murray."

"Hi, Matthew. All well?"

"As good as it gets, my friend. It looks like the gold is all taken care of, and De la Hora has taken off by ferry, of all things, to an island off the coast and from there by plane to Vancouver, as far as we can tell. Strange route. I don't know why he didn't just take the plane from here."

"Maybe he's just being extra cautious. The route he's taken means he doesn't need anything special for ID, maybe a false driver's license for the plane. They might be a little more suspicious at the airport—who knows. If he had crossed the border and gone the Alaska route, he would have needed a passport."

"I think you're right. I plan on having him followed in Vancouver. Can you arrange that? I want to see how he plans to get out of the country. I may need your help there as well."

"No problem, Matthew. Have you got a fix on the timing for the gold to be shipped?"

"Make it three months from now. I'll nail down the date later. De la Hora left a couple of guards at the camp that we'll either have to deal with or get them caught at the border as illegals. What do you think?"

"I like that plan more than a blood one. We can hold them indefinitely in Canada and then extradite them back to the States for the lawyers to deal with when we're ready."

"What do you have in mind for the ship's destination?" Matthew asked.

"Well, my plan is to get it over to the port at Dardanelles Strait, fairly close to Istanbul, where the Istanbul Gold Refinery is located. We thought that would be an ideal destination for the storage of the gold, so it can be refined on an as-required basis. But the refinery can only refine 120 tons a year, and I doubt they would give up their entire annual capacity to one customer. So it will likely have to be spread around if our client wants more than the Istanbul refinery is willing to process.

"Anyway, that will be their problem to manage, and they can always send a load out to somewhere like Valcambie, in Switzerland, which can handle up to 1,200 tons a year. Nice problem to have, and when you think of the mathematics, that each one hundred tons represents something over five billion dollars at, let's say, seventeen hundred dollars per ounce, it's worth the worry. Not bad, eh?"

"Sounds good, Murray. At what point do we pull back?"

"When the gold docks in Turkey. You can be sure our client will be waiting with open arms, and the Israelis will be there with them to help in the dispersion efforts. That means we need to clean up everything behind us before the gold arrives. I think we have plenty of time, don't you?"

"I do. There are a few loose ends to attend to here, but I don't foresee a problem. Would you make sure Emma and her guys are still with us until everything's out of the camp? I'm going to rely on them to get rid of the guards at the port and the camp. I think that's a total of four. Now, we could treat them all the same as we discussed before and follow them to the US-Canada border, then have them picked up. What do you think?"

"I'm with you, Matthew. It's a better plan than a violent one, where we may lose people ourselves or just not be able to deliver. This way they'll never know what hit them until the Immigration guys pick them up."

"Good, that's settled. It means I don't have to hang around here or come back unless Emma calls for help. We'll let her team handle things from here. I suspect she should put a man out at the camp for a while to keep an eye on things and change him out every week or so until the loads are out of there."

"Good idea, my boy. I'll get it arranged, but you need to stay on alert in case something goes wrong. I don't think the Mafia boys are going to give up that easily, but that business in Rome is going to keep them busy for a while, so maybe they'll cut their losses. I doubt if any of them really appreciates what Toodoggone is all about anymore, so it would be best to keep De la Hora out of the way. Otherwise, he'll educate them."

"Understood, Murray. I'd better head out. I need to catch the last flight out from here to Vancouver."

"Catch you later, Matthew. Stay in touch, and let me know what happens with De la Hora."

"Will do."

Matthew heard from Lester and Switch while he was waiting for the plane at Prince Rupert. It was a relief to know that the eyes on De la Hora were working well. At least it confirmed his flight to Vancouver.

46
Global Revisited

Matthew's arrival in Vancouver was met by an overcast sky, rain, and the chill of winter as September started to roll in and the leaves began to fall. He thought about the gold loads coming out from the camp. It was a good time of year for the campaign. The ground was firming up with the temperatures dropping, and the tractors would make better time coming out from the forest.

He made his way over to the Opus where he had reserved his usual room at the top. It was his first opportunity in a while to eat a decent meal and relish some liquid refreshments. He was tired and didn't go out that evening. Instead, he spent a few hours in his room by the fire going over his notes for the future and what he had to do with Global the next day.

Matthew had called Burvill the day before from the Prince Rupert airport to let him know he would be in their offices at 11:00 a.m. the next morning.

He called Murray again and asked if things had been set up with Emma and whether the tail had been put on De la Hora in Vancouver.

"We tailed him from the south terminal at the Vancouver airport to his hotel. It looks like he met with the Global guys last night and spent some time at their office. We understand he's scheduled to check out tomorrow and has a cab booked to pick him up at 11:00 a.m. to take him to the Crescent Beach marina on the Canadian side of the border. That's about thirty miles away from the city. No idea what all that means, but it must have something to do with boats. We're not sure what his plans are from there, but I'll keep you posted. We're having our agents running passenger flight lists out of Seattle as well as Blaine."

"Boy, that's an odd one, Murray. I wonder if he's going to try to make a run for it to the States by motorboat into Blaine from Crescent Beach. He must have got wind of the Chicago boys being caught at the border. Could you get one of your tails down to the marina before De la Hora gets there and do some snooping around? I know that marina well, and it's all in the open, so if there's any unusual activity, they're going to see it."

"Sounds good. I'm on it. As for Emma, she sent two guys into the forest to set up at the camp. My guess is they'll stay there for the duration, but that's up to them. She has a couple of her guys down at the port keeping their eyes on things there. We still don't know if any more Mob boys are going to turn up. I don't think so. If they do, they'll likely wait until after De la Hora has called in to let them know what's going on."

"OK, Murray. I'm meeting with Global Gold in about twelve hours, and I wasn't planning on telling them anything about Toodoggone. My guess is that they got all the news they needed from De la Hora last night. I want to look into their eyes and try to figure out what they know and how much notice we need to take of them. At this point they're going to know that Toodoggone is closing down with the gold all moving out. That means it may be up for sale in a few months' time, and perhaps De la Hora is in there somewhere. I don't think we care, do we?"

"No, I don't think so, Matthew. Of course, that's not to say we won't get involved again sometime in the future and perhaps with different people— you know, ORB stuff. But at this point we'll just leave it alone."

"OK, my friend, I think I'm going to get some sleep. Call me any time if there's anything I need to know. I'm particularly interested in what De la Hora is going to do down at the marina tomorrow. I think he'll make a dash for the States, so we need to be prepared. We don't need to stop him; we just need to know where he's heading. If you find out he has an airline reservation, make one for me, and I'll be sure to be there."

"OK, Matthew. Take care. I'll talk to you later."

Matthew headed for a shower, shave, and bed. He was snoring by midnight.

*   *   *

Matthew woke up to the sound of a message coming through on his cell phone. It was from Murray.

"Target reserved on United flight from Seattle SeaTac to Rome at ten-thirty tonight."

"Thanks," Matthew wrote back. "Reserve me a seat in Business. I'll be there."

He called room service to get some fuel into him. Meanwhile, he looked outside his door and there on the handle was his suit, shirt, and tie freshly pressed from the overnight service. He had left a bag at the hotel the last time he visited.

At 10:30 a.m. Matthew got into a waiting cab and gave the driver the address for Global Gold.

"Good morning, sunshine," Matthew said, greeting the receptionist. He felt sorry for her, likely unaware she was a downer for those who hadn't visited before. Matthew knew better and had no expectations. "Would you let Mr. Burvill know that Mr. Black is here to see him, please? Oh, and don't bother about refreshments. I had coffee before I came." There was a touch of sarcasm in his voice, but the words went right over the receptionist's head.

"Mr. Burvill will be out shortly." She didn't look up from her desk. This time she seemed to be involved in messaging a personal associate, judging by the speed of her texting, short breaks, and more texting. Her face gave nothing away.

It was twenty minutes before Burvill came out. There was no hand shaking or vocal greetings, just a wave toward the same room they met in previously.

"Well, Ian, what's been happening over the last two weeks? Everything solved? Got all the answers? Ready to deal?" Matthew put on his friendliest, if not somewhat sarcastic, voice.

"Listen, Black," Burvill replied, "it looks to us as though you've finished with the stock buying. I believe you've run Peter dry. It also seems to us that whoever you represent is going nowhere with this foolish attempt to buy Toodoggone by bullying Global—or should I say our shareholders—into relinquishing its hold on the property."

"Oh." Matthew appeared taken aback, but it was a ruse, and his mask didn't give anything away. "I thought we were close to getting a deal done."

"What on earth would give you that idea?" Burvill asked with a twinge of a twisted smile in one corner of his mouth. It was a clear indication that he was trying to hide something that would give him great pleasure if, or when, he revealed it.

"Oh, I don't know. Call it a gut feeling. At some point along the way, I thought you would conclude that you would be better off without the Toodoggone property. After all, it is, as you say, a minor or bit player to Global's bottom line, and perhaps you see that this 'emotional' tie to it is really for naught. Am I right?"

Burvill still hadn't wiped the smirk from his face. "Tell you what, Black. Perhaps you're right. How about you make an offer and leave it with us for consideration?"

"Boy, you really have turned a corner, Burvill, old boy. Has it been keeping you up at night, and now you have the urge to get rid of it? Well, it matters not. The important thing is that we all get what we want, so here's our offer, including a few caveats and timelines." Matthew placed a folder on the table and pushed it across to Burvill.

Burvill was stunned, and his face showed it. He didn't look at the offer though, merely tucked it under his arm. "Well, well, Black. This is a surprise. We'll take a look at it and get back to you within, say, two weeks?"

"That sounds fine, Ian. Now let's be friends and shake on it." Matthew reached across the table and held his hand out. Burvill was hesitant, but now was not the time to show his displeasure with the situation. De la Hora had given him enough information for him to know the property would be cleared out by the end of the year and that the portal would be sealed off. By that time, it would be too late for anyone else to go into the property, and it would remain that way until May.

Burvill shook Matthew's as vigorously as he was able.

"Great. Hopefully you'll like our offer. I look forward to your response. Here's an email address you can use to contact me."

Matthew pushed a white business card across the table with nothing on it except an email address. Burvill took it without looking at it and put it into his breast pocket.

"Goodbye, sunshine," Matthew said, smiling at the unsmiling, miserable girl behind the desk on his way out. She actually looked up at him as he said goodbye, then went back to whatever she was doing.

When he was at his gate at the airport, Matthew called Murray for an update.

"Any word on De la Hora?"

"Yes, something quite unusual, and we can't make it out. Two of our people went down to the Crescent Beach marina early this morning. There were a couple of guys down there in a sailboat. Our guys couldn't get too close because the slip gates were locked, but they saw a black plastic canister sitting on the dock with what looked like oxygen tanks and some other paraphernalia. My guys are going to stay around to see what happens. This may not even be connected to De la Hora, but I'm guessing it is. I'll let you know as soon as I get an update. Where are you now?"

"I'm at the Vancouver airport. My flight leaves in about forty minutes. I get to SeaTac in about an hour and a half from now. Then I'll just be waiting around for De la Hora. I kind of know what he looks like from observing him at the camp. He has no idea what I look like though."

"I was talking to Emma an hour ago, and all's well up there. They're waiting for the second load to come through. Then things should settle down to a regular schedule. Any news from your two Native friends?"

"Nothing. I don't expect to hear anything for a while, but I'll call them when I get to Rome."

"Good man. Talk soon."

47
Goodbye, De la Hora

The twenty-seven-foot-long Catalina sloop moved as fast as it could away from the Crescent Beach marina, located just north of the US-Canadian border, about forty kilometers south of Vancouver. The little boat was pushed by a six-knot tailwind and the ebbing tide. Though not a beautiful yacht, it was a sound and inexpensive "Volkswagen of the sea" that drew little attention and performed in an incredibly mediocre but reliable way.

For over forty years the Catalina Company had churned the proven fiberglass hull off the factory benches and into the hands of sailing novices and lovers around the world.

The laws of the sea wouldn't allow the twenty-seven-footer to go any faster under sail than the mariner's physics equation dictated for its length, or about seven knots providing it was not pushing into a headwind. Planing boats were a different matter, but keelboats had to abide by the laws of physics when it came to speed with a keel.

The little boat, with both sails hard to the wind and taking advantage of everything it could, plodded through the swells and troughs, dragging its payload just shy of the ferry traffic and the coal tankers at Roberts' Bank, not to mention the knot of local commercial fishing boats hungry for their take as they cast their nets across the bay.

The boat braced against the tidal currents swirling around the headland of Point Roberts, that tit of United States territory that had been forgotten by the British in the nineteenth-century Oregon Treaty when it established the forty-ninth parallel and ended up on the western side of the international border to become part of America.

The sloop set a course to the next headland across Mud Bay to Blaine, where the American coastline took over and headed south.

The sloop's keel was just over six feet below the water line. Two thousand pounds of lead attached to the hull with stainless-steel bolts and galvanized zinc wrapped around the propeller shaft, relying on the galvanic series to protect itself from the saltwater. Old style.

Twenty-five feet behind the rudder was a black plastic canister—a little longer than a coffin and only slightly wider—tied by a nylon rope to stainless-steel hooks attached to specially fabricated brackets bolted to the underside of the hull. The canister was weighed down sufficiently to ensure it never appeared above the surface but traveled a foot or so below. The closeness of the canister to the boat's stern was such that it wasn't likely to show up as a separate vessel from the sloop but, rather, as a life raft. In the canister one could put anything one wanted—camping gear, liquor, supplies, spare parts drugs, rare commodities, stolen treasure, bodies—and the quick-release, engaged from the side storage in the cockpit, would ensure that one would never be caught with a haul by raiders in the event an emergency arose, although that could mean the temporary loss of the payload, which could be retrieved later using the proximity transmitter inside the canister. The activation of the quick-release also activated a small float to mark the container's location.

Angel pushed the tiller hard to starboard as the mainsail came around, and they moved to a port tack. Marley looked around in all directions with the five-by-thirties and saw no other boats in the area except for the one heading toward them in the distance. Only radar would be able to detect them. They had made this run for two weeks now. Canadian sailing neophytes going in and out of the slip from across Boundary Bay and into the Strait of Georgia, never quite making the islands. Always out for just a couple of hours on the chuck. Nothing too strange for a couple of casual sailors and too boring for the coastguard to follow. There were bigger fish out there for them to catch.

The Hunter 41DS moved gracefully toward them on an intersect course and under full sail as it exited the marina at Blaine, just on the south side of the US-Canada border and a little more than half a mile dead south of the marina at Crescent Beach. It's crew of two were in complete control as they moved toward the Catalina. Howard watched the sloop from the cockpit as they advanced toward it while Drake kept his eye on the horizon and the ocean around them for obstacles or other boats as he held the wheel on a starboard tack and listened for his associate's instructions. Deadheads—vertical floating logs—were the biggest problem, but horizontally floating logs let loose from the tugs that hauled them were a close runner-up.

When there was fifty feet between them, Marley reached down into the side storage panel in the sloop's cockpit and pulled the chrome lever. Their course never changed. The water line gave nothing away. The submerged plastic canister continued forward under its own momentum toward the Hunter, and the Catalina tacked to port and veered back toward the way they came, this time closer to shore as though they were out having a pleasant couple of hours on the chuck before heading home.

Drake lowered the hooks and net from the Hunter, catching the canister as it attempted to go by, then fastened it to the cleats on either side of the rear cockpit. Howard sailed the Hunter another hundred feet before they adjusted their course and followed the coastline farther south, staying on the American side of the invisible international boundary. It would be a few hours before they reached their mooring on Whidbey Island. They settled in with a beer and relaxed as the sails embraced the north westerlies and pushed them south at a steady nine knots.

*   *   *

Marino De la Hora was a small man, but he was broad and getting extremely uncomfortable in the confines of the plastic canister as he controlled his breathing in response to occasional bouts of claustrophobia. He was loaded with Ativan to keep him sedated, but he knew he would be able to stretch in a short while. He had felt the contact with the hooks and knew—as much by intuition—that his people had done well. He would be back in America in a short while. It was time to move on. His escapades had not been successful, but he needed to get away and wind down for a few months until his next assignment—if he ever got one. This one had been too close. Matthew Black had caught up with him and snagged his prize project before he could complete his assignment, but he also sneered at the thought of being discovered by such an amateur.

Drake and Howard dragged the container up onto the beach in a secluded cove on the west side of Whidbey Island. Drake snapped the line to the oxygen tanks that provided the precious food to De la Hora's lungs during the sub-sea trip and had been designed to stabilize the canister during its passage. He wrenched open the latches as De la Hora pushed upwards on the lid and reached up to the two pairs of helping hands held out to him. He breathed deeply and managed to step over the side of the container with a little help, stretched his legs, kicked back at the canister with his right heel, and smiled at his saviors.

"Fuck! Thank Christ that's over! I almost suffocated in there. What a shit-hole." De la Hora gasped and coughed as he stretched, reached out for the proffered cigarette, lit it, then took a deep breath. "Never again!"

De la Hora took another drag of his cigarette and then flicked it away and started forward, slightly unbalanced. "Let's get going."

Drake and Howard led De la Hora to a waiting Range Rover hidden behind the trees on a short track off the main road, dragging the canister behind them. They heaved it onto the truck, covered it with a tarp, and strapped it securely in place. De la Hora climbed into the back seat, lit another cigarette, and slouched back against the comfort of the black leather while reaching for the vodka offered to him.

"Thank Christ I'm outta there," he said as he took another drag, followed by a slug of vodka.

The Range Rover slipped onto the main road and headed south toward the Whidbey Island ferry that would take them to the mainland just north of Seattle and down to SeaTac airport. From there De la Hora would board a flight to Rome and then on to Napoli, where he would brief his people on his escapades and wait for the next challenge—unless they decided otherwise, given the circumstances of his catastrophic failure, which was highly likely.

* * *

Murray had made contact as soon as his men called him about the activity at the Crescent Beach marina.

"Damn me, Matthew, De la Hora climbed into that canister, and they lifted him into the water behind the sailboat. It sank to just below the water-line, and they spent a little time checking things out before heading out under their own power. That's a hell of a long way out to the chuck from there. About half an hour of gunning it before you can put up a sail."

"Boy, now there's a plan," Matthew replied. "Any idea where they're headed?"

"It has to be somewhere close to Seattle, although that could be any number of places. We've put a small fixed-wing up to follow them. I don't really think it matters much as long as he ends up on that flight, do you?"

"No, but it would be interesting to know where he lands and what his two accomplices are up to. They must be Mob members or associates, and I hope they don't end up at SeaTac on the flight or even go as far as SeaTac. Maybe run a check on them from a description from the marina operator."

"OK. You'll have to figure things out if De la Hora isn't by himself at the airport. My guess is they're both homegrown and will stay in the US."

"I think you're right, but let's follow through."

"I agree. Talk later. I'll call before the flight if anything crops up that you should know. Ciao for now."

"Are you going to be in Rome?"

"Yes, I'll be there in a couple of days to follow up on a couple of things with the Vatican."

"OK, cheers for now."

* * *

Moving through SeaTac airport, De la Hora had a sense of being followed, as he always did given his neurotic disposition, but he stayed in the main traffic areas for safety and lounged casually against a partition with his small carry-on bag set on the ground between his feet. He wore dark glasses to hide his constantly moving eyes as they searched for any telltale movement that might indicate a problem. His newspaper was half lifted to his eyes, and his posture gave nothing away.

De la Hora felt nothing as the stiletto made its way through the partition behind him and found his heart. His bulging eyes were hidden by his glasses, and his gradual stoop ended after a short fall as a second stiletto found its way into his neck just below his skull—enough to hold him in place for a short while.

A suit-clad figure came around the corner of the partition and stood in front of De la Hora as though in quiet discussion. Fingers went through the pockets of his pants and jacket, taking everything they could reach and then traveling down to the carry-on. It took all of thirty unhurried seconds for the figure to complete his work, lift the bag, turn, and saunter away with a backward wave to his "friend." De la Hora stayed in place, supported by a pair of sturdy points that had been neatly covered by a coat draped over the top of the partition and hung casually over the hilts of the weapons. He had nothing on him that could be used as identification, and he would stay where he was until the cleaners came by and asked him to move a little, so they could do their job.

Meanwhile, Matthew flashed his passport to the airline attendant, together with his ticket as he joined the line to board the flight to Rome.

"Thank you, Mr. Black. Have a pleasant flight." The attendant smiled in a carefree way as she reached out for the next ticket. Matthew casually walked down the skyway, tucked his passport into his suit's breast pocket, and settled into his window seat at the back of the Business section.

"Just a small Chivas on the rocks—and light on the rocks," he told the passing attendant. A smile crossed his lips as he looked out over the airport and wondered what he would be in for next.

"Amateurs," he said under his breath.

48
Rome

Matthew's flight touched down at the Leonardo da Vinci-Fiumicino Airport in Rome ten minutes earlier than scheduled and waited on the Tarmac for twenty minutes for a gate to open up.

Matthew headed to the airport's exit while negotiating the crowds coming from all angles, with everyone in a rush to get in or get out. Customs was a breeze, and Matthew sailed through with no hold-ups. He located the Viatar car service, the driver holding a sign over his head while he waited for Matthew in the arrivals hall.

They arrived at the Portrait Rome hotel on Via Condotti forty-five minutes later. The old converted townhouse was located in the heart of the Eternal City and was one of six boutique hotels owned by the infamous Salvatore Ferragamo family, who started life as designers and makers of shoes, bags, clothing, watches, and all the accessories that went with them. The Ferragamo family had lived in the Chianti region of Italy for many years and owned a small village, Il Borro, there while they continued with business and entertained tourists. Over the years they had acquired other properties and converted them to upscale hotels, six in all.

Portrait Rome was within spitting distance of the Spanish Steps and all that went with that location, including the high-end stores lining the myriad of narrow streets with cafes interrupting pedestrians constantly along the way.

It was early afternoon when Matthew took in some of the sights in the neighborhood. He thoroughly enjoyed his visits to Rome, especially when he was accompanied by the lady of the moment. In this case it was all business, at least to start with, but perhaps he would be lucky enough later to get to enjoy the city.

Murray had set up a meeting at 10:00 next morning up on the terrace restaurant. He and Matthew were meeting with Misha and Eric, their clients from Turkey, and Yousef, the Israeli watchdog.

They all arrived at about the same time and settled around a table for six and set for five. Coffee, juices, and menus were handed around while they caught up on their more personal exploits until the waiters were out of earshot and breakfast had been ordered.

September was a beautiful month in Rome, with the paler sun giving way to high clouds, a gentle breeze, and an aroma that promised autumn was on its way. It was coming into sweater season in the early morning and later evenings. Murray's group laughed and talked until Murray brought some order to the meeting.

"I think I've been in contact with you enough over the last several months for you to be up to date on where we're at and where we're going with the project. It's coming to that time when we'll pass the baton to you all." Murray raised his eyebrows as he looked at the three client representatives.

"I think we know enough, Murray. We've been in touch with our respective governments." Misha looked over at Yousef, who nodded in agreement. "And we believe they're ready to do their duty and manage the receipt and distribution of the gold."

"You may know that the amount of gold we're talking about is far too much for any one refinery to manage," Murray said. "We haven't been in contact with any of them, but our research confirms the facts."

"Yes," Eric replied, nodding, "we're very aware of the limitations, especially on those of the Istanbul Gold Refinery. But we're thinking that we'll split the gold between several refineries across Europe, especially Switzerland. We've also discussed a timetable that indicates repatriation may take up to five years, so we're not having to race to get this finished. Our mutually interested friends in Israel," Eric nodded at Yousef, "have a substantial account of those who lost their lives—and their gold, of course—to the Nazis. We also have documentary evidence from the archives of most of the invaded nations for them to establish claims. At this time no one other than the secret services of our countries—Turkey and Israel, that is—are aware of where the bounty has come from or where it is. All they really know is that we're trying to deliver it back into the hands of those it belonged to."

"What are you going to do with the pope, Murray?" Misha asked.

"Well, once the gold has been shipped from Canada and is on its way to Istanbul, I'll give him the signal to resign. But that's still several months into the future. The gold shipment will arrive, if all goes well, by mid-December. That's when you need to be prepared to offload and get it through customs. You may be able to deliver it all to the Istanbul Gold Refinery for safekeeping and have them process a certain amount each year, but again, it's up to you to make those arrangements.

"Now we'll follow through with the loading and shipping of the gold, managing the Mob members who are left at the site by having them detained by Canadian Immigration officials."

"What about De la Hora?" Misha asked. "If he gets back to his people, he will undoubtedly motivate them, especially when they have a better understanding of the enormity of the gold value and the fact it was snatched from under their noses. I don't want to think about the storm that could follow."

"He has been dealt with, Misha," Matthew stated succinctly.

Misha and Eric raised their eyebrows in a questioning manner.

"Care to share, Matthew?"

"Not really, Eric. I think the less you know the better your sleep will be at night."

Their breakfast arrived, and they happily tucked into the delights that only an open-air Roman meal could bring as they looked out over the rooftops to the Colosseum and the history beyond.

* * *

Murray and Matthew said goodbye to their clients later that afternoon. Murray was heading back to Cyprus, his home.

"Great job, Matthew. Hopefully everything will work out from here. Meanwhile, both of us need to stay in contact with Emma and your Native friends. I'm going to stand the other guys down. If there's the slightest cause for concern, we'll contact each other, right?"

"You bet, Murray. I think it was a job well done with only a couple of injuries, and none of them ours."

"Oh, I meant to ask you, what's happening with that agreement you conjured up for Global Gold?"

"Ah, that." Matthew rubbed his chin. "Well, I think they're going to have some trouble with the offer as time goes on. I did it in two stages. The caveat is that they're interconnected—accept one provided you accept the other. The first stage is the promise of three hundred million, payable upon execution of the final agreement plus a 3 percent NSR, with the offer of a board position."

"That sounds pretty good. Don't know where you're going to get the money though. That's your business, but I admire the spirit. What's the second stage?"

"That's the kicker. Once we have all the gold out of there and we get an indication of acceptability of the first stage, the Native band, represented by Lester, Switch, and their sister, Sam, will be responsible to raise the necessary funds or renegotiate the price. They have one year from the date of acceptance of the total offer to deliver the funds or get an accepted alternative financial agreement. If they don't deliver, there will be no penalties or legal repercussions against anyone on the potential purchaser's side. The overall caveat is that there will be no consideration of an alternate offer."

"Wow, a bit of a blow, I would say," Murray commented.

"It'll give them something to think about. Perhaps they'll help the Natives raise the funds. After all, the Canadian federal government sponsors a lot of costs for Aboriginal Affairs, and this is just a drop in the ocean. If successful, it'll give the Natives something to sink their teeth into and better understand business. It's really a win-win, but it's going to cause Burvill to froth at the mouth while he gets a grip on it."

"Well, keep me in the loop on that one, my man. Sounds like a zinger with a sting and a reward. Take care. Oh, by the way, make sure you get that money for the shares back from Global. We're in the hole for about two million dollars."

Matthew smiled as they shook hands. "No problem."

Murray headed out to a cab and then turned back. "Oh Matthew, there's a little surprise for you in your room. Enjoy." Murray grinned and then waved as he climbed into the cab's back seat.

*   *   *

"Emma—for God's sake. How the hell? Murray, that bastard. Trust him."

"That's no welcome," Emma responded as she sat up in bed, the remnants of breakfast around her, and her clothes spread around the room.

"Well, I can't think of anything better, but trust your dad to get it done this way. The man has no limits." He plonked onto the bed and slid a hand behind Emma's back, pulling her toward him. "Rome is going to be delicious."

They both laughed.

49
The Transfer

The Office, as it was most often referred to, was one of the several high-security agencies within Israel. This one was specifically charged with the responsibility for repatriating the Nazi gold to the descendants of the Holocaust survivors once it had been returned. They were exempt from the Basic Laws of Israel. However, its activity was subject to secret procedures that had never been published. Its director answered directly to the prime minister.

The Office was created specifically to coordinate with the Turks and now ORB as things started to close in on the gold's whereabouts. It was not an easy operation. Turkey and Israel were on opposite sides of a religious equation, each side totally incapable of trusting the other. In fact, some 20 percent of the spying that occurred in each country was dedicated to following the operations of the other. It likely increased from the point when the nuclear threat from Turkey seemed imminent, and Israel became even more jittery. It was impossible to have constructive dialogue with each other, so it became necessary to create a specialized group within each government to leave the politics to one side as they managed the gold situation.

Over the years, the Office had collected, cross-checked, and collated the thousands of records of Holocaust victims and their families and extended families. They had been responsible for the tracing, extraction, and extermination of many of the Nazis who had been responsible for the war crimes, but their goal was to repatriate the gold. However, it had been impossible for them to act alone. The Turks had been a godsend, and now ORB had moved in to help.

The Office was formed in 1946 at the recommendation of the Israeli prime minister and supported by the Allies, who wanted to track and recover the Nazi lootings. In 1951, it was made part of the prime minister's office, reporting directly to the prime minister.

From there things took off, but every time a lead was followed, it was dashed by government, false leads, mysterious circumstances, and, of course, the Vatican and the Mob, both of which were insurmountable problems. Yet they eventually realized that both groups were central to the disappearance of the majority of the gold. Israel had zero chances of breaking through their barriers. Their religions and cultures were diametrically opposite.

Over the years the Israelis had tracked and discovered relatively small amounts of looted gold. Their problem was that they could never lay claim to it. The gold was claimed by the Allies, and whenever they were about to lay their hands on the gold, it was spirited away.

There were many theories, stories, and possibilities without proof, and lost leaders. All of them were followed up by the Israelis, but it wasn't until the Turks got involved that things seemed to move along more constructively. Perhaps it was their thinking outside of the box, or perhaps it was the fact that they still held the secrets to some of their own banking during the war that had helped the Nazis get the gold out of Germany, Switzerland, Turkey, and the Vatican. They were not even in their frame of thinking at the time, although they had their suspicions, but they had no insiders who could help.

At some point the Turks also seemed to come to a grinding halt in their endeavors. They appeared to be close to the target but couldn't go the extra mile. The task required the help of a professional group who could more easily open doors to the places that neither the Turks nor the Israelis could go—the Vatican and the Mafia. Israel was quite content to let them in the door, although they kept a close eye on their activities. Yousef was only one of a number of Israeli agents assigned to the project. They kept as close as they dared to Matthew and even tracked Murray and his people.

The meeting in Rome confirmed the schedule. The gold would most likely arrive in Istanbul by mid-December, or the end of the year at worst. Those dates were determined by activities some 7,000 miles away in the backwoods of Canada. It was out of everyone else's hands. All they could do was watch and wait.

* * *

On January 1, two weeks after the gold arrived in Istanbul, the Vatican confirmed that Pope Germane would resign the papacy the following month as a result of his advanced age of almost eighty-six years and his continued exposure to injuries and sickness. According to a statement from the Vatican, the timing of the resignation was not caused by any specific illness but was to "avoid the exhausting rush of Easter engagements."

* * *

The Turks, supported by the Israelis, moved the gold into the specially constructed storage area at the Istanbul Gold Refinery. The area was surrounded by spiked barbed wire, electronic surveillance, dogs, and guards, and all of it was contained in steel boxes inside an impenetrable warehouse. Occasionally, armored trucks would file in, load some of the gold, and move it to other refineries for processing.

* * *

Emma and her team maintained oversight on the comings and goings from the De la Hora camp as well as the port. There was no telling up to the time of the ship's departure whether any of the De la Hora crew would pull a fast one and syphon off some of the gold. No one tried, but Emma's team kept a close eye on them all.

She had sent people up to the cabin that Matthew had used on the other side of town and cleaned it of anything that may give rise to questions. It was a neat job, and Emma gifted the Native band with anything they recovered that could be useful to them—all in the care of Lester and Switch.

Once the last of the Mob men came out of the bush, the Canadian Immigration people pounced, and Emma at last saw them being hauled off in a reinforced SUV. She didn't bother to follow it.

It was the same down at the port. Once the ship was fully loaded, Emma instructed the captain on what course to sail. They would leave on the next ebbing tide. Meanwhile, the Canadian Immigration people surrounded the Mob guards and hauled them off to face an indeterminate incarceration in some remote prison facility in nowhere BC.

* * *

Lester and Switch, along with their sister, Sam, were struck dumb by the prospect of owning a gold mine smack dab in the middle of their territory, their sacred lands. The land that they and their fellow Native bands had been protecting from environmental damage all these years.

The Canadian government would be only too pleased to provide them the money for the property purchase, although they naturally would want their share of the proceeds as payback. But it was a ten-year agreement, and that was good with the Natives.

Now there they were, searching for development permits and seeking management to build and operate a gold mine. They believed they could do it without causing too much damage to the environment, just like a White man would claim.

Lester ordered beers for everyone as he swung through the doors of the Zoo the morning after the feds promised to fund the purchase. Fortunately for him, there were only three people in the bar at that time, including the bartender, until Sam stepped through the door and plunked herself down next to them in the well-worn booth.

"Looks like we're gonna' 'ave to work fer a living, you two." Sam looked at her brothers as she grabbed the bottle in front of her and sipped her beer.

"What? I don't think so, sis. We'll jus' let the feds do that fer us. We jus' gotta sit back with some good lawyers and let them do it all." Lester was clearly thinking, but this was only his first beer of the day.

"I wuz thinkin'," Switch said, "why don' we jus' sell it?"

"Now that sounds like an idea," Lester said. "Then we really don' 'ave to work. Whatcha think, sis?"

"I like it."

They tipped their bottles together, smiled, and chugged their beers.

* * *

It was a beautiful spring day in Vancouver as Matthew and Emma sat on his balcony overlooking the ocean.

His cell phone rang.

"Black."

"Just to confirm, the Global shares you held have all been sold back to them, at a 20 percent premium."

"Sounds good."

Matthew went back to enjoying his spring day.

THE END

Ref.: George Taber's *Chasing Gold*. I have never read such an incredible and fact-based account of gold movements throughout the world as a basis of supporting wars from the Spanish Civil war of 1936–1939 to the end of WWII. Germany was at the center of the movement. They craved the financial security of gold to further its cause and its future. They used it to rebuild their wealth and military might. They used it so maliciously that it became their downfall through their rape and pillage of countries and the Jewish nation. They used it regardless of their lack of understanding that the rest of the world could not, and would not, allow them to become the supreme leaders of the world on the basis of materialism alone.

Printed in the USA
CPSIA information can be obtained
at www.ICGtesting.com
LVHW091456301024
795099LV00001BA/127

9 781038 3011